DB Bell was born in the North of E
and worked in the South of Englar
eventually returned to the North,
partner, and with whom he has a grown up son.

Having read many crime novels he wanted to write a book that contained strong women, and men who are rather less so, and this is his second such novel.

His first book is the precursor to this one, is called "Badminton Coaching and Murder at Basingrove School, and is also available from Amazon Books.

To Carole, who carried out the proof reading.

January 2023

Death in the Barn

[A liaison (unexpectedly) dangereuse]

An
Inspector Roberts
Investigation

D B Bell

Chapter 1

With the crates unloaded and stacked, and the barn doors closed, the three bejeaned men's job was done. They turned to check that the bolt was fastened, that the padlock was on, and that the lights were off.

'Il n'y avait personne pour nous déranger cette fois-ci,' said one of them.

'To be honest, I am disappointed that she wasn't there,' replied another, 'because she could have bothered me anytime she wanted to!'

'Me too. We should have had fun with her before she died,' said the third.

'How many shots was it? Three each? And so much blood!'

They laughed heartily, they slapped each other on the back, and then headed for their truck.

'I'm going to Paris love,' announced Akmal as they were eating breakfast.

'Are you? That's really annoying. Why are you going away *this* time?'

'I've had a message from work telling me that I'm needed in Paris again.'

'Really! And when are you going?'

'Later today.'

'Later today! Great. Our weekend plans are blown then,' said Tegan.

'Afraid they are Tegan, sorry.'

'Fine. It's a lovely Spring Saturday and suddenly you have to go away. We've been planning that weekend break in Oxford for ages.'

Oxford was only a one-hour drive from what was their expensive and stylish home in Iver Heath; it was a city that they both loved, and with which they both had happy memories. Their intended B&B was one that they knew well too, but with Akmal about to leave for Paris, Tegan would likely have to spend her weekend break there alone.

'Are you not going to protest then?' asked Akmal.

'No Akmal. I will just take my toy boy to Oxford with me instead.'

'I thought that I was your toy boy?'

'You often mention that Akmal.'

'Yeah, but it's true isn't it.'

'I'll replace you with a "real" plastic toy boy if you are too long in Paris!' she said as she gave Akmal's nose a kiss.

'I'd better be back tomorrow then.' They both laughed and enjoyed a quick hug.

'What time did you say you were leaving?'

'I didn't, but it will be at about 10.30am.'

'Time for a quick shower then,' said Tegan, with a broad grin.

Their clothes were off before they had reached the shower room and they emerged at about 10am looking "refreshed".

Akmal was born in England but his parents had arrived in the UK from Africa in 1993. Now aged 21, and at around 6 feet 5 inches tall, Akmal was a big man; the rest of him was in proportion to that height, which made his head appear to be unusually small. This effect was made worse by the fact that his whole head, and face, was covered only by a short stubble.

'Do you want your hair and stubble trimming today then love?'

'It doesn't need it today Tegan, sorry, and anyway, when you do that, we usually get carried away, and we end up in bed. I haven't time for that now! I note that you never let me do *your* hair for you, I would enjoy doing yours as much as you clearly enjoy doing mine.'

'You're going nowhere near my hair Akmal!'

Unlike Akmal, Tegan would spend quite large sums at the hairdresser, and this was despite her very glossy, mousey coloured hair being fairly short. At twenty-seven years old she was a little older than Akmal, but most people thought that she looked younger than he did. Like Akmal, she had also been born in the UK, but she had lived some of her early life in Scotland, and her parents were Swiss. She was very tall at 6 feet 1 inches and her figure was classic hourglass.

'So, for how long will you be in Paris?' she then asked.

'I don't know Tegan, but I'll message you when I get there.' After a very, very, long embrace, he was off, case in hand. They were so confident in their relationship that they didn't need any parting words, no 'look after yourself', no 'write often', no 'be back soon', no tears, in fact no "Brief Encounter"

3

style moments at all. Tegan just closed the door after him and that was that.

It isn't far from Iver Heath to Heathrow Airport and, though he had been a little late leaving, Akmal was already parking his Range Rover in the airport car park at 11.30am. After a quite uneventful flight, his plane landed at Charles de Gaulle Airport at 3.15pm (UK time). Once he was off the plane and he had collected his luggage, he went to Cafe Eiffel, where he had arranged to meet his associate Marie.

'Bonjour Marie.'
'Ah, Bonjour Akmal. Ca va?'
'Tres bien merci, et toi?'
'Rather familiar,' she thought. But then she had already worked with Akmal a few times so she let it pass. 'Bien monsier. Eh bien, *comment était ton vol?*'
'I'm sorry Marie, you've gone beyond my French now. Can we continue in English?'
'So you 'aven't been practising our language? Shame on you.'
'I've been too busy,' he lied.
'I asked how was the flight?'
'It was good actually, quite smooth and no problems. I had a bit of a sleep on the plane in case you keep me busy well into the night. So what do we do now?'
'We 'ave some coffee and you can enjoy some proper French food, and then we go to my hotel room.'

Back at their home in Iver Heath, Tegan wasn't very happy about her spoiled weekend away. She and Akmal had been together for almost three years and they loved nothing better than a weekend away except, perhaps, for a good argument. They would argue about anything, why Akmal lounged about in just swimwear (and a dressing gown, *usually*), the new colour for the garage doors, whether Doctor Who should be played by a woman, whether men should wear blue socks (Akmal hated blue socks) or even whether the coffee tasted good today, which it invariably did. But these were very Italianesque arguments, and they would always end up laughing at each other.

There had been no arguments today though, but, quite soon after Akmal's departure, she had telephoned *her* associate, Gustav Reyes.

'He's gone to Paris again.'

'Has he now. For how long this time?'

'I rang the airport and asked for the Airport Parking company. I told the chap there that my husband had parked the car and that he had forgotten that my purse was in the boot. When I asked whether I could come to collect it he told me that he couldn't allow anybody that hadn't actually parked the car to go anywhere near it. He said that the face recognition technology wouldn't allow it anyway. I moaned that I would have to wait two weeks for my purse, and I couldn't manage without it. He replied that I'd have to wait for at least a month because that's how long Akmal had paid for.'

'So, we easily have four weeks?' asked Gustav.

'We do,' Tegan replied.

'Get yourself here then, ASAP.'

Meanwhile, Akmal had been making himself comfortable at Marie's hotel in Paris. His was the room two doors down the corridor from Marie so they could meet up, accidentally or otherwise, on the stairs or on the way out. At about 6.30pm they "bumped into each other" on the way down to dinner.

'Akmal, bonsoir, puis-je me joindre à vous pour le dîner.'

'Avec plaisir,' replied Akmal.

'Très bien Akmal. You have a little more French than I thought!'

'I always recognise an invitation to join a beautiful woman for dinner! That's about the limit of my French though,' he confessed.

They wandered into the restaurant together. The hotel refectory had a very classic French looking interior with decorations that had been elegantly applied in the 1930s, and these had been so well maintained that there had been no need to replace them. The waiter approached and provided them with menus.

'I'll have Soupe à l'oignon, followed by Boeuf Bourguignon. What about you Marie?'

'I'll also have the soup, but I'll follow it with Poulet Rôti.' After a substantial pause they both enjoyed a small Crème Brûlée.

'Do you know Marie, as we came into here I felt as though I had walked back in time. I wonder whether it even smells the same as when it was newly built?'

'I imagine that it does Akmal. Maybe you should make a mental note to bring Tegan here one day.' They continued chatting gently over dinner, in English, sounding just like a British married couple having a meal out together.

Neither drank wine, which had annoyed the waiter tremendously, but Marie did order a bottle of the "house wine" to take back to her room, which is where they retired to after their meal had ended.

'Wine Akmal?'

'Yes please.' They sipped their wine for a while but then Akmal announced that business had to begin.

'Where am I off to this time?' he asked.

'Canada, Montreal in fact, and we leave tomorrow.'

'That's a long way off,' said Akmal. 'And you said "we", so you are coming too? That's unusual for me, and don't they speak French in that part of Canada? That could be really awkward with my level of the language.'

'That's exactly why I am coming with you this time, *so that I can help you with anything that you don't understand.*'

'OK, but how will that work out? I usually do these things alone and I'm not used to having an assistant.'

'I know you are, but a non-French speaker will stand out even more in that part of Canada than they would in France, *and* I will not be *your* assistant thank-you very much!'

'I apologise for the use of the word assistant, but why will my lack of French stand out more in Canada than in France?'

'France gets many tourists who speak English, so French people are used to being surrounded by English speakers. France is so beautiful that many English speaking people holiday here, including Americans and Australians. In Canada they also get many tourists, but fewer of them speak English, in fact a large proportion speak French, so you would really stand out unless accompanied by a French speaker.'

'OK. So, who will we be?'

'We will be a couple having a last attempt to patch things up before we start divorce proceedings. You will be Akmal Ibori, and I will be Marie Ibori, soon to revert back to Marie Bernard. I will be French; you will be an Englishman born in Africa.'

'Which part of Africa am I from?'

'Why does it matter?'

'The men in some countries of Africa are bigger than those in other parts.'

'We can see that you are a big man Akmal.'

'Not everywhere you can't!' Marie laughed.

'Ah. Male pride again. Will Lebanese do?' Akmal took out his phone and did a quick internet search which started with the word "Africa" and ended with the word "sizes".

'Yes,' he replied. 'That will do nicely.'

'So, you are Akmal Ibori, originally Lebanese but you moved to England shortly after birth. We met and married when you were living in France two years ago, but we then moved to England about a year ago. That seems to have been a mistake, and our marriage hasn't gone well since then. You like other women too much and I have had enough. Despite my annoyance, you will be trying, but failing massively, to win me back.'

'Can't you be the baddy and like other men too much?'

'Not this time Akmal. It will be useful to this mission if you are a bit of a flirt because that will give you an excuse to talk to lots of other women in my presence.'

'Sounds really odd. Not our usual sort of mission. So, to even things up, will it be you that will talk to the men?'

'Yes, if it seems appropriate.'

'So, what's the deal with the job?'

'It's late now so I will leave full details until the morning. Here's your dossier though, in case you aren't as tired as me, with UK time being an hour behind ours in Paris. It has all of your details in it, and a brief summary of the job you have to do. It looks fairly complex, and there are two parts to it, so it might take the full four weeks to complete. One important thing is that, unusually, we do have another squad working alongside us this time. They will leave from Spain soon and we will meet them in Canada.'

'So now there's three of us! I would still prefer to work alone.'

'Most of the area around Montreal is French speaking so I need you to be helped by a French speaker, but don't worry, the actual *work* done will be only handled by you. Your associate is English/French bilingual, so she will fit in there, but even she is to have a nonactive assistant.'

'You said "she".'

'She is indeed female, but she would murder you as quickly as look at you so no funny business with her. She is happily settled with a boyfriend I gather, so keep your hands off of her.'

'I wouldn't cheat on Tegan, but aren't I supposed to be a womaniser in my role?'

'Yes, you are, so maybe do just a little flirting with her, but no more than that. Anyway, we aren't to contact each other initially unless an emergency crops up. You and she will have one task each to complete, and you must initially work independently because both jobs involve the same company. It's all in your dossier.'

'This is all going to be really odd for me, but we'll see how it works out. When you say "emergency" are you expecting any fisty-cuffs?'

'This one is potentially more dangerous than our usual operations Akmal, but more for her than for you, so there's no need to be afraid.'

'I'm not particularly afraid, but that sort of danger isn't what I signed up for. I'm too young to die!' he joked.

'Mmm,' said Marie. 'We'll continue in the morning because it's your bedtime, and I now need to contact the Lebanese authorities to make sure that you can indeed be listed as Lebanese. I must then ring and speak to my wife.'

'OK. Say hello to Simone for me, and tell her that if ever she takes a fancy to men, then I'm available.'

'I know that you fancy Simone, but she's definitely not available and *you've* just said you wouldn't cheat on Tegan. Anyway, I will shoot you if you try to convert Simone!'

'I know you will. I'll see you in the morning.'

Just then Akmal's phone rang.

'Why haven't you called?' raved Tegan. 'You spoiled my weekend away and you haven't even messaged me.'

'Sorry Tegan. I've been with a client since I got off the plane and I thought you'd be in bed by now. It's noisy there, what's going on?'

[Tegan was actually calling from an aeroplane.]

'It must be interference. You know how bad reception can be in this part of Oxford.'

'Sorry. Have you had a good day?'

'Yes, it's been nice not having you around to bother me. I am a little envious of you though. The weather will be lovely in Paris right now, so I'll bet you've taken those swim shorts with you, the ones that you love so much, the ones that you annoy me with by even wearing in the house.'

'You know me well Tegan. You know, I don't like wearing clothes so the shorts are handy at home, and yes, I do have them with me, but I've also brought my Speedos, so you can't bin those while I'm away either!'

'I don't think you'll get away with wearing budgie smugglers in your hotel love, especially when out of your room, like in the restaurant!'

'Very funny. You really hate them don't you?' He laughed. 'You know that I didn't intend to wear them indoors, but if the weather is nice, I might actually use them for their intended purpose, and swim in them!'

'Well, that would make a change. Who is your client? Does she want to buy anything yet?'

'How do you know that it's a she?'

'Just a guess, but then you usually tell me all about your contact if you are meeting a man.'

'Marie is "on my hook". Her company don't usually buy Chinese made refrigeration, but they need a large quantity quickly, and they hope that we can do some tailor-made stuff faster than the competition.'

'And can you?'

'It's what we are known for and why I make so much money.'

'OK. Well, I'm tired now so I just called to say I love you, as the song goes.' Akmal began to sing Stevie Wonder's hit back to her, but Tegan winced and made him stop.

'OK! That's enough. You have a voice like sandpaper against a cheese grater.'

'You say the nicest things.'

'But not today, yes, I've heard that one from you too. You must be getting old Akmal.'

'Remember that I'm younger than you.'

'Thanks for reminding me. See you soon?'

'Hopefully. I Love you.'

'And I love you too gorgeous. Goodnight.'

'Goodnight Tegan.'

Tegan arrived in Barcelona early on Sunday morning. She was met by Gustav at Aeropuerto de Barcelona airport at about half past midnight (UK time) and thirty minutes later they had arrived at his flat in Badalona.

'How was the flight?'

'Not too bad at all. To get a direct flight I needed to drive to London Gatwick which is a fair old distance. It took me an hour and a half to get there, it being Saturday. Akmal only had to drive to Heathrow, which is less than thirty minutes away.'

'Are you tired?'

'Very. I just want to sleep. Is my usual room ready?'

'It is indeed,' said Gustav.

Once in her room, Tegan partially unpacked. She removed a small device from her suitcase and switched it on. She entered some data that she found on her mobile phone and waited. After a while she smiled.

'So he is indeed in Paris,' she thought to herself. She turned off the device, packed it away, and went to bed.

Chapter 2

'Where am I off to this time?' asked Tegan, as she and Gustav breakfasted together.

'You have a ticket to fly to Montreal, Canada,' replied Gustav.

'Oh. That's further afield than we usually work so what's the deal there?'

'I'll give you your usual dossier of information to read on the plane.'

'Yes, security, I was forgetting, it's been a while since I went out on a mission. When is the flight then Gustav?'

'Your flight is scheduled for 2.15pm this afternoon but with recent problems it's likely that it will leave later than that. It's a direct flight though so you'll probably be in Montreal around 11pm tonight, which is about 5pm Montreal time. I'll fill you in with some personal details now, but you can read the full dossier on the plane.'

'Who will I be for this mission?'

'You are Tegan Durand, born in Switzerland and currently resident in the UK, and you will be an accountant for the non-existent firm of Appleby Brothers. Though fictional, this company does appear online, it does have a headquarters, and somebody will be there to answer any queries should anybody ring to confirm that you are genuine. If they want to check whether you are available, the staff there will be able to confirm that you work for them, but they will divulge no information about you personally, and say that you are currently out of the office. If anybody calls who is desperate for accounting services, our staff will direct them to the real accountancy firm for whom they also work. I know that you are an accountant anyway so that cover seemed a good idea. You are visiting Montreal because you have separated from your long-term boyfriend and you are looking to have a holiday before making a new start with somebody else.'

'So, I'm on holiday and looking for a new boyfriend?'

'Yes, in essence, that's what you are doing.'

'That sounds like fun. Out of interest, who would have carried out this job if I hadn't been available?'

'Now why would you want to know that?'

'Just curious. I wondered whether the job has been waiting for *me*, or whether I just happened to become available for a job that is already prepared.' Gustav looked at her curiously.

'It did look for a while as though I would have to do the job myself, so I'm glad that you became available.'

'So, it's just a coincidence that I am doing this particular assignment?' asked Tegan, with an odd level of insistence in her voice.

'It is a coincidence Tegan, but you will have access to another operative this time, should an emergency arise. He is playing the role of a womaniser, so you will fit much better than I would because you may need to develop a rapport with him. He doesn't yet know any of this by the way.'

'Do we know anything about the chap I will work with?'

'You should know better than to ask about an active participant Tegan.'

'Wow. That's me told then. Will we lunch at the airport?'

'Yes, we will eat there, so I want to leave here at about noon, and it's only a few minutes' drive. You will be met in Montreal, in the usual manner.'

'OK. I'll go and freshen up, and I'll see you later.'

Meanwhile, Akmal and Marie had met up in the hotel restaurant for breakfast. After opting for what he considered to be a typically French breakfast (croissants and hot chocolate), Akmal had asked Marie about their flight.

'When do we leave then old fruit?'

'Old fruit? You can pack that in for a start.'

'We are supposed to be divorcing so I might keep calling you "old fruit", just to get that reaction!'

'Tu êtes un pillock. Pas étonnant que je vous divorce!'

'Thanks. I think I got the message there. It sounds like this cover might work out after all.'

'Peut-être.'

'The plane?'

'The flight is scheduled for 12.20pm and we should be in Montreal at about 8pm, which is 2pm in Montreal. The airport is just around the corner from here, so we'll leave at 11.00am. Get packed before then, but you have a few hours free if you want to explore, or if you need to buy anything?'

'What's the weather like in Montreal in May?'

'The current forecast is for rain over the next few days with temperatures around 15 degrees max. Why do you want to know?'

'I've brought my Speedos for swimming and sunbathing in, but it sounds like I won't need them in Montreal.'

'You'd better not wear Speedos anyway. Don't forget the reason you gave for wanting to be from the Lebanon. *They* might reveal that you really aren't Lebanese.'

'Charming. I think I'd better go and incinerate them then.'

'Bonne idée. See you at 11.'

Akmal and Marie's flight was delayed slightly, and they left Charles De Gaulle airport at 12.45pm.

Tegan's plane was only slightly late taking off, and her plane left Barcelona International Airport at 2.35pm.

Though neither yet knew about the activities of the other, Tegan and Akmal had both spent their flight studying the dossier that they had been given. The dossiers were identical, and made for interesting, but slightly confusing reading. Their mission, which they were to work on at the same time, but individually, was centred on some unusual activity around Montreal.

- A significant number of fake audio systems have been sold worldwide. This wouldn't seem all that unusual in this day and age but these, like the ones made by the original designers, were made in China and were very very similar to the real things, so close in fact that it seems that they must have been made in the same factory. The fake systems were copies of the "RUMP Audio TR450 *Høyeste*", which is one of a series of compact hifi units that are designed in Norway but made in China to an extremely exacting specification. The genuine systems would retail at about $26,999 Canadian dollars, are beautifully finished and, once one is ordered, it's audio performance would be tailored to the customer's own specific requirements. Only about 500 are made per year, and each is made unique by the addition of an embellishment such as a jewel, a child's thumb print image, or artwork, also tailored exactly to what the customer wants. They are bought by the world's elite, especially younger people like football players and contemporary singers. In audio terms they sound like units that are much bigger, and visually they look astonishing. The copies though are very very good, and are only distinguishable because they don't have a serial number that corresponds to RUMP's database. Customers who had inadvertently bought them also found that the unique sound tailoring wasn't quite what they had expected, but they couldn't find any way to return them or to communicate with the company from which they were bought. The fakes had been purchased from a website that had nothing to do with RUMP Audio and the genuine company have had to fend off many complaints and attempted lawsuits.

- Fake weapons have also been found which are copies of those made by RUMP's firearms subsidiaries. These fakes work pretty well for copies, but an exploding pistol brought one of the fakes to the authorities' attention and others have been taken away from individuals who have been arrested on firearms charges. Intelligence suggests that around ten *thousand* of these fakes are in circulation. RUMP doesn't market firearms under the "RUMP" name; they have a range of brands that they use and apply to each type of weapon. They mainly specialise in rifles for the American market, so Canada seems like a good place to headquarter the fake company. The authorities haven't been able to extract any data about the fake company from the dark web, where they are sold quite freely, and nobody seems to know where they are made.

- Nobody has yet been able to take down the fake websites that sell the RUMP audio products. This is a major concern for the authorities in Canada because there is obviously a very able and sophisticated team preparing the sites, and the potential for destructive internet activity, such as ransomware seems high.

Both Tegan and Akmal had wondered how the company had got the name "RUMP". This was simple enough, the company was founded by the acquisition of twelve failing companies, most of which were wound down by their new owner, a woman that bears the name Erica Trumpe. She hadn't wanted to be confused with the big American Corporation, or the ex-President, or the snooker player, of a similar name, so she lost the T and e and continued with the rump of the twelve companies. The name was born. Some had suggested to her that "RUMP" wasn't a brilliant name for an audio company, but she would always point out that most HiFi systems have names that can sound odd, especially when read by those that speak a different language. She would add that style and quality always sells, which in these instances was absolutely true.

Akmal and Marie's plane touched down in Montreal at 3.25pm Montreal time.

Tegan's plane landed there shortly afterwards, at 4.10pm.

Both Tegan and Akmal had spent some time on the plane reading the dossier, but also a substantial amount of time asleep; they had been exhausted by travelling so much and they knew that their sleep might be irregular for the next few weeks. Marie on the other hand had managed to read an entire novel.

Akmal and Marie left the airport quite quickly, they only had a relatively small amount of luggage to collect, and passport control was surprisingly fast. Tegan had to wait a little longer for her luggage, and passport control had a longer queue, but even she was on her way by 5.15pm. She had been met by a young woman called Camille Belanger who had caught Tegan's attention by waving a card on which had been written "Tegan v Tegan v Tegan". This was the organisation's way of announcing that they worked for the organisation, with minimum attention being drawn to the greeter or the agent.

Both agents and their partners been booked into the same hotel in Saint-Jérôme, a suburban town about 60km northwest of Montreal. Marie collected a hire car from the airport while Camille used a car that she had bought from a used car dealer in Montreal. Akmal and Marie arrived at the hotel first, and Marie forewarned him about their sleeping arrangements.

'Akmal, we are to stay in a room *together*, but don't worry, we have single beds. We have been provided with a very large room to give us the maximum amount of privacy during the operation, and the two beds are positioned so that they don't face each other. The room has a large and very modern en suite bathroom with a shower, a bath, and a full range of other washing facilities.'

'You didn't tell me *that* before we left! I wonder what Tegan would make of it if she knew?' Marie didn't reply to that. She was to play no part in the job that Akmal was to carry out, but she was expected to guide him in the ways and the language of the region, and to help with his cover. Marie and Akmal's room was on floor one and Marie began her part by instigating a minor argument at reception.

'I told you to behave!' shouted Marie. This was in response to a broad smile that Akmal had worn when a very pretty young woman had handed him their key. As if to annoy Marie more he responded by saying to the young woman 'Don't mind her, she's my soon to be divorced wife.' The young woman smiled back at Akmal and glared at Marie.

'Upstairs now!' said Marie.

Tegan and Camille arrived about thirty minutes after Akmal and Marie, and they had been provided with almost adjacent rooms which were rather smaller than that shared by Marie and Akmal, but they too had rather large en suite bathrooms and very large built-in cupboards.

'Remember that we are posing as "best friends from uni" and that we're in Montreal to catch up with the past, and to possibly meet new boyfriends. We have just broken up with long term partners, so no mention of Akmal in other people's presence Tegan.'

'Fair enough Camille. So, we chat up every handsome dude that we meet?'

'Not everyone Tegan! Have some pride!' They laughed loudly, attracting a stare from the concierge.

Camille and Tegan were booked into rooms on floor two. A young porter had greeted them at the main door of the hotel and taken their bags up the stairs and put them directly into their rooms, earning a pretty good tip for his trouble. Tegan waited for the porter to return to reception before going up to her room while Camille remained at the reception desk to fill in the paperwork and sign them both in.

'Are you on holiday?' asked the receptionist.

'We are old uni friends, and we are here to celebrate the breakup from both of our former boyfriends. We hope to find some new, better ones here!'

The receptionist smiled. 'Then have a nice stay.'

'I am sure that we will,' replied Camille. On the way to her room Camille spotted Tegan chatting to a man on the stairs. When she saw Camille Tegan said goodbye to him and joined her to go up to their room.

'Who was he?' asked Camille.

'A man from England who is staying here on holiday. He's looking for a new girlfriend. He was nice actually.'

'And?'

'And what?'

'Will you be "seeing" him?'

'No. He's going home tomorrow. I couldn't cheat on Akmal anyway, but I suppose I have just cemented our cover.'

'We'd better go up,' said Camille with a smile and they walked up the remaining very plush stairs to their rooms.

'I'm looking forward to going in to freshen up,' said Tegan.

'That's a good idea, I'll do the same,' responded Camille. 'But join me later though. I could use some company for a while.'

'Look Camille, my door's open,' said Tegan as she looked over at her room. 'That porter can return his tip. Anybody could have got in.'

'Tegan, relax. It's only a few minutes since we left reception and anyway, we'd have heard somebody break into your room, it's as silent as the grave in here and you were chatting to a chap on the stairs. You will remember to come along later won't you, but not too much later.'

'I'll be along in an hour or so. Get the drinks in.'

'Will do,' said Camille.

After over an hour and a half had passed Camille had become impatient, so she went and knocked on Tegan's door.

'Tegan, the drinks are getting warm!'

'I'll be with you in a few minutes,' was heard from the other side of the door.

'OK,' shouted Camille.

Tegan joined Camille about ten minutes later. She appeared damp, as though just out of the shower.

'I really needed to freshen up,' declared Tegan. 'I hate aeroplanes.'

'Must have been very grubby to need such a long shower,' thought Camille, feeling anxious now for some reason.

Marie and Akmal stayed in their room on that Sunday evening, having eaten on the plane. Akmal telephoned Tegan at about a quarter after midnight UK time (7.15pm in Montreal) using his own phone, but he activated the "fake origin" app that the company had supplied. He dialled Paris into the app then telephoned Tegan. Tegan spotted that the call was from Akmal and activated her own cloaking app before answering.

'Hi Akmal. You've left it a bit late to call, haven't you? It's past midnight you realise and it's past one in Paris. You should be asleep. I hope that you don't want any kinky late-night chat because I am tired.'

'And I love you too Tegan,' replied Akmal. 'I just called to say hello. I'll say goodnight then.' He hung up and turned off his phone.

'Problem?' asked Marie.

'No. I think I've called her at a bad time. I will phone her again when I have calmed down, probably by next Thursday.'

'Never mind, you've got me and I'm here for you!'

'You are married, and to a woman! You wouldn't be chatting me up now, would you?' Marie knew that Akmal fancied the pants off her.

'Just trying to get you excited Akmal!'

'You might be succeeding there Marie, but we'd better get some sleep before I try to convert you!'

'Goodnight Akmal.'

'Goodnight Marie.'

It was while Camille and Tegan were about to discuss arrangements for tomorrow's breakfast, and for the week ahead, that Akmal had made that call to Tegan. Having only heard the conversation at Tegan's end, Camille asked Tegan whether everything was OK. They had discussed Akmal on the way to the hotel and Tegan had done nothing but gush with enthusiasm for Akmal, so she had been surprised by Tegan's brusque response to him on the phone.

'Is it wise to upset Akmal?'

23

'Perhaps not but I am tired, and I know him well. We'd have been on half an hour if he had started, and don't forget that he left first. He can expect me to be a bit narked.'

'Does he often jet off to Paris at short notice?'

'Not really. About twice a year.'

'Why does he go?'

'It's with his work. He's a salesman specialising in refrigeration, so sometimes he has to go to their other branch to sort things out. He gets paid well for his trouble.'

'I suppose he spends the money on football and drink like most men.'

'Actually, I'm the football fan, and I play for Ruislip ladies' team. He usually buys me something nice with his extra money.'

'I don't think you've much to complain about there then Tegan.'

'I take your point. I am tired though.'

'Fair enough,' said Camille. 'Shall we meet for breakfast in the hotel refectory at 8am!'

'Definitely. I will see you in the morning.'

With that, Tegan returned to her own room and left Camille to herself. It was only late evening in Montreal, but Camille was asleep as soon as her head hit the pillow. She slept heavily and her alarm got her out of bed at 9am. She ought to have woken at least two hours earlier than that, and she hadn't been expecting to sleep that long, so she was pleased that she had remembered to set that alarm.

Chapter 3

Monday dawned bright and clear, and Marie awoke to find Akmal already awake and stretching while still in bed.

'Shouldn't you be getting up?' she said. 'You have work to do.'

'And good morning to you too my love! Yes, you are right, I suppose that I had better get up, but this is a lovely comfortable bed and I'd like to stay in it all day. But then I'm pretty much awake now, and my nagging wife is demanding that I get up, so there's no point in lounging around.' Akmal threw back the covers, got out of bed and stretched again. 'I like to stretch in the morning because it helps the circulation get moving.'

'Akmal, you have nothing on,' said Marie.

'Whoops, sorry, I forgot. He grabbed the duvet and wrapped it around himself.

'But then you aren't bothered surely, not being interested in men.'

'That doesn't mean I want to see a *naked* man in my room.'

'Whoops, I really wasn't thinking there. I'm sorry.'

'Surely not.'

'I do apologise Marie. I never wear anything in bed, and I hadn't thought about things like this. I'll get some sleep shorts or something.'

'Good idea.'

He donned his boxers and trousers and began to find a suitable business shirt. When he stood up from rummaging in his suitcase, he turned to see that Marie was now out of bed, completely naked and heading for the shower.

'Now that's just not fair,' he said.

'C'est si facile de taquiner les hommes,' she replied with a laugh.

'So, you deliberately get out of bed naked, especially when you are as gorgeous as that, and it's to be taken as a *tease*, but I get out of bed naked, totally without thinking, and you are offended! Either way, after that display just now, I think I need to take a *cold* shower today, and before you I think.' Marie laughed heartily. She noted that he had understood the French.

'You'll have to wait until I've finished,' she replied and dashed into the en suite bathroom. Akmal's face had become a picture of misery.

Akmal sighed and while Marie was in the en suite getting ready for the day ahead, he opened his laptop and set to work. His job today was to find out from where the website selling the RUMP HiFi originated, and to try to use that knowledge to infiltrate the company behind it. The company selling the fake hifi equipment wasn't pretending to be the "RUMP" company itself, but an official retailer for "RUMP" equipment. The fact that "RUMP AUDIO" didn't have any official retailers was handy for the fake sellers because nobody would be directed to any other retailers by RUMP's own website. That way, unless a customer checked with "RUMP AUDIO" themselves, they wouldn't know that it

26

shouldn't be possible to buy from anybody else. With a profit margin of $18,000 Canadian Dollars per device, it was a lucrative business.

Canadian authorities had advised Akmal's organisation that they believed that the fake company had so far sold 550 units, meaning a loss to "RUMP AUDIO" of over nine million Canadian Dollars (over 6 million US Dollars) in just six months. After quite a lot of work by them, and using data from defrauded customers, it had become their view that the fake company was based somewhere near to Montreal, though customers' units were shipped directly from somewhere in China.

Marie emerged from the shower wearing a huge towel and was pleased to see that Akmal was working.

'Nice to see that you already busy. Will you explain to me what you are doing Akmal?'

'Yes, provided that you show me proof that you are an employee of the organisation!'

'Do you want a thick ear?'

'No thanks,' replied Akmal, and he gave up trying to be clever. 'I've just done a routine search, and the search engine took only seconds to find that the hifi in question can be bought from "RUMP AUDIO" directly, or from an apparently Vancouver based company called "Equipe Audio (Canada)" but look at this Marie.'

He opened the "Equipe Audio" website and showed her a fairly bland page that carried pictures and prices of the equipment that they sold. 'Not a great webpage is it! It seems that they offer quite a range of equipment, from basic to prestige, with a big thing being made of their ability to sell

"RUMP AUDIO" devices. They boast of being the only Canadian retailer to offer this brand *and* that they can offer a small price reduction because of their low overheads.'

'So that's the company behind the HiFi fraud.'

'So it would seem Marie. I'm surprised that people would buy expensive kit from such an apparently mundane company. Watch while I open my tracer app.' Marie wondered whether he had any clue that the app was probably the work of his girlfriend. He opened the tracer app that was installed in an encrypted part of his laptop, disconnected from the hotel's wifi and then connected to the local 5G network. 'The app needs to be left running and my stomach is rumbling. The tracer app can take a long time to run so can we head down for breakfast now?'

'Remember that we have a twin operative looking into the weapons angle and that secrecy is initially paramount if we are to make real money out of this case. The other operative is to have first breakfast sitting. We can eat from 8.30 onwards. What time is it now?'

'8.10.'

'I will get dressed. Remember that there are biscuits over there.'

'Fine. I'll try to resist them.' Akmal watched his tracer program for a while, deep in thought. Marie emerged quite quickly, looking as beautiful as always.

'Look Marie, about earlier when I got up with, you know, nothing on. I was insensitive and I'm sorry. I genuinely forgot that you were there, and that I was naked. Remember that I usually come on these missions on my own, so I don't normally need to think about sleepwear. I am truly sorry.'

'Don't worry, I have seen naked men before and you are no different. You've seen one naked man you've seen them all. Anyway, we are supposed to be married so it's perhaps appropriate that we have seen each other without clothes. Perhaps we should have sex to make sure that we really know each other.' Akmal couldn't believe his ears. There was no way he would cheat on Tegan, but then he realised that she was still teasing him again anyway.

'Yeah, thanks but no thanks, and anyway, where's *your* apology? I didn't expect to see a naked woman in my room today. Shouldn't you say sorry too?'

'Were you offended or upset when you saw me sans vêtements?'

Akmal became flustered. 'No, but that's not the point,' seemed to him to be a reasonable reply.

'You wouldn't pass as Lebanese by the way,' said Marie with a very serious face.

'Charming. You missed nothing then, and when did you get so good at estimating sizes? Anyway, I thought you women weren't interested in studying naked men, even straight women tell me that!'

'I lived a while in Lebanon. There wasn't much else to do there.'

'Isn't it breakfast time yet?' pleaded Akmal.

'Yes, it is.'

'Thank God for that.' They went down to breakfast, in elevator number 3, without a word passing between them.

At the same time, Tegan and Camille were returning to their rooms in elevator number 1, and Tegan went to her room alone. She had breakfasted on pancakes and maple syrup and, together with lots of very dark coffee, had enjoyed them tremendously.

'You have to be in Canada to enjoy those properly,' she thought to herself.

Once in her room she extracted the "device" from her suitcase. It had been built by her whilst she was at uni about eight years previously and she had designed it to make access to the so called "dark web" much easier for anybody that wanted to search for illicit materials. Once it was built, she realised that she could make a small fortune by retailing the device, but she acknowledged that she would need to continually update the software to make it useable into the future. It would, of course, have been very valuable to the less honest members of the world's community so she considered very carefully what she might do with it once she had no further use for it. In any case her use of the device hadn't gone unnoticed by the organisation, and they had contacted her in 2015 and made her an offer to buy the device, which she accepted, although it had really been a lease. Tegan, together with all of her software updates, had also become a part of the package. She had rebuilt the device a number of times to embrace improvements in chipset speeds and die sizes and, though it was now hundreds of times more powerful, it was also much smaller and more portable.

Operationally, it was understood that the organisation would never call on her for her services, she would always let them know when she was available for work. She was doing rather well financially from this but had only been able to solve about sixty percent of the tasks she was given. It was unusual for her to be working so far from home, and this time she didn't seem as comfortable as she had been in previous operations.

To prepare for this particular mission, Camille had read about the dark web. She was surprised to read that a recent study into the dark web had shown that the number of listings that could harm an *enterprise* had risen by 20% in only 3 years. Of all the listings they found (excluding those selling drugs), 60% could potentially harm enterprises, and it was these people that the organisation had been set up, very many years ago, to identify, and hopefully to resolve. She noted that, whilst accessing the dark web isn't all that difficult for anybody with some IT knowledge, (normal search engines don't produce hits from it), actually entering and communicating with sites or their owners can be extremely difficult. She concluded that this was why Tegan was so valuable because she had kept up with dark web developments, and updated her device accordingly. She wondered by how much things had grown since that study was done.

Tegan connected the device to the organisation's supplied phone using a standard USB C cable and, once energised, the device used the phone's nice large screen as an input output device. Tegan recalled the contents of the dossier and entered the relevant search criteria. The device asked whether it should use wifi or 5G, to which the reply was '5G'. It then asked how many search results were required and she entered 'ALL'. She hid the whole lot in a cupboard and went to find Camille.

Meanwhile Akmal had enjoyed a breakfast similar to that eaten by Tegan and had returned to his room with Marie. Once there he switched on his laptop.

'Look Marie, the tracer app has finished and provided an IP address for "Equipe Audio". The IP address is the internet's way of finding a server, like a street address finds where you live Marie. I'll just communicate with it by sending a 'ping' to that IP address.'

'With you so far, but what's a ping Akmal?'

'A ping is a small program that asks a web server for a reply, but does nothing else. It allows an operator like me to read the IP address. Look Marie, there's been an immediate response. Excellent. Now let's see how good their security is.' He pinged the address again.

'Do you see that Marie? There was no response this time. This is exactly what I had expected. The fake RUMP retailer's server has realised that the site had just been pinged but not accessed, and so it has changed its own IP address. Their server is sufficiently intelligent to recognise the difference between a potential customer and the ping program and so it has instantly changed its IP address.'

'So, customers who would like to buy audio equipment can't now be directed to their website because the IP address has changed?'

'Unfortunately, that's not the case Marie. It's just like the fake company has moved premises. Same company but new address. The server has assigned the new IP address to "Equipe Audio", like I would tell the post office if I changed address, so customers can still buy their products, and this way the company can still operate fully while anybody that tried to find where the website was based would be unsuccessful.'

'So, every time anybody tries to find the company server they just move. Can they keep doing this forever?'

'Not forever, but for long enough. I was fully expecting this response because the Canadian authorities would have already tried the same process. Like many websites, the company supplying the HiFi gear has no premises address on their website. Once an order is placed by a customer, the equipment will be despatched directly to them from China, and monies will go into a holding fund. That fund will be emptied regularly but money will go via so many "banks" and systems that its destination is impossible to trace. All that the authorities know is that the website operation is somewhere near Montreal. They weren't sure whether the company itself was based near to the server and that's why they called us in.'

'Seems fair enough.'

'Watch, I will now activate a different part of the program and leave it running. This is the clever part and I'll show you the results when we get back.'

'Back from where?'

'We are supposed to be on holiday Marie!'

With little else to do while the program ran, he and Marie drove into Montreal to see the sites, to eat and to shop. They were blown away by the size of everything and quickly forgot that they were not *really* there on holiday!

Camille and Tegan had spent the morning staying fit. They ran for about five kilometres, swam for about thirty minutes and then did some muscle work at the gym. Feeling much better for that they had eaten a large and leisurely lunch. Tegan ended up going back to her room at 2.30pm, coincidentally about the same time that Akmal had been browsing sleep shorts in a large Montreal men's outfitter! He ended up buying seven pairs of the very plainest; he didn't want any more daft comments from Marie.

Back in her room, Tegan looked around at the fairly drab surroundings she found herself in. Though thoroughly modern, the room's total lack of character had become glaringly evident in the bright afternoon sunshine that streamed in through the large windows that hotel rooms seemed invariably to have. 'It could be worse,' she thought. 'I don't intend to be here very long, so I suppose that the décor isn't really that important. Anyway, I'd better get on with looking at these search results.'

Tegan opened up the device and found that it had come up with twenty-four possible matches. She wrapped up a parcel of twenty of what appeared to be the least likely suspects (or those that were definitely too far away to investigate) and despatched them to the organisation. This was done via the usual secure channels. The organisation had been primed to receive those and it was expected that one of their members would begin work on them immediately. Tegan then studied the remaining four results and realised that all four were within driving distance.

'Time to hire a car,' she said to Camille after strolling the few steps to her room and entering without knocking.

'What's wrong with my car?' asked Camille.

'Something plush and environmentally good is better for me I think,' replied Tegan.

Meanwhile, Akmal had returned to the hotel, and he found that his laptop had finished its work.

'Look Marie, the app's done well. The company's new IP address has been found but this time the app has locked it and the complex route to the company's server has been unravelled. The company is indeed based somewhere near Montreal, in Saint-Laurent in fact.'

Akmal was delighted that the app had worked first time; he hadn't expected their server to be as basic as it obviously was. He realised that he could use that vulnerability in his "negotiations" with the company.

'I am going to communicate with them now and I think it best if you don't watch this. It might break a few laws and it's best if you don't know about it!'

'OK, I was getting bored with it anyway. I'll read a book.'

'Bye Marie.'

'Bye Akmal.'

Akmal set about sending the fraudsters a note. He used the organisation's "Direct Message" system which was a program that emulated a piece of software that was similar to a trojan horse virus and is often used by criminals to produce "ransomware". This usually locks computers on a network until a ransom is paid. This system allowed Akmal to send a message that wouldn't stop the company's website from operating but would make sure that all terminals on their server would see just his message instead of their desktop. Nobody at their end would be able to remove it or allow them to process orders. He wrote them a "letter" and wrapped it inside a very decorative envelope that would float on their screens until somebody opened it. It read as follows:

35

'Hi Folks.

My name is Ibori, and I am on holiday in Canada. I am from Europe, and I am quite well known there because I take fair to middling websites and make them super cool and exciting. Most companies that I work with find that their income doubles after I have finished my work on their website. I am very very good.

Be warned that I only provide my service once, and I only offer it once. This is your chance to double your profit, which I estimate will take your income to eighteen million Canadian Dollars every six months. That's more that twelve million US dollars.

You already know how good I am. I have found out where you are, who the real owners are, and I have stopped your server from changing its IP address. If I tell the authorities your new IP address, they will find you easily and that will be curtains for your operation. In fact, they are possibly searching for your IP address at this very moment, waiting for it to freeze. It will then only take them about 24 hours for them to find you.

So, I will offer my services for twenty-four hours. If I haven't heard from you within that time, I will leave your server locked. I might even take it down or completely lock it up for you, depending on my mood. I have the power to put a program onto the web that will prevent any new website with your "name" on it, or any site selling any of the very lucrative "RUMP" devices (that I note you sell illegally), to cease to function within minutes.

I already have a fantastic new website to demonstrate to you, one that will make your current operation look thoroughly immature. I am free tomorrow afternoon, can deliver by tomorrow evening and then I will disappear. I will expect to meet your entire operation in one go, all of you in the same room together. I am not faffing about waiting while you call others to discuss my offer. ALL OF YOU!

*Just to be clear, I am not cheap, but I only require one payment, in cash, upon completion of the work. To be even more crystal, you can't get out of this. You are entirely web based and any new server output you produce will be quickly removed, by me, if you don't play ball. I have given you a unique identifier and neither you nor anybody else can remove it. I also have some very **serious and powerful friends** who won't let you try to come after me so don't even consider arranging for me to be "met" after our negotiations come to an end.*

Click the link at the end of this note and tell me where and when you want to meet, provided that it is tomorrow afternoon. If you want to meet in your premises just say so, I know where you are already, so you don't need to reveal anything in your reply. Just say "our place".

I look forward to hearing from you and remember that your operation is now being closely monitored by me and you won't have any customer access until this meeting is arranged.

Ibori.

Chapter 4

Camille had her head in a book when Tegan walked into her room. Slightly disturbed by the sound she jumped massively and the book that she had been reading fell to her side, and her place was lost.

'Thanks Tegan. I've lost my place now and I was just getting to a good part.'

'Sorry Camille, I thought you were expecting me, so I just came in. I am beginning to believe our cover story I suppose. Is it a scary story?'

'Yes, it damned well is,' replied Camille. 'Never mind, I suppose I'll get back into it tonight. What are we up to next then Tegan, that's if you want me to come with you.'

'Of course I want you to come with me. You can watch my back for me.'

'Just let me get ready,' said Camille, still rather annoyed with her.

Camille and Tegan drove out of the local car rental depot in their shiny silver Toyota Prius at about teatime, and, with Camille driving, they set off to study the area. All of the companies that Tegan's device had identified as potentially suspicious, and therefore been flagged as worthy of a visit, were in Montreal itself, rather than being in towns close by.

All they had to do was to drive along Saint-Patrick Street and each of her suspects was in a street or avenue off of that.

Tegan had committed a sort of hit list to memory; these were companies that seemed to have the ability to hide large consignments of weapons without raising any suspicions. She decided that it would be wise to visit the *least* likely company to be a weapons storage venue first, and she gave directions to Camille.

"Curioso Pet Supplies (Canada) Ltd." wasn't far from the car hire company and the journey only took just over ten minutes. Camille parked some way away from the Curioso Pet Supplies premises, deciding not to use their car park in case there were security cameras, and they didn't want the Toyota to be recognised.

They studied the outside of the building before going in and then she and Tegan entered, through a sort of air lock, into a large industrial looking building containing many cardboard boxes, and a counter bearing the label "TRADE ONLY". There was nobody at that counter and there was no bell or other summoning device.

'Bonjour,' shouted Camille. No reply.

'Hello!' shouted Tegan. No reply to that either so she and Tegan felt empowered to look around. They could see no security cameras and none of Tegan's portable devices had sounded any warnings. They found that they were able to walk freely amongst the boxes, so they studied those, visually and by noting their smell. Having examined about ten percent of the stock and finding that everything definitely smelt of pet food, and none of the boxes seemed unduly heavy, they decided to look behind the Trade counter. They found nothing but bills and receipts and they, on examination, seemed genuine enough. This had taken them over half an hour, so they decided not to push their luck too much, and to leave the place until somebody was actually there. They had just reached the door as a man entered wearing overalls.

'Hi. Can I help you? I am sorry I wasn't here when you arrived, but Louis isn't in today and I had to deliver an order.'

'Hi,' said Camille. 'Don't worry about not being here to greet us, but we are considering opening an online pet care centre and are trying to find out where we can buy stock to retail on that site. We wondered whether you could maybe help us.'

'We only sell very large quantities of pet food so we would only make a contract with a company that could order at least $4,000 Canadian dollars' worth of stock each week. Will your site be likely to sell that amount?'

'We don't know yet but that seems unlikely.' She gave the young man a very winning smile and asked whether they could talk to him about what was likely to sell well. He replied that ordinarily he would love to do that because he lived for animal care, but with Louis unavailable he couldn't at the moment.

'When will Louis be back do you think?'

'Don't know. He's supposed to be my partner but he's never here and he's likely off with a woman or on a beer binge.' He looked haggard as he said that but added 'Sorry ladies, that's none of your business and I apologise for saying it. You could call in tomorrow if you want.'

'Perhaps we will. You look busy so we'll leave you to it.'

'I am!' He showed his "to do" list to Tegan. It looked very full indeed. Back in the car Tegan turned to Camille.

'My French is good but there were a few bits there that were a bit fast for me.' Camille recounted the conversation and they both agreed that this looked an unlikely venue for hiding crates full of weapons. Normally the "front" operation would be extremely well run and operating on relatively light trade so that no suspicion would fall on them. This place clearly didn't fit into that category.

'They could of course be banking on that,' said Camille.

'I'll look into the foundations of this business when I get back to the hotel and see what I can dig up. Perhaps Louis is not all he seems,' replied Tegan.

'It's 5pm now,' said Camille. 'I'm starving. Can we leave things until tomorrow now and organise dinner?'

'Oui, bien sur,' replied Tegan. 'Somewhere nice I think!'

Back at the hotel, Akmal and Marie were also discussing their need for food and were considering going down for dinner.

'Our time slot is 6pm until 7.30pm if we want to eat here,' said Marie.

'I am starving, so we'll stay here if you want, and can we order from our room so that it's ready when we get downstairs?'

'Certainly can.'

'Tourtière sounds nice. It says here that it's meat pie.'

'Typical Englishman, pie and mash at all times, except when you are eating boiled meat!'

'Actually, it says here that it comes with roasted vegetables or salad. I think I will have both.'

'Then I will not be a typical French woman and have the same as you. I don't have meat pie at home. It will make a change.'

'Will you suggest a dessert?' asked Akmal.

'Pouding chomeur is a bit heavy after meat pie but you will only get it in Canada.'

'OK, Order me that please. I will shower and then we could go down together.'

'I will go down first if you aren't out of the shower by six. Remember that we aren't supposed to be getting along,' said Marie.

'Good point. I'll take my time then.'

Akmal and Marie needn't have worried about meeting Tegan and Camille because they had found a quiet restaurant in Montreal for dinner. They both had a Canadian salad followed by a rather decadent Blueberry Grunt with fresh cream rather than ice cream. They sat in the lounge area of the restaurant after eating and discussed their day's work.

'I feel that there is something suspicious about that pet food store,' said Tegan. 'It seemed OK while we were there but now I think that the apparently frequent disappearance of the partner needs investigating,'

'Good, but that's enough for me for today. I'm tired, probably jet lag!' said Camille.

'You haven't flown very far Camille duBois! I should be the one who is suffering jet lag and I'm fine. Incidentally, that waiter over there keeps looking over at you. Do you know him?' asked Tegan.

'No I don't, I've never been to this part of Canada before. Should I look over at *him* for a while then?' laughed Camille.

'Why not. We are after all supposed to getting new boys after our breakups.'

'Actually, he looks quite nice. I like a slim man with dark hair. Why don't you go and ask him to come over.'

'I think I'll do just that.' Philippe arrived promptly.

'Madame?'

Camille ordered two more glasses of wine and asked the waiter to bring them over personally. When he did so the conversation flowed and it turned out that, like Camille, he was originally from France and they both had family near Paris. They swapped phone numbers and he and Camille arranged to have a night out the next day.

'That was fast work Camille!'

'Might as well have some fun while I'm here,' said Camille as the waiter disappeared to serve other people. 'We'll have to get you fixed up now.'

'Perhaps I'll hit it off with this young man that's supposed to be working alongside us here. We ought to meet soon I think.'

'He's probably hideous,' said Camille. They both laughed.

'We must wait until the organisation says we need to meet though and that might be ages yet.'

'Has Akmal telephoned since Sunday?'

'No. He'll be in a huff. Typical man thinks about nothing but sex. He'll be in touch eventually. I wonder whether Philippe is a typical man?'

'I hope so!' said Camille, and they laughed again.

Back at the hotel, Marie and Akmal had enjoyed their dinner and decided to take a bottle of wine back to their room in case they should be spotted by their opposite numbers. When they got back there Akmal opened his laptop and found that Equipe Audio had replied. They had summoned him to be at their office, alone, at 12.30 pm the following day. That meant that he had work to do, and it had to be done that night, so the wine would have to wait.

Chapter 5

Tuesday dawned clear and bright and, while he was still in bed, Akmal heard a beep from the organisation's phone. It seemed that everything Akmal had requested from the Montreal authorities was to be provided so he began his usual preparation for his meeting. He showered and then covered himself in his very expensive cologne, which always told the client that he was a successful man, which indeed he was. He then donned his formal business suit and, at 8.40am, he and Marie headed down to breakfast.

'What will the condemned man be eating today?' asked Marie.

'Better be something hearty,' replied Akmal. 'It might be my last.'

'Don't be so melodramatic.'

'You started it.'

'It's always my fault, isn't it? I don't know why we ever got married.'

'Neither do I. You are too old for me anyway.'

'Tu est un...' The caustic comment was cut short by the approach of the waiter.

'Madame, Monsieur?'

'Crêpes sirop d'érable et café s'il vous plaît,' said Marie.

'We had pancakes, maple syrup and coffee yesterday,' said Akmal.

'And can you order anything else in French? You are a typical Englishman; over a year of marriage and hardly a word of French have you learned.'

'J'aurai la même chose s'il vous plaît,' replied Akmal.

'Oh very good,' snarled Marie.

'Avec plaisir,' said the waiter as he left them to it.

'I think that we did a good job there,' said Akmal.

'I think we did too. I am actually enjoying this so perhaps I'll leave the organisation and go on the stage.'

'And spoil our marriage? I'd never see you!'

'Pah,' said Marie.

After breakfast, Akmal spent a while doing more careful reading of his research into the owners of "Equipe Audio". The company was led by two men and a woman, comprising a Mr. and Mrs Laguardia and her brother. They were registered as British, but they had all lived in Canada from a very early age. They had parents of four different nationalities including Italian and French and they were all multilingual. Akmal hoped that they wouldn't start speaking Italian because he really couldn't fathom that at all, even though he could do the gestures! There was no family for any of them left in Britain as far as he could tell, but he was a bit worried that he might not be safe when he returned home. He was an industrial trouble-shooter not James Bond, and he was glad that Marie was with him. She would have given 007 quite a run for his money, or so he had heard. He considered that she could probably disarm anybody with her caustic tongue!

He opened his proposed webpage and decided that he was pleased with his work because it looked superb, rather better than that belonging to "RUMP" themselves. He made a mental note to show it to them one day. He then made sure that his tracking chip was working (the scar from its insertion had faded now so if anybody looked, they wouldn't find anything) and he prepared to leave for his meeting.

Marie drove him to a random point outside of Montreal and then returned to the hotel. Akmal then walked the mile or so back in the city and strolled up to the entrance of what looked like a derelict house in a very deserted area. There was no sign of occupation but there was a faded 'For Sale' board and a shiny modern doorbell that seemed to have a camera attached. He rang the bell.

Akmal was concerned when there seemed to have been no reaction to the doorbell, even after his fourth ring, but, after about five minutes, the door was eventually opened.

'Come in. Ibori I assume?'

Akmal entered a hallway from which he could see three rooms. All doors in the house were open and he noted that there was very little furniture in the house. He heard nothing from his detector devices, so he assumed that there were no alarms or outside agencies expecting him. Besides his laptop he only had his organisation phone with him, and he knew that that wouldn't ring just yet.

'Yes, I am indeed Ibori. Good afternoon Mrs Laguardia. I hope I can be of some benefit to you.'

'So do I,' she replied, and she led him into a small windowless room where three men sat on spindly dining chairs. She waved an arm and introduced three men.

47

'My husband Lorenzo, my brother Pierre, and Fernando, who is our technician.'

'Good to meet you,' said Lorenzo. May I know your first name Mr. Ibori?'

'No. That isn't my style, and you couldn't pronounce it anyway!' He had expected the gathering to laugh at that, but nothing stirred at all.

'How do you want to begin?'

'I think you need to show us your goods,' said Fernando.

'I will if you like but I thought we were here on business,' said Akmal with a very cheeky grin.

'This is no game. Get on with it or get out,' said Lorenzo.
Akmal, who was pleased that they all spoke English, opened his laptop and showed them his proposed webpage. Fernando studied it first and, after asking a few questions, showed it to the others.

'How will you deliver this webpage to us?' he asked.

'Once I see the money I will install it for you immediately, and then unlock your servers from my ransomware.'

'You know that what you are doing is illegal, and we could turn you in to the Canadian authorities?' said Lorenzo.

'You won't do that though will you. We are both doing what we do best, even if we are bending the law a little.'

Fernando studied the webpage further.

'Can I see it in action?'

'Certainly. It will take just a few minutes.' Akmal made a show of typing into his laptop and showing Fernando his progress. After 5 minutes the webpage was up and running, though it wasn't actually on the internet, just connected to their servers.

'It's good,' said Fernando.

The others studied the webpage. It was glossy, professional and very easy for customers to use. Between them they placed a number of fake orders, watched for the results, and then declared themselves happy with what they had seen.

'Get the money,' said Fernando to Pierre.

Pierre disappeared for a while and returned with a number of supermarket carrier bags. Akmal counted the cash very carefully.

'That's perfect. I will connect you to the internet and you can begin operating as soon as you want, and I hope that you will do very well with your new website.' He pressed a few keys on his keyboard and Lorenzo declared that the webpage was working, and Fernando confirmed that he now had full control of the server.

'I'll be off then,' said Akmal.

'Won't you stay, have some refreshments?'

'I have other business to attend to,' replied Akmal, and he rose to leave.

'Where can we find you if we need anything else?'

'You can't. You won't see me again. If you do try to find me, or any of my family, your business will be toast. Clear?'

'But what if our new system develops a fault?'

'There is nothing here that Fernando can't fix.'

With that, everybody agreed that business was concluded and Akmal was escorted to the door, but as he stepped out through the front door, police officers appeared as if from nowhere, and all five of them were arrested. They made a show of arresting Akmal as though he had been the target of their operation and even put him in the van before the Lorenzo's. Akmal feigned absolute anger and annoyance in the van. He made it clear that he was furious and demanded to know which of them had "dobbed him in" to the police.

None of the gang protested that it might actually have been Akmal who had told the police about them, which left Akmal a bit surprised and slightly anxious.

They were all processed at the nearest police station but, after a few hours in a cell, Akmal was collected by a member of the Canadian British Embassy. After the official had made it plain that Akmal was still under arrest, he was taken away to the embassy itself, and then he was flown from Toronto to Ottawa and the operation, as far as Akmal was concerned, was over. During the journey to the embassy, he learned that the Lorenzo's had told the police that they had been approached by a hacker who had frozen their website. They said that they would lure him to the empty house and that the authorities would find him there at around 11am. Since the three of them had been running a legitimate business alongside "Equipe Audio" they weren't concerned that the police might also investigate *their* activities. They had had no idea that the police were working with Akmal (and the organisation) and that they themselves had been the real target of the police operation.

The Embassy official told Akmal that arrests had been made in China to coincide with today's activities. The Chinese authorities had located a gang that had coerced a number of Chinese companies, that normally made products for Western companies, to make extra goods. So, for every mobile phone or TV or hifi product that they made for a big-name company, they would make another two. The quality wouldn't need to be as good because they would be sold through a third party at a knock down price, so these additional two were often rejects from the assembly line.

Officials at the British Embassy had booked Akmal into a hotel in Ottawa and, once he had arrived there, he felt that he could relax for the first time since arriving in Canada. He removed most of his clothes and donned a dressing gown. This was much more like it. He actually preferred to just wear a dressing gown at home, but Tegan had objected to that, giving the likelihood of visitors as her main concern, so he would often put on swimwear in case the dressing gown fell open. He had decided against being quite that undressed today, but he would soon be home and he could go back to wearing whatever he wanted, and Tegan could spoil him after his exhausting week.

Unfortunately for Akmal, developments meant that he wouldn't be going home any time soon and, though he didn't know it yet, Marie was to re-join him in Ottawa late on Wednesday night. Before setting off she had wondered how he would take the news that his work in Montreal was not yet finished.

Chapter 6

Back on Tuesday morning, while Akmal had been preparing to meet the Equipe crowd, Tegan and Camille had been following their now usual morning exercise routine. It was a chilly morning, so they had run a bit further than the day before, and then really enjoyed their swim. They had emerged feeling invigorated, but Camille was a bit disappointed that Tegan hadn't asked her about her proposed night out with Philippe, and she certainly didn't want to be first to raise the topic, or to be first to volunteer any information. She actually hadn't made any plans, and she had no idea what Philippe may have intended to do, but she wanted Tegan to at least show some interest.

'Back to my room for a chat?' asked Camille after they had finished their coffee.

'Why not,' replied Tegan, and they returned to Camille's room chatting and looking to all the world like old school friends.

'What have you found out about our friend Louis Albert Belanger?' asked Camille, trying start the conversation.

'I told you yesterday all that I knew.'

'Haven't you found out anything new today?'

'There's plenty of time. Be cool. Enjoy yourself a bit more.'

'You won't be back in the arms of Akmal for ages at this rate,' laughed Camille.

'A change is as good as a rest for both of us. I'm enjoying being away from him to be honest, but just for a little while. He went away to Canada first remember, so I'm not fretting over *him*, but he'll be all over me when he gets back and that will be fun. It usually is anyway.'

Something there didn't sound right to Camille, but she couldn't work out what. She didn't think it worth worrying about it though because her job was to facilitate Tegan, not to do her job for her, or concern herself with her love life, so she decided to do exactly what Tegan had suggested and relax.

After a very leisurely lunch, Tegan fired up the Prius and she and Camille headed for their next suspect company. This was *Trinitaires Boulevard Paint Supplies* which was also in Montreal, so the journey was similar to yesterday's. They were both fairly quiet in the car on the way to Newman Boulevard.

'What do we know about this company?' asked Camille.

'Run by a pair of brothers, François and Étienne Lavigne, born and bred in Montreal. They seem totally legit, but we'll have a look anyway.'

After about fifty minutes they drew up close to a very large painting and decorating store, parked, and entered by the "Trade Only" entrance. They gave a similar story to the one they had used yesterday: they wanted to set up a business that specialised in home and small business design and so they would need access to regular amounts of paint, wallpaper and other sundry decorating supplies. They were met by a tired looking young woman.

'Can I help you?'

Tegan recited her prepared description of what they wanted.

'Have you got a trade card?' demanded the young woman.

'No. We are still planning our new enterprise and want to know exactly what the costs and supply chain might look like before starting the business,' replied Camille, sounding very businesslike.

'I need to see a trade card,' said the woman behind the counter.

'And I want to see your boss,' said Tegan with a ferocity that surprised Camille.

'Perhaps there is more to this woman than I have been led to believe. I'd better be careful,' thought Camille.

'I'll get him,' replied the young woman, and she disappeared into a small office to return with a tall, good looking young man. He was wearing a very well-tailored business suit.

'May I help you?' asked a busy looking François.

Tegan repeated her enquiry.

'We only deal with trades people, so you will need to return once your company is up and running, and you can then register with us as members of a trade.'

'I apologise for my friend's aggressive nature,' said Camille. 'While we are here, may we browse some of your products, just to get us going.'

'In business I mean,' she added provocatively.

'OK. But no more than ten minutes and you'll have to wear a protective helmet because most of our stock is in the warehouse.'

Wearing bright yellow plastic helmets, they were shown into the warehouse, which turned out to be enormous. Tegan had insisted on exploring every part of the warehouse and François obliged without complaint. Eventually, they had seen enough, and they headed for the reception area. As they were leaving Tegan turned to François and said 'Dinner tonight?'

'Are you asking me out for dinner?' asked François.

'I certainly am.'

'And can my wife come too?' asked François.

'Sorry no,' said Tegan.

'Then it's also no from me,' said François.

Camille didn't know where to look as they left. 'Is Tegan for real?' she thought to herself. 'Something doesn't seem quite right with this assignment anymore and I'll be glad when it's over.'

'So, what do you make of that place?' Camille asked Tegan once they were back in the car.

'Seems above board. I'll do some more checks, but they seem OK.'

'They didn't seem to be very busy. Isn't that a bit suspicious, especially since their warehouse seems to be so huge?'

'That's a good point,' replied Tegan. 'I'll think about that while we're driving.'

Camille drove the hire car back to the hotel, both of them remaining silent during most of the remainder of the journey.

'I am disappointed that François wouldn't come out for dinner,' said Tegan, suddenly. 'It would have made a change for me.'

'And was it only dinner you wanted?'

'Probably, but he is rather gorgeous so anything else would have been nice. I would have enjoyed digging the dirt with him and maybe uncovering something useful. Even if he isn't involved in the fake weapons scam, he might have heard something on the grapevine.'

'Fair enough,' said Camille as they approached the hotel.

'When are we going for dinner? Asked Tegan. 'I am starving.'

'Had you forgotten that I am going out with Philippe, so you are on your own tonight?'

'Yes, I had. Have a nice night then and I'll see you in the morning,' said Tegan as they entered the hotel.

'I'll do my best.' They both laughed. 'You're not suggesting that I might *not* be back in my room tonight, are you?'

Tegan looked at Camille. 'Philippe isn't my type but there's something cute about him. Go for it girl.'

Despite the tacky comment, Camille was beginning to wonder whether Tegan wasn't of French origin after all!

Camille had arranged to meet Philippe at 7.30 pm. They decided to be inconspicuous and meet outside the restaurant where he worked, and she was there on the dot. She had chosen to wear something typically French, and she looked beautiful in a shiny burgundy blouse over one of those French pencil skirts that reach down to just below the knee. It was a mid-grey colour and the combination looked stunning. She had adorned the ensemble with a single diamond on a very fine gold chain and, with her glossy shoulder length hair, she looked as though she had just stepped out from a New York fashion magazine. Philippe arrived shortly after her and Camille was very disappointed to see that he was wearing a white tee shirt and jeans, and that his feet were kitted out with a pair of white trainers.

'Hi Camille,'

'Hi Philippe.'

They greeted each other with a peck on the cheek, and then Camille realised that she had been a bit hasty in her disappointment with Philippe's outfit. The white tee shirt bore the emblem of a famous French fashion designer, it was of a very good quality and was tailored to fit his athletic torso perfectly. She hadn't noticed his athletic build while he was working but now she was impressed to see that he looked after himself. The same applied to the jeans which must have been made to measure because there wasn't a loose bit anywhere. It was as though the denim had been sprayed on, and she was relieved to see that it was very stretchy denim otherwise they would have had to eat standing up! He smelt rather nice too and he had obviously spent a while tidying his beard, though she wasn't sure how successful that had been.

'Where are we going?' asked Camille.

'Down-town if you agree. I have booked a quiet Indian restaurant and we can go to a club afterwards if you like.'

'Sounds lovely Philippe.'

Philippe hailed a cab, and they were at the restaurant within minutes. The menu arrived promptly, and they both settled for a glass of Indian beer while the courses were prepared.

'I don't often eat Indian food so I will have the same as you Philippe.'

'OK Camille. This means that you will have butter chicken as a main, followed by Kheer, which is essentially rice pudding with many added spices. Do you think that will suit you?'

'We'll soon find out!' It turned out that Camille found the combination to very refreshing, as well as filling. 'I never thought rice pudding could be so light and flavoursome,' she said to Philippe, as she put down her spoon.

'I love Indian food. It's probably because of my heritage.'

'Which is?'

'My father was from Northern India, and he moved to France in 1989 where he met and married my mother, who is French. I moved to the USA with my dad when I was two. My parents had split up and she stayed in France with my sister who was six at the time. I do still visit them.'

'And your dad?'

'He was shot in a drive by shooting ten years ago. I was at uni in Montreal at the time, so I stayed here. My full name is Philippe Agarwal by the way. I would love to have an Indian accent, but I was born in France and speak American English with a French accent. I wish I had learned to speak some Indian but there are so many regions there that I gave up attempting. My dad always said to concentrate on "International English" and I would get along well, which has been true.'

Camille studied him for a moment and recognised that the dark hair, bushy straight eyebrows and well-groomed beard should have made her realise that he was of Indian descent. She really had no interest in his heritage but, whatever his origins were, she did think him rather handsome, and that was all she was interested in right now.

'What did you study at uni?'

'Thermodynamics and math.'

'Wow. Yet you are a waiter? Did you not pass?' She suddenly realised that that had been rude and turned away from him.

'I passed with honours, but I worked as a waiter when I was a student. I love being a waiter and my dad left me a great deal of money, so I don't need to earn lots. I enjoyed doing my degree, but I really don't fancy any of the jobs that go with the qualification.'

'It sounds like you really enjoy your life. A bit of a playboy perhaps?'

Philippe suddenly looked embarrassed, but Camille decided not to pursue that idea further.

'No, not really. I am actually quite shy. What about you then? You seem very mysterious. A beautiful French maiden turns up in Montreal and chats me up. Does she have a boyfriend? Does she live here? Does she earn a living?'

'Wait, slow down. Yes, I am from France, and I did live there. My name is Camille duBois and I am here with my old uni friend Tegan, who is looking for a new man because her previous boyfriend has gone off with somebody else, at least she thinks he has because she doesn't hear from him at all. I am 27 and live just outside Toronto with two cats and a goldfish. I haven't a steady boyfriend because the right man just hasn't come along yet. I am a stenographer and I work in the law courts there. I moved to Toronto five years ago after completing uni. My parents are both French and they still live happily in a small town near Paris. I don't have any great wealth.'

'Wow. You have passed my interview Miss duBois and I would like to offer you the post of my escort at a night club for this evening.'

They both laughed heartily.

'I would be delighted to accept your offer.'

Philippe paid the bill and they ventured on to a very glitzy nightclub where they stayed until 1.30 am. Philippe turned out to be quite witty and Camille spent a lot of the evening laughing, at least when she could hear him.

'I will hail a taxi and accompany you to your hotel,' said Philippe.

'There's no need. I can manage myself.'

'Is this the brush off then,' asked Philippe, looking like a little boy who has lost his new toy.

Camille took him by the waist and gave him a very deep kiss. After she had removed the odd bristle from his now very untidy beard, she answered his question.

'No, it isn't. I want you to realise that I don't need protecting, but you can take me back in a taxi if you wish.'

'I will. Provided that you agree to see me again.'

'Of course.'

The taxi driver took a longer than necessary route back to the hotel, by which time Philippe's beard had become really flattened down, and was adorned with most of Camille's lipstick.'

'Call you tomorrow?' he asked as she left the taxi.

'You'd better!' was her reply.

Chapter 7

Camille woke with a start. She glanced at the bedside clock and realised that it was already 9am. 'Better get up,' she thought. 'I wonder what Tegan is doing?'

After a quick shower, and a brief application of makeup, she went along to see whether Tegan had had breakfast. There was no reply to her knock at her door, so she decided to go down for breakfast. Tegan was nowhere to be seen while she ate so Camille assumed that she was out for her morning exercise.

Back in her room, Camille was getting changed for her own morning routine when her phone rang.

'Bonjour.'

'Bonjour Camille. C'est moi, votre rendez-vous chaud de la nuit dernière.'

'Philippe! It's so lovely to hear you, and you were indeed a hot date. How are you this morning?'

'I am well, despite our late night. How about lunch today?'

'I'd love to join you for lunch. Do you want to come here or shall I meet you somewhere?

'How about the restaurant where I work? I will get a discount on the bill.'

'You know all the chat up lines!' said Camille. Philippe was confused by this because, though he a was witty sort of chap, he wasn't good with sarcasm, but he laughed anyway.

'Twelve-thirty OK?'

'I will see you there. Casual dress today?'

'Definitely,' replied Philippe.

Camille went out for her run and swim and was back at 11am. She had another brief shower and then donned a pink rugby top and a pair of very dark blue jeans. She then went along to find Tegan. This time, Tegan *was* in her room.

'Camille. I didn't want to disturb you this morning in case you were tired after your night out and I didn't want to intrude if you weren't alone either. How was it?'

'How was what?'

'Your night out silly!'

'It was lovely. Nice meal then a night club. We had fun.'

'Will you see him again?'

'That's what I came to tell you. I'm meeting him for lunch, so you are on your own this afternoon. What will you do today?'

'I am going back to Trinitaires Boulevard Paint supplies. I want to chat up François again, and maybe meet Étienne Lavigne too. I won't write them off as villains until I speak to them both. There might be more to them than we think.'

'OK. But be careful, and record the conversation since I won't be with you. You know the organisation's rules.'

'Yes, I will Miss duBois. Thank-you for reminding me.'

'That's my job Tegan! I will take my car so you can use the Prius.'

'Where are you off to with Philippe?'

'That's my business,' said Camille, with a cheeky grin, and with that she was gone.

Camille met Philippe at the restaurant. Philippe told her that she looked beautiful, and she had to admit that Philippe wasn't bad in tee shirt and sweatpants either. They had a delicious lunch, and then began to smooch a little. It was a sunny day, so they decided to stroll along Rue Fleury, and then to maybe go on somewhere else afterwards.

'Are you enjoying Montreal?' asked Philippe. In response Camille took his hand in hers.

'I am now,' she said.

'Good. I am finding life much nicer since you chatted me up at work,' responded Philippe.

'That's the second time you have said that Philippe. *You* spotted *me* remember.'

'Did I?'

'Yes. Tegan saw you looking at me and we ordered more wine so that you could come to the table and that I could see you at close quarters,' said Camille. Philippe took on a troubled look.

'Now don't take this the wrong way Camille but I was actually looking at your friend.' Camille removed her hand from his.

'So, it's actually Tegan that you fancy, but you got me instead!'

'No, No. No. I don't fancy Tegan at all. That's not why I was looking at her, and anyway, I hadn't thought that anyone as beautiful as you would be interested in a little French waiter like me. I assumed that you would have a hunky husband or something. I still can't believe that you agreed to go out with me at all. You are the most beautiful woman I have ever seen, and I can't believe my luck that you are out with me now.' Camille could see how upset he had become, and she put her hand back in his.

'So why were you looking at Tegan?'

'Because she must have escaped, and I was glad to see that she was OK.' Camille stopped walking and turned to Philippe. She held him by the shoulders and looked down to stare straight into his face. She adopted the sort of facial expression that teachers use when they need the truth from a naughty boy.

'*What* are you talking about?' Philippe now looked really anxious.

'It's probably nothing.'

'Tell me.'

'I saw a woman in a car on Sunday night, just before eleven o'clock. I had been sent to deliver some food to your hotel when I was almost run over by a blue car that was leaving the basement garage. It was dark but a flash, maybe from another car's headlights, illuminated the blue car and in the back was a woman that looked just like your friend. Her mouth was taped over, and she was staring out. She looked terrified. The car sped on and it was clear that the driver hadn't seen me because he nearly knocked me down. So, when I saw somebody that looked just like her on Monday night, I kept staring in the hope that I could attract her attention and ask her about it.' Camille was quiet for a while.

'Are you sure that it was Tegan in the car?'

'No. That's why I was staring. She certainly looked very like your friend. I only had a glimpse of the woman in the car but the fear on her face has etched her face into my memory.'

Camille stood a while, deep in thought. Perhaps the odd things she had noticed now made some sense. Perhaps the Tegan she had been helping since Monday wasn't actually the Tegan that she had picked up at the airport.

'Of course,' she thought, 'Akmal had left for *Paris* on Saturday, not *Canada*. That's what seemed wrong yesterday. Tegan shouldn't have made a mistake like that, especially since she had used organisation technology to check that he really was in Paris.' And it was now almost three days since Tegan had potentially been seen driving away.

'When do you need to be back at work Philippe?'

'I need to be at the restaurant at 5.30pm.'

'I am just going to make a call to an associate. If she agrees, could we all meet at your house?'

'Of course. It's at…' Camille cut him short.

'We know where you live,' she said.

'We?' Philippe was now starting to look even more concerned.

'Don't worry. I'll be back in a minute, don't go away.'

Camille left Philippe sitting on a low wall and used her organisation phone to speak with Marie. Marie had been surprised to hear from Camille so soon because any contact between them hadn't been part of the first phase plan. Camille outlined her conversation with Philippe and Marie agreed that all three should meet. Camille returned to Philippe who was looking very concerned.

'Could my associate and I meet with you at your house later today, say 3pm?'

'Yes,' said Philippe. 'What is all this about?'

'All will become clear when we meet. Shall we go to your house now?'

'Why?'

'We have an hour before we all meet up. I can think of something very pleasant to do in the meantime.' Philippe's eyes widened.

'It's just up here.'

'I know,' replied Camille.

Chapter 8

Marie arrived at Philippe's house at 3pm precisely, by which time Camille and Philippe were fresh from the shower. After the introductions, Philippe went to make coffee while Camille and Marie chatted quietly. Once the coffee had arrived all three began to talk, with Marie opening the discussion.

'Philippe, would you tell me exactly why you thought that you recognised our colleague Tegan when she and Camille arrived at your restaurant on Monday night?' Philippe looked like a little boy that had been caught eating sweets at bedtime.

'I was at work in the restaurant on Sunday night, and I was sent out with a food delivery to the hotel that Camille is staying in. I have a little bike that has an insulated box so that the food stays hot. I was nearly at the hotel when a car came out of the underground car park at a high speed. I think something must have run out in front of the car because the driver slowed down and swerved, so as not to run it down perhaps. I had to pull over to let him pass, because he clearly hadn't seen me, and he almost knocked me down, and as the side of the car drew level with me another car's lights shone directly into the rear window of the car. I saw a woman in the back seat who was looking distressed. There was tape over her mouth, and she raised her eyebrows when she saw me. I think that she hoped I could help her. When I saw your friend Tegan at the restaurant, I thought it was the same woman.'

'Did you call the police to tell them what you had seen?'

'No. I hadn't caught the car's registration number or it's made. It was just a medium sized blue car. They wouldn't have taken me seriously if I had called them.'

'When you saw us at the restaurant, Tegan called you over because she thought that you were looking at me,' said Camille. 'When you got closer to her, did you still think it was the same woman?'

'I'm sorry, I didn't take much notice after I got to your table because she introduced me to you Camille, and I was a bit smitten by your...' Camille cut him short at that point.

' So you still aren't sure that it is the same woman.'

'No.'

'Thanks Philippe,' said Marie, 'Can I ask you a few more questions?'

Philippe looked at Camille, who smiled at him.

'Yes, of course.'

'Do you have a criminal record?'

'No, of course not. What is this?' Camille told him not to worry.

'Do I have permission to access your social security details and your housing and employment record?'

'Yes, but why?' Marie ignored that question and there was a pause of about 10 minutes while she accessed the details she wanted. Philippe and Camille cleared away the coffee things and put them in the dishwasher while she did that.

'What's going on?' Philippe asked Camille.

'You might have helped solve a little problem I have had for a few days.'

'Is it about your friend Tegan?' Camille put her finger to her lips.

'Be patient,' is all she said. Marie called them back.

'Philippe, can you explain why you didn't work for nearly 4 months two years ago?' Philippe looked highly embarrassed. Marie glared at him.

'I spent those four months with a very attractive super model on her yacht.' He looked anxiously at Camille.

'I thought you said you weren't the playboy type?'

'She was very persuasive, and I was young!' said Philippe.

'Really?' said Camille.

'Do you have any proof of this four-month stint on a yacht?' asked Marie without batting an eyelid.

Philippe extracted his tablet from a drawer and showed Marie some video clips, some filmed by a TV network and others he had done himself. Marie smiled as she watched them. 'Did you spend all of the four months wearing almost nothing?' Philippe didn't know where to look but Camille rescued him.

'Marie, are you happy with Philippe's version of his life?'

'I am, but I still need to know why the affair with the model ended.'

'I had to leave when a strapping young man arrived to repaint the handrails of the yacht. He wore very little while painting, it being rather hot where we were berthed. It wasn't long before she got to know him very well and I was sent packing.'

'Were you disappointed?' asked Camille.

'It was always clear that I was a temporary plaything. I was glad when it was over to be honest.'

Marie and Camille retired to the kitchen leaving a very bemused looking Philippe wondering what on Earth he had got himself into. After five minutes or so they returned and sat down facing him.

'We would like to offer you temporary membership of the "organisation".'

'What?' said Philippe, now looking rather more concerned than bemused.

Marie began the introductory speech that she had now delivered on, to her mind at least, too many occasions.

'The "organisation" was set up in 2010 in response to the fake goods retailing epidemic that is now sweeping the globe. Many companies spend millions researching and developing products that end up being copied or sold through illegal or inappropriate channels and this corporate fraud costs legitimate companies billions each year. We spend a lot of money ourselves finding sales that look illegal or disreputable, both online and from retailers, and we make contact with the reputable companies that are losing out. We make a hefty charge for this service, but most companies are satisfied with the results that we produce.'

Philippe now looked a little happier and Marie continued. 'It is looking increasingly likely that one of our operatives has been compromised and may be in real danger, or worse. We believe that you might be the right person to help us to sort things out. You might be in danger yourself during the operation, but you will not be working alone, and you will be paid handsomely.'

'Wow. And are you also an operative Camille?'

70

'No, I am a facilitator. I usually work in the background to make sure that the operative can work without issues such as language problems, and to help them to stay out of danger. I seem to have messed up that last bit with Tegan.'

'So, Marie, are you an operative or a facilitator?'

'I am actually a senior director of the company, but I sometimes work as a facilitator. I am here currently with another operative whose work was carried out unusually swiftly. He will now be called back to help resolve the issue with Tegan.

'So, you do have other men in the "organisation",' asked Philippe brightening up a little.

'We do, but we find that women are often better at gaining the trust of the bad guys. People are less suspicious of women generally, but we employ men if we want to infiltrate a company on a higher business level. Boardrooms are often still dominated by men, and a well-dressed male can still find it easier to be believed in that situation.'

'So, am I to be the well-dressed businessman?'

'Not quite. We think that your wealthy playboy past might help us in other ways.'

'Ah, my "playboy past". That does sound intriguing, except that I have just met a gorgeous French woman! I wouldn't want to upset her.'

'I hope you mean me!' said Camille.

'If that's fine with you Camille?' said Philippe.

'Of course it is.'

'Then do I need to sign anything or fill in any forms?'

'No. This conversation has been recorded and it acts as your contract. You begin immediately.'

Chapter 9

Marie had booked her flight out of Montreal before meeting with Philippe and Camille, just to make sure that she could be with Akmal quickly. She was really concerned about Tegan, and it was obvious that Akmal would be the best person to help find out whether the woman in Montreal was indeed a fake Tegan, but she wouldn't let on to him that it was *his* Tegan that they would end up looking for until the identity of the woman in Montreal was certain.

Marie was on the plane at just after 5.30pm and she arrived in Ottawa at about 6.15pm. She was now heartily fed up with travelling, especially by air, but she realised that it had to be done. She had known Tegan for a long time, and she was really worried about her. On arrival in Ottawa, she telephoned Akmal.

'Akmal, I am in Ottawa, I'll soon be on my way to your hotel so please stay in your room until I arrive.' He had sounded disappointed by the call because he had thought that he could go home soon, the memory of Tegan's comment about a plastic toy boy still running around in his head.

'Marie! I didn't expect to hear from you so soon, so what's this about?

72

'I'll tell you when I get there, just stay put and I'll tell you about it soon, but it is quite a serious matter. Hang up now, I won't be long.'

At about 7.30pm Marie was knocking on his door. It was opened by a rather dishevelled looking Akmal.

'Hi Marie. So, what's this serious matter that gives me the pleasure of your company again?'

'Let's sit down first. You can offer me coffee if you like.' Knowing that Marie would detest the coffee that is so often available in hotel rooms he telephoned room service and ordered black coffee and cakes for two. They exchanged pleasantries while they waited for the coffee to arrive. He told her about his ordeal with the Canadian police, who he described as "A fearsome bunch with enormous weapons". Akmal decided that Marie must have a very filthy mind when she roared with laughter *and* had to explain the innuendo to Akmal.

'I wish I had been a fly on the wall when you worked in Lebanon!' he said.

'Your wildest dreams couldn't have coped with seeing what I got up to then,' she replied. Just then the coffee arrived, which turned out to be very good, the cakes being rather less so. 'There's another job for you to do back in Montreal, or rather Saint-Jérôme. Our room is still available, and we can continue our previous personas as members of an arguing married couple.'

'That's disappointing, I was looking forward to going home. So, what does the job entail? Have you got my usual dossier?'

'There is no usual dossier this time because this is not a usual job, and nothing must be put in writing.'

73

'Sounds ominous. Is it really that serious?'

'We don't know for sure but potentially it is. I don't want to say any more until the operation begins, but we fly back after breakfast tomorrow.'

'OK. Where are you staying tonight?'

'In here with you.'

'But it's a double room, with a double bed.'

'Good thing you bought the sleep shorts then,' laughed Marie. Akmal looked a little sheepish and was now worried about whether Marie really had been up to some seriously peculiar practices in Lebanon. While many would have been excited by such things, Akmal felt that he was too young to die from some form of curious kinky torture. 'You can behave can't you? If not, you'll be sleeping on the floor,' said Marie.

'Fine. But can I trust *you*? No pretending to feel around in the bed for the TV remote during the night. I've had that one played on me before.'

'Really?' said Marie. 'I hadn't thought of that one,' and she carefully placed the TV remote in the middle of the bed before covering it with the sheets. Akmal didn't know where to look and he went to the bathroom to get into his sleep shorts.

'Men are so easy to tease,' thought Marie, but then she was suddenly struck by how difficult this operation might become when Akmal knew the full details, and she thought she should perhaps go a little easier on him. Not only would he discover that Tegan was in the same organisation as him, but also that he might permanently lose her, or have already lost her, for the very same reason.

Chapter 10

Helen Morgan was outside tending to her garden when she noticed that there were lights on around the old barn that lay near the top of the hill which rose majestically behind her house. She was surprised by this because the old barn didn't have electricity, at least it hadn't had electric power when she was last up there back in 2012. It was late on Wednesday afternoon and she was feeling perplexed. 'Now why would anybody want to put power all the way up there? Nobody has used the barn since old Ned died and his family couldn't have sold it because the entire estate is locked in legal wrangles about who it's true owner is.'

Ned wasn't actually the owner's real name – he was only called "old Ned" because he had looked old when he was 20, and he never really changed. He had never married, and he had died aged 59 leaving nothing. No bank account, no national insurance number that anybody could find, no money, nothing. He had lived a solitary, self-sufficient life and, apart from the odd visit to his nearest bar, he was rarely seen. His cottage hadn't been upgraded to have electricity either, so seeing a light on anywhere near that barn was truly unusual.

Helen loved her garden and she had worked in it all that afternoon, but it was becoming quite dark by the time she was finishing up. That light in the barn kept praying on her mind but she decided to have dinner and try to forget about it. After dinner though she looked out of the window to check on that light, but it was still on, even clearer now in the total darkness of the hillside.

Helen had moved from Wales to Canada when she was 49. She had followed Tegan, her daughter, to Sainte-Agathe-des-Monts when Tegan was 22 and newly married to Jed Palmer, who was a Canadian native. They had been a handsome couple, Tegan a classic Welsh maiden with long dark hair and a fair skinned beauty that cosmetics companies would have paid millions for. Jed was part Native American and part Austrian, and his dimpled chin and angular jaw had made him resemble many of the film stars of the 1960s. They had settled in Sainte-Agathe-des-Monts in 1992 and set up a business selling agricultural products, which did very well in the early days, but had become swamped by larger concerns in the early 2010s. They had two children, neither of whom resembled either parent. They were named Helen, after their grandmother, and Tom, after their Canadian grandfather.

'Now what can that light be on for?' she wondered. 'It must be somebody up to no good. What should I do about it? I can't phone the police. What would I say? "There's a light on in a barn." They'd say so what? It's 2022 they'd tell me, and we have electricity now. They'd tell me that it isn't like the dark ages back in Wales and that I should just go to bed.'

Helen had never lost her Welsh accent and she was popular with the locals who loved to hear her speak. She had felt fortunate that most people where she lived could speak English because, though Helen *was* bilingual she couldn't speak French. But then nobody near to her could speak Welsh, which was *her* first language. So, curiously, everybody in her locality spoke to each other in their *second* language, which was English, but their first language could be any one of many. They were a happy community and, though Helen yearned to be back in the *Welsh* Valleys, she was content to see out her days in these.

She went to bed that night and tried to sleep, but she couldn't forget the light in the barn, and she got up every fifteen minutes or so to look out of the window. At 1.15am she looked out and it was still on. She wasn't in the habit of looking out of that window in the early hours, and she couldn't be sure that it hadn't been there yesterday, but, whether or not this was a new light, it was there now, and her curiosity was getting the better of her. She got up and made a pot of tea, but it was no good, she would have to investigate this new phenomenon.

Helen was now 75 and had remained very sprightly. Her husband Rhys had died from cancer while Helen still lived in Wales, so she had followed her daughter to Canada but, to maintain her independence, she had bought her own house just up the valley from Tegan. Unfortunately, following a very tragic air accident that resulted in the death of both Tegan and Jed, she was now totally on her own, though she did get the occasional visit from her grandchildren, Helen and Tom. Tom would visit with his husband and adopted daughter, who loved her grandmother, and Helen would be accompanied by her husband. The last time that Helen had seen her granddaughter she had learned that Helen junior was pregnant and that Helen "would be a great gran by Christmas".

She dressed quickly and fired up the Toyota. She had owned the old truck for nearly twenty years and it had never let her down. Tonight was no exception and moments later she was driving, rather slowly, up towards the barn. As she neared her destination she dropped the headlights to dim level and crawled into the yard in front of the barn. She stopped the engine and turned off all the lights.

She gave her eyes five minutes to get used to the darkness and got out of the truck. Despite them being closed, light was coming out through the barn doors because they were so old that the wood was well rotted and they were full of holes, some quite large. There was also a floodlight illuminating the area behind the barn.

'You couldn't store anything securely in there,' she thought while she wandered about. 'But why would you have a light on when there's nobody here?'

Indeed there was nobody there, at least not as far as she could see. There were no vehicles other than her own and she couldn't hear anything moving.

A sudden sound made her jump. It was the noise of an engine! Suddenly in a panic she made for the safety of her truck but, once she was back in the cab, she realised that, though she could hear an engine, nothing had turned up. She wound down the window.

'It's a generator,' she thought. 'Of course, many people in the hills have generators because running cables up there isn't

78

always feasible. Most systems have a battery backup so the generator must have kicked in because somebody had left the flood lighting on!'

She got back out of the truck and headed for the barn door. She peered through one of the holes and was surprised to see that the barn had been swept clean and that it contained some packing crates. "Columbian Coffee" was stencilled on the side of one of them, so she assumed that somebody was using the place as a storeroom. There were a lot of those crates and she realised that there was quite some money's worth in there.

'But why would anybody want to store coffee all the way up here?' she wondered. 'Perhaps it's stolen, or counterfeit, or stuff that hasn't passed safety standards, so it's up here waiting for disposal.' She pondered the crates for a while and lapsed into a sleep like state. She realised that she was very tired and, especially since she had just seen movement in a bush near the barn, she decided that it was time for bed again. She climbed back into her truck and headed back home, even more slowly than when she was on her way up there. She was asleep as soon as her head touched the pillow. Her visit to the barn played a large part in her dreaming that night and she had visions of everything that she had seen up there. She had obviously remembered it all, vividly and in great detail. Unfortunately that detail hadn't extended to spotting the CCTV cameras that hung from three poles around the barn and from one of the trees at the entrance to the yard!

In Ottawa, Akmal and Marie both woke up the next morning after having slept surprisingly well. Marie hadn't been molested during the night and she had also behaved herself. When Akmal had woken up he found that Marie had her arms around him but, with the impending "mystery" operation on his mind this had comforted rather than excited him. Though he was a big man he wasn't at all aggressive or skilled in combat, and he was worried about what was to come. He hadn't signed up for this sort of hard edged stuff. He was a technician, not a combater, and he was worried by the lack of a dossier. He had already decided that he would go back to Montreal with Marie, but to ask to be released if it seemed to become too dangerous. He gently climbed out of bed and was showered and dressed before Marie had herself got out of bed.

'I'll see you downstairs. I'm going down to breakfast so I'll expect you to join me.'

'Good idea,' replied Marie, looking very serious this morning and obviously still tired.

'Will you be able to find the dining room?' asked Akmal. Marie gave him a look and he decided just to leave her to her ablutions.

Marie joined Akmal while he was drinking coffee. As she ate he asked her just how serious this assignment was.

'It might end up being nothing but it could be potentially deadly. Sorry about this Akmal. I know it's more than you usually deal with but there are others there to help you, and we really really need your input into this one.'

Akmal had seemed even more anxious with that reply. Marie noticed that anxiety and suggested that he go up and pack because their plane was due to leave at 11.30am.

Chapter 11

That same morning Helen Morgan awoke at 10.30am, which was very late for her. Annoyed with herself she began her morning preparations and it was while applying her lipstick that the events of the previous night came crashing back into her mind.

'Those lights and the coffee crates! Why were they there and who put them there?' She put down her lipstick, thought for a while, and then made some decisions. 'I think that I might go into town later to do some shopping, and maybe make some enquiries while I'm out.'

She ate her breakfast of coffee and pancakes with some relish that morning because she felt starving after her previous night's excursion. She set out for the shops at noon, but called on her friend Gareth on the way down.

Gareth had also been born in Wales but he, at the age of 65, was just a youngster to Helen. He had been a Welsh International Rugby player back in Wales and, like Helen, had left his home nation when his daughter emigrated to Canada. His wife was "even younger" than him, being only 56, but she was away on a university course at the moment, so Helen was sure that he would be pleased to see her today.

She knocked on his door at 12.20pm but, after giving the door a second loud rap, she spotted his dark hair in amongst the bushes of his garden. 'Bore da Gareth,' she shouted, realising that with that Welsh greeting Gareth would know instantly who it was. Looking slightly sheepish, he appeared a few moments later. Continuing in English he greeted Helen with a kiss on the cheek and a broad smile.

'You look as gorgeous as ever Helen. How do you do it?'

'You aren't doing so badly yourself Gareth,' she replied. 'What were you up to in the garden?'

'A surprise for Delphine, for when she comes back from her uni stay. It should be nicely settled in by then, but you won't say anything to her, will you?'

'Of course not,' said Helen, and offered to make him some coffee. Gareth had never quite got the hang of making good coffee so he accepted her offer with a wide grin. He still couldn't understand why North Americans had cream with their coffee and neither had Helen, so they both sat down with large mugs of black coffee, a jug of milk and a Danish pastry. These pastries had been made by a store in Sainte-Agathe-des-Monts, so they weren't very Danish, but they were enjoyable none the less.

'So, to what do I owe the pleasure of your company?' asked Gareth. 'There's usually a reason for your visits.'

'Can't I just visit a good-looking Welshman while his wife is away?' teased Helen.

'Of course you can,' he replied, 'but I really don't believe that's why you are here.'

'Actually, I want to ask your advice.' She told Gareth about her adventures of the previous night.

'Another mystery for you to solve then eh? You are not still watching the late Angela Lansbury in that series of her's are you? You know that they don't make it now don't you, and the ones that you watch are all repeats?'

'I haven't watched that for years Gareth. Actually I had thought that you would enjoy another episode of mystery cracking. You enjoyed it last time.'

'And nearly got killed for my trouble! What are you thinking of doing this time?'

'I just want to go back up there and I thought you might like to come with me. There's something wrong around that barn and I can't quite put my finger on what. I don't like mysteries as you know, I'm not just being nosy.' Gareth thought for a while. He *had* been a bit bored while Delphine was away and decided that it might be good for him.

'OK then, if you're sure. So let's think about what you *did* see. While you were up there, did you notice how much CCTV they had and where the cameras are?'

'No I didn't. Damn. I must be getting old. Perhaps that's why the place was so well lit, and they probably saw me, and my Toyota. Damn it.'

'Helen, I'm surprised at you. They are likely to know you've been there so let's hope it's all legit, or you might be receiving unexpected callers.'

'Whoops. You're right, and now I feel a bit scared. What if they, whoever they are, do find out who I am. But then they only have my registration number so they won't know where I live, or even that it was me driving. I'll be OK. Anyway, it might have been taken over by really lovely people, and they would thank me for being vigilant.' She relaxed a little.

Unfortunately for Helen that relaxing had been rather premature and, even while she was speaking, a truck was driving into her yard. Fortunately though, she had installed one of those internet enabled doorbells, and just as she had finished her speech her phone bleeped. She fished it out from her handbag and watched the footage of her caller. She replayed it for Gareth.

'Well, I don't know about you but I don't think I like the look of those two. I *do* think though that you might be at risk so you had better go and collect a few things and come and stay here for a few days. We can keep an eye on your callers using your doorbell.'

'Does that mean that I can share your bed?' asked Helen, brightly.

'Now then, much as I might like that, I am a married man, so you'll be up in the attic room. You haven't changed though have you Helen?' Helen grinned mischievously.

'It was worth a try anyway.' Helen was known to be a bit of a flirt, but no man had ever found out what would happen if they *had* said yes to her.

Gareth fixed some lunch for them both and then Helen was despatched to collect everything that she would need for a two week stay. It took her a while to retrieve those items and Gareth kept a close eye on her doorbell app in case anybody else turned up. After turning off her water, and her heating, she set off back to Gareth's house and was there by tea time. Gareth put Helen's Toyota into his garage and they headed out for the shops, catching them just before they closed. Included in their shopping list was a large pack of high power flash-light batteries, and some bullets for Gareth's gun.

Marie and Akmal's flight back to Montreal had been delayed by bad weather, and then affected by turbulence, so they were pleased to be leaving Montreal airport at just after 3pm on Thursday. They had spoken very little during the flight and they had tried to watch an in flight movie, but both had had little interest in it. They returned to their hotel by taxi and Marie was careful to ensure that they didn't bump into Camille or Tegan. They didn't tell reception that they had arrived.

That same afternoon, "Tegan" was at Champlain Boulevard Autos Ltd with Camille. They had spent a few minutes browsing some slightly used cars, all of which were convertibles, when a middle aged podgy man approached them. 'Is there anything that I can help you ladies with?' he asked brightly.

'I am looking for something a bit special,' said "Tegan". These all seem a bit dull. Is there anything else that you might have hidden away?'

'Hidden away? You sound like a spy! There are some cars in the workshop but they aren't yet prepared for the showroom. There's a Mustang and a 2013 Camaro SS Convertible in stunning black. Both need a polish, but you could come back and look at them tomorrow if you want.'

'We really want to see them today because we have others to see tomorrow. I am happy to see the unpolished ones.'

'Our technicians are out at the moment and the receptionist isn't in today. I don't want to leave the showroom unattended. Sorry.'

'Show us where the shop is, and we'll just have a look. We won't touch anything, promise.'

'You'd need to wear overalls to go in there. Company rule.' This didn't put "Tegan" off, much to the dismay of the salesman.

'You must have a spare set.'

'Yes, but if I wear mine and you wear the spare set, the showroom will still be unmanned. Sorry but you will have to come back tomorrow.'

'What if I buy you dinner tonight?' The salesman looked shocked.

'What is this? I have no intention of going to dinner with either of you so you can come back tomorrow, that's if you really do intend to buy a car. Otherwise please leave because I see other customers coming in.'

'OK. We *will* leave now, and we will try to get back tomorrow. Thanks for your time.' As they left, Camille gave "Tegan" a quizzical look. In response, "Tegan" replied: 'Camille, watch the doors because I'm going into the shop. He just told us that the workshop is empty, so keep a lookout because I am going in search of treasure.' "Tegan" boldly entered the back door of the garage and began her search. The place was untidy with spanners, screwdrivers and some car parts on the floor. It certainly looked as though the technicians had left in a hurry. She considered that this might be because they had been called out to an emergency, and that the car on the lift was not needed urgently, or that the garage didn't do any work on cars at all, and that it was actually a front for more sinister things. Now fired up, she looked around the walls for signs of concealed cabinets, but found none. There was only one toilet. 'Typical sexist bunch!' she thought, but she explored that anyway and found nothing. The cistern was quite disgusting but only contained water. There were no doors leading anywhere else so "Tegan" decided to re-join Camille.

'Anything?'

'Nothing. I'll go round the back and see whether anything seems obvious.' "Tegan" explored the area to the rear, which was quite vast. The dumping area showed a great deal of carelessness; she found a box of used syringes and needles and there were the remains of car parts, broken spanners and a very peculiar smell that "Tegan" recognised, but couldn't place. She was just studying a pair of very dirty boxer shorts and various other sundry items, and wondering what sort of parties had gone on here, when a very strong arm took her around her throat.

'What the hell are you doing round here' said a voice. "Tegan" wrestled herself free and turned to see a woman dressed in overalls.

'I'm just..,' uttered "Tegan", stopping when she saw that the owner of the powerful arm belonged to a woman. Following behind the mechanic was another woman, dragging Camille behind her like a sack of potatoes. Camille had tape over her mouth.

'Now, whose talking to me?' said the bigger of the two mechanics, who turned out to be called Pixie, or so she claimed. This was despite Camille having tape on her mouth, so she was clearly addressing "Tegan".

'We came to look at some cars but your boss said that he was busy so we were just having a little look around.'

'Like hell you were.' Pixie's assistant pulled the tape from Camille's mouth and loosed her grip on her.

'Names, now.'

'Stephanie.'

'Denise.'

'Right Stephanie and Denise, what the fuck are you really doing here. And don't bullshit us because we aren't in the mood and we've got work to do. *And* that dude in the showroom isn't our boss.'

'So are you car mechanics?' asked "Tegan".

'You ain't listening are you. Trixie, get the rope.'

'No. There's no need for that.'

'So, do I need to ask you again? Trixie here can be very violent.'

'Alright! We are looking for a crate of weapons that are being illegally sold. We work for the authorities. Show them your card Stephanie.'

'Bullshit.' Camille then showed a card to Trixie.

'Is that the best you can do? I've seen better forgeries made at elementary schools. Now talk.' There was silence from "Tegan" and Camille, so Pixie and Trixie dragged them into the workshop and tied them up before the mechanics resumed work on the car.

'I need the toilet,' said "Tegan".

'You'll have to piss yourself. Just don't make too much mess.'

'It's not that that I need.' Pixie swore profusely.

'Fine.' She undid just enough of "Tegan"'s restraints to allow her to go to the bathroom, and escorted her to the door. She had to let "Tegan" go into the toilet on her own because it was too small for two, but after 5 minutes "Tegan" emerged, free of restraints and brandishing a small Taser de poche. Within seconds Pixie was on the floor, convulsing uncontrollably, and Tegan was heading for Trixie.

'You, release my friend, *now*.' Trixie looked at Pixie writhing about on the floor and decided to do as she had been told. As soon as Camille was free, "Tegan" struck Trixie with the same Taser, and she and Camille fled the scene.

Once back in the car, Camille drove like a mad woman, and followed a very roundabout route back to the hotel.

'What the hell was that about?' asked Camille once they had recovered their composure.

'They certainly aren't gun runners,' said "Tegan". 'Based on their reaction to what I said we were doing, and what I found in that waste behind the garage, those two women are running some sort of brothel. I found some interesting receipts buried in the rubbish. It seems that they buy quite a lot of condoms and men's kinky underwear. I suspect that they are running a mixed sex brothel, catering to all sexes, everything in between and even those that don't identify themselves at all. You wouldn't believe what you can legally buy now, based on the receipts I just saw. Quite a few items were rather soiled so I'm glad I got to use their toilet. I wasn't keen on rummaging around to get my Taser before I had washed my hands.' Camille shuddered.

'I suppose that we should say that it's all in a day's work, but I'm glad that it's you doing the searching. I'm just the facilitator remember.'

'Yes. Maybe I could do with another operative to help me.'

'You seem to be managing just fine. For a while I thought that we were done for in there. Thanks for that rescue "Tegan".'

Chapter 12

Once back at their hotel room, Marie and Akmal had begun to unpack their things. 'I am starting to feel as though we really are a married couple,' said Akmal.

'Well I'm not,' replied Marie. 'But then I am married so don't forget that Akmal.'

'Is it cool being married? I have been thinking about asking Tegan to marry me, even though she seems a bit annoyed with me at the moment.' Marie didn't reply to that and decided to cut the conversation short as a knot had appeared in her stomach.

'We have a job to do here so this isn't the time for sentimental chit chat. We start tonight, just after dinner.'

'So when am I going to find out what we *are* here to do? This all seems a bit cloak and dagger, and far too serious for my pay grade to be honest.'

'All will become clear after dinner. Shouldn't you be changing before we go down? It's getting near dinner time and I'm starving.' While Akmal was showering Marie messaged Camille on her 'second' SIM card.

'Is 6.30 OK?'

'6.30's fine,' came the reply. Akmal didn't enjoy his shower. He had thought that he might be heading home by now, and his mind went back to some of the times that he had shared his shower with Tegan. He had thought it a bit kinky when she had first suggested it to him, but it had become one of their little rituals. He really was missing her, much more so than usual. He wondered why that might be and he decided, after some thought, that it was Marie's constant teasing that was getting to him. He decided to try to get on with the task in hand and he wondered, for what seemed like the millionth time, what it could be.

Akmal returned to their room looking very smart.

'I have reserved our table tonight Akmal. I thought that it might make a change to be able to choose where we sit, so follow me when we get to the restaurant.'

'Whatever you say.'

'Remember that we are supposed to be an arguing couple,' added Marie.

'Is that important tonight? I am getting tired of the pretence, and that's alongside the mystery of not knowing what I'm doing.'

'Be patient.'

'OK. I'll try to be, but I am becoming more than a bit anxious now.'

Marie had booked a position so that, in the restaurant, they were two tables away from Camille and Tegan, and after they entered the restaurant, Marie sat with her back to Camille. That meant that Akmal could clearly see Tegan. They sat studying their menus for a while, but Akmal seemed distracted. 'That woman over there looks a bit like Tegan,' he whispered to Marie.

'You just can't help yourself can you,' said Marie, loudly. 'We are supposed to be patching things up and you just can't help looking at other women can you! If you fancy her so much then bloody well go and see how you get on. See if I care, and I will enjoy watching you return with your tail between your legs.' Akmal looked astonished. He gave Marie a quizzical look, but she just carried on.

'Go on, go and talk to her. I can see where you are looking and there's two of them. Go and chat them both up, try to get them both into bed and I hope they slap your face you swine. Go on, get it over with, see whether either will put up with you for more than five minutes, then come back to me like you always do.' Akmal could feel other diners' eyes boring into him, so he slowly got up from his chair and then went over to join Tegan and Camille, adopting his best "pulling" face.

'Can I join you ladies?' he said brightly as he approached Tegan and Camille.

'Certainly,' said Camille, 'There's only two chairs but I'm going to powder my nose so you can sit down here. Make less of a spectacle of yourself! Understand though that I want no part in being chatted up. Tegan here will entertain you, at least for a while. I would be careful what you say though, she has a temper.' Akmal sat down, facing the newly introduced "Tegan".

'Hi Tegan. I'm Lethabo. It means happiness. My girlfriend is called Tegan, which means Pearl. Pearls and happiness go together don't you think, and isn't that a coincidence?'

'Is that Tegan over there, or is all that a part of your chat up line?' Akmal spotted his error immediately and realised that he had better resume his persona.

'No, that woman over there's my wife. We married in haste. Tegan is the woman I go to for proper sex. Another coincidence eh?'

'So, you think that I could be your substitute for this woman who just happens to be called Tegan? Really, that's not a great chat up line either.'

'No, I just wondered whether we could eat together, get to know each other a bit, *then* maybe more.'

'As it happens I am on holiday with my friend because I need to help her get over her breakup with her idiot of a boyfriend. My boyfriend is called Akmal by the way. He looks a bit like you as it happens, but I don't think he'd appreciate your approach to me now. We could have sex if you like but you might have to face him when you get home. You are English right?'

'How did you know?'

'The accent. West of London I think? That's where we live too, and my boyfriend is clever and he will soon find you. You won't be able to hide from him.'

'That's a no then?'

'No it isn't; you can come up to my room later and we can have fun, but it's you who'll have to live with the consequences.'

'Why does there have to be consequences? Can we not just have a quiet, comfortable relationship? The only people who would know would be me and you.'

'And my boyfriend.'

'You don't need to tell him.'

'We tell each other everything.'

'That's a shame. I wish I could say that our conversation has been a pleasure, but I can't. I'll get back to the ball and chain then.' Akmal gave "Tegan" a winning smile.

'Good idea. Nice to have met you.'

'Likewise.' Akmal returned to his table and sat down in front of Marie, who shouted at him.

'You are a bloody idiot you know. You don't look after yourself, you don't smell that great and you don't even get a proper haircut. And who the hell is this Tegan you just mentioned? I heard you! With your looks I suppose that you made her up to try to get me jealous. Wait till I get you home and into court you snake.'

'Can we just eat now?'

'Fine.' There was no more response from Marie and they both ate in silence. Akmal returned to their room immediately after eating and Marie, making a statement of severe annoyance, followed him after about ten minutes. "Tegan" made no attempt to follow Akmal as he went upstairs. Once they were together in their room, Akmal gave Marie a few minutes before he began the questioning. 'Alright Marie, what's going on and who is that Tegan woman in the restaurant, the one that looks just like *my* Tegan?'

'We are moving out tonight so you need to get packed.' Akmal was becoming really angry now and he felt that he was entitled to some proper answers. As a result his normal reserve vanished.

'That isn't what I asked you so, again, what the fuck is going on? You get me to face a woman that looks like Tegan, get me to chat her up, and it turns out that she is even called Tegan. Now none of that can be a coincidence.'

'I will tell you tomorrow.'

'You will tell me now or I will find that Tegan woman and lean hard on her until *she* tells me what's going on. As I was heading back up here I hid behind a curtain and telephoned *my* Tegan using my cloaked sim card, but, once my call had been connected, I heard a phone ring *in the restaurant behind me*. I saw that woman answer her phone, but I just left mine in my pocket and waited for her to ring off. It's time for some truth now Marie.'

'Alright Akmal. You'd better sit down.' Akmal sat on the bed and watched Marie intently as she began to speak.

'Akmal, the woman you call "your" Tegan is one of our oldest and best operatives.'

'What? You are mad, she would have told me if she was. I know that she is a brilliant technician, but she left all that behind after she finished uni. She never goes away on her own and I haven't seen her do any work from home, so how the hell *can* she be an operative, unless she works from home when I am out?'

'Have *you* told Tegan that *you* do this Akmal?'

'No, but I didn't want to worry her, and I only do this to buy the nice things that we now both take for granted. Anyway, this is all supposed to be secret so why would I tell her?'

'Akmal, how did you meet Tegan?'

'It was a blind date. My friend Paul arranged it.'

'Akmal, it wasn't a blind date. Tegan first saw you while you were both working. Do you remember your first assignment? It was in Paris, and you managed to successfully delete all those fake websites without the fraudsters knowing about it? You won't know that it was Tegan who initially found those websites by using her device, and it was her, and

I, that went out and picked them up afterwards. As a new recruit you got the organisation's thank-you dinner, so they paid for you to attend a post England/France football match party. You had no idea that I was there, or that I was accompanied by Tegan. She saw you chatting to a bunch of England fans and she was quite taken with you, so much so in fact that I gave her enough clues to find you when she got back to England. She is a superb operative, and very few would have found you from the clues I gave her, but find you she did, and it was Tegan who got *your* friend Paul to organise the blind date. Nothing blind about it at all. She told me that she had fancied a toy boy and that you looked like you would do. You were still eighteen then, and she was twenty four.' Akmal recalled his conversation with Tegan before he left home.

'I don't believe a word of that, and anyway, like I said, she never goes away.'

'But *you* do! She only makes herself available to us when you go away.'

Akmal stood up and paced around for a while. He began to look very worried as the penny began to drop.

'So Tegan is one of your best operatives. I'll deal with that bombshell later, but you wanted me to meet the woman downstairs who is also called Tegan. What's that about and why has she got Tegan's phone?'

'Akmal, she looks like Tegan but she isn't your Tegan. You agree with that don't you?'

'She does look a lot like Tegan but she certainly isn't my Tegan.'

'So work it out Akmal,' said Marie, patiently. Unfortunately, he had already worked out the worst case scenario and he was desperately hoping that he was wrong.

'So the Tegan I live with has been working for the organisation for years, and that woman downstairs is pretending to be my Tegan?'

'Yes', said Marie. 'We definitely have been employing "your" Tegan for years.'

'But I assume that *my* Tegan boarded a plane to get here, and is the mystery operative that I was due to meet if I didn't complete my mission. So the woman downstairs must be an imposter, and so surely we need to tell the organisation so they can find out what's going on.'

'Akmal, we can't. There's something else you need to know. Sit back down.' Akmal sat down, looking really anxious now. 'Go on.'

'We have a witness who thinks that he saw Tegan on the Sunday that "our" Tegan touched down in Montreal. Akmal, he saw her in the back of a black car and her mouth was taped over. He says that she stared at him and looked as though she was trying to get help.'

'Then we need the resources of the organisation to help us find her. She could be anywhere, or dead, but we have to find her.'

'Akmal, don't you see? We think that the false Tegan might be a *member* of the organisation. The first that anybody knew of *your* Tegan's association with this particular job would be just after you arrived at Heathrow last Saturday morning, because that's when she would have phoned her contact. Tegan only works for us when you are away, so the only way that this swap could have been arranged so quickly is if

97

somebody had already been prepared, and briefed, to replace her. Tegan is by far the best operative for the role she was to carry out here, and somebody must have realised that our fake Tegan looked so much like her that she could get away with foiling our efforts. They must have made sure that Gustav, Tegan's contact, had the dossier for this case, and that eventually Tegan would get the job. The fake Tegan knows too much about us, and about Tegan and her skills, to be anything other than a member of the organisation.'

'Shit,' said Akmal. 'So somebody that looks like Tegan has been recruited by somebody at "head office" to foil this job, expecting Tegan to be the one given the job in the first place?'

'Yes Akmal. We also feel that the imposter must work for the retailers of the fake weapons too.'

'Weapons? I thought we just did corporate stuff. So Tegan was put on the trail of gun smugglers? Is the organisation mad?'

'Believe me Akmal, if you had seen Tegan in action you would know that she can handle herself amazingly well. She must have been caught unawares last Sunday to have been taken as easily as she was.' None of this was giving Akmal any comfort.

'So Tegan is a real female James Bond who foils gun runners and takes down assassins.'

'Yes Akmal. You wouldn't stand a chance against her in combat.' Akmal sat silent for a while and thought about the woman he loved, about how foolish he must have seemed to her when he had talked about protecting her when they went out, and he felt embarrassed when he thought about some of their conversations. He wondered how things would be between them if they ever got back together. After a few more

98

minutes in these thoughts he suddenly said, 'Microchip. Marie, I have a microchip so that I can be located in an emergency. Surely Tegan will have one too. Can't we ask the organisation to locate her for us?'

'Listen Akmal. I can access operatives positions and I can assure you that trying to locate the real Tegan was the first thing I did. Unfortunately, the GPS locator system finds our Tegan exactly where the false Tegan is. Either her chip has been removed and put into the false Tegan's ankle, or they have a way of reprogramming the chip so that false information is sent out from it. Remember those electronic displays that supermarkets use now, the ones that look just like a label but shop assistants can reprogram from using a wireless directional programmer? Well it seems that they could be able to do that to our microchips because I can't see how they would have had time for surgery on Sunday night. Our Tegan went into her room and the fake Tegan must have emerged quite soon afterwards. This has been a sophisticated switch Akmal, and we will need all of our best people to find her. I hope that you are up for this?'

'Of course I am. When do we start and what is our plan? Hang on a minute, you said that our Tegan only works when I am away, so do you think that *I* was put on the case that I have finished just to release Tegan so that she could be swapped out?'

'To answer your second question first, yes, somebody had probably got you onto your case so that it would be Tegan that was put onto the fake weapons case. It did seem to be a rather simple problem for your skill set Akmal, and it seems odd that I was posted to be with you since you usually work alone.'

'But aren't you with me because I don't speak French?'

'How often have you needed my French speaking skills since you got here Akmal?'

'Actually, not often at all. Ordering food seems to have been the most common place I would need your help. So, you've been engineered into this too, to get you out of the way perhaps?'

'Yes Akmal. And to answer your first question, we are leaving the hotel tonight. Though the fake Tegan knew that another operative was staying in the hotel, she didn't know who it was. Now that she has met you, she might realise that it's you who is also on a case and take some action against you. So, we will be leaving at about 1am and staying with a man called Philippe Agarwal and his new girlfriend Camille. They are both members of the organisation, though Philippe is a new acquisition.'

'And are these two reliable? Can we trust them to be who they say that they are?'

'We have no choice but to trust them. I have worked with Camille on many occasions, and I think we can be happy with her. Not so certain of Philippe because he was only recruited to the organisation after the Tegan switch.' Akmal looked very tired all of a sudden. He realised that the new Tegan must be the person that he spoke to last Sunday, and that was why she didn't want to talk for long. The task ahead of them was going to be difficult and he wondered about his own safety as well as that of Tegan. His mood gradually changed from anxiety to fear.

'Is there a chance that this might be the end of the organisation in its current form?'

'Yes Akmal. That seems, at the moment, to be a possibility.'
Before repacking his case Akmal turned to Marie.

'So why did the organisation put us both together on these concurrent missions? What's that about?'

'The organisation doesn't like conflict and having two operatives that live together, but who don't work together, doesn't sit well with them. They decided to let you two meet whilst on assignment and let things sort themselves out.'

'And what if that that meant we separated or only one of us could continue?'

'Either of those would be their preferred option I'm afraid Akmal!'

'And presumably you would prefer to keep Tegan?'

'Yes Akmal. Now finish your packing.'

Chapter 13

Gareth and Helen had returned from shopping at about 6pm and, after putting away their shopping, Gareth set about preparing dinner. 'Let me do that,' said Helen. 'I have already disrupted your day so it's the least I can do.' Gareth agreed and allowed her to take over the preparations. A little later, and after boredom had set in a little, he wandered into the kitchen and noticed that, while preparing their omelettes, Helen had made some welsh cakes. The smell took him back to his youth in Wales and he suddenly felt very comfortable.

'If you ever want a job as a live in housekeeper the job is yours,' he said as Helen emerged from the kitchen.

'I don't know what your Delphine would think of that idea, but I might take you up on your offer when I'm in my dotage,' she said with a laugh.

'I doubt whether you will ever enter a dotage!' responded Gareth. He moved into the dining room and Helen joined him with the food. Gareth poured them out a glass each of a Canadian dry white wine, the mushroom omelettes were superb and the dessert of Welsh cakes and maple syrup went down very well indeed.

'Best dinner I have had for ages,' he said to Helen as she began to clear away the things. 'Leave those Helen, I will put them in the dishwasher later, but now I want you to come and sit down while we finish this bottle of wine.' Helen did as he said and sat down opposite to him in Gareth's smart, modern lounge.

'This room's lovely,' said Helen. 'All Delphine's work I suppose?'

'Yes,' replied Gareth. 'I am so lucky, and I will be glad when she gets back.'

'What is she up to at university then Gareth?'

'It's the final step of her course on interior design. This bit has to be done as a practical course and she will be graded on her work at the end. She's been away two months already, and I'll be glad to see her when she is finished.'

'Your house is so lovely that I can't see why she would need to do a degree in design.'

'It's not quite a degree Helen, but remember that Helen is younger than me, and she would like to further develop her career in interior design, so she would benefit from this qualification. She's only in Toronto but we agreed that she should complete the course without coming back here for breaks. It will help keep her in the mindset of a student, she said.'

'Away from us oldies you mean,' said Helen.

'Definitely,' replied Gareth and they laughed.

'Now, back to this barn of yours. Describe the doors to me. What size are they and what sort of locks were fitted.'

'Now, it's not *my* barn, but you are right in your assumption that I want us to go up there and have another nosey around. The doors are about 8 feet high and each one of the pair is about 3 feet wide. There seemed to be only a bolt, about 8 inches long, that was held in place by a hefty padlock, but the bolt and hasp seemed only to be held in place by screws. They would easily be removed from that rotting wood. We'd only need a crowbar, or even just a screwdriver, and that bolt will be off.'

'Good. Now what about security cameras?'

'I told you earlier that I didn't look for those, sorry Gareth, but I wasn't expecting any security when I went up there, it is just Ned's barn after all.'

'Considering the visits you had earlier today, I think that something's up round there. We'd better take quite a few torches and stands.'

'Agreed,' said Helen. After the pleasantness of the meal and the sedative effect of the wine, they both fell asleep.

Without checking out, Marie and Akmal left their hotel at 1.15am carrying only light luggage, and they departed on foot. It was now Friday morning and Akmal was so tired that he began to feel as though he had been in Canada for months, rather than just five days! They walked about a half a mile along a tangle of local streets before getting into a taxi that took them to the "Rockaberry" restaurant in Monkland Village. They headed toward the restaurant, but then backtracked as soon as the taxi had disappeared. They then had a thirty minute walk to Philippe's house. There they were met by a very fresh looking Philippe. A very tired Akmal's first words to him were to ask why he looked so awake.

'I am a waiter so I don't get up early. I have only been at home for thirty minutes myself. I am Philippe Agarwal by the way and you must be Akmal Ibori?'

'I am indeed.' Akmal invited Marie to introduce herself.

'We have already met,' said Marie.

'I'm beginning to wonder whether I know anything at all about this organisation,' said Akmal, with some despondency.

'I'm Marie Bernard,' said Marie to Philippe, just to make Akmal feel better.

'I need to sleep,' said Akmal, so Philippe showed them to their room. It was a spacious and stylish room with twin beds which, unfortunately, was a pair of large bunk beds.

'You can sleep on the bottom bunk because of your bulk. I don't want to wake up to find you on top me,' said Marie. Akmal gave her a look and she realised the ramifications of what she had just said. For the first time in ages they both laughed.

Back at Gareth's house, Helen had woken first. It was 2.35am. 'Gareth. Wake up.' Gareth woke slowly and it was clear that he had been dreaming.

'Helen, what are you doing here?'

'Wake up Gareth. We have work to do.' After looking at him she decided that they both needed coffee. An hour later they were dressed in their black "work clothes", and Gareth had a holdall containing everything that they might need for their night's work. They set off in his new Ford pickup at 4am. It was still very dark but the lights on the truck were very bright, and finding their way up there wasn't a problem. They parked about 200 yards short of the barn and they approached it together, deliberately using a rather dim torch to light the way. Gareth used his low light camera to view the spot that Helen was illuminating with that really dim torch and, and once in the barn's yard, they were, between them, able to spot 3 security cameras. Hoping that this was all there was they set out with 3 really bright led torches that they had previously fixed onto tripod stands. Within minutes, all three torches were set up to direct a very bright beam into all three cameras. Though the cameras would have "seen" the figures setting up the torches, all that they would had recorded was the sight of black clad figures in balaclavas, who could have been anybody. Helen and Gareth realised that the alarm would likely now be triggered, but they didn't intend staying long.

Working quickly now they headed for the barn and, within seconds, the hasp was off the barn doors and they were both inside. They hadn't had to use the crowbar; Gareth had only had to unscrew four rather loose screws and they were in. Now using the crowbar, they quickly ascertained that the coffee crates contained a variety of weapons. This had rather disconcerted them, and they decided that this was more than they were expecting, so they set about leaving but, as they were considering what do next, they heard a noise. They stood in silence, breathing shallowly, and there it was again.

'That sounds like snoring,' whispered Helen. 'Perhaps it's a dog, and if it is I hope it's chained up.'

'I think that a dog would have woken up by now and we'd hear it barking. We'd better see what it is.'

'Are you sure Gareth?'

'Yes. We can't go without finding out what this is. We'll only be back up here again tomorrow night, as well you know!' Helen nodded, realising that he was quite right. Cautiously and quietly, they approached the source of the sound and, behind a curtained off area, they found a woman in what appeared to be a makeshift bed. She seemed to be attached to the wall by a pair of chains and a leg cuff. Gareth looked at Helen.

'What the hell is going on here?' he whispered, 'Do you think we should wake her?'

'She's chained up, and I don't think that she can harm us, so I think that we should.' At that point the woman woke up anyway and looked at the unlikely pair in astonishment. It wasn't long before she realised that these two might be able to help her, they definitely didn't look like henchmen!

'Please, get me out of here, and quickly. They aren't far away and they will soon know that somebody is here. I don't care who you are, just get me away from here. *Please!*'

Without any further thought, Gareth used his crowbar to get the shackle from the timber wall, and then the three of them, looking an unlikely trio, prepared to flee the scene. Helen said that they should leave the torches shining into the security cameras as they departed, to which Gareth agreed, and Gareth's decision to refasten the hasp onto the barn door was also met with *her* approval. The whole process had taken less than 5 minutes, and as they ran to Gareth's truck the woman, trailing one of her chains and carrying the hasp, began to explain that she had been abducted by the crew that used the barn to store those guns and that she needed to ring for help as soon as possible. Once in Gareth's truck they headed back down the mountain, but Gareth didn't drive straight home. Instead, they headed for a secluded clearing that he knew wouldn't be visible from the road. There they got out of the truck and, using the trucks dim dip headlights for illumination, Helen began to question the woman, leaving the leg cuff in place, with Gareth standing on the chain so that she couldn't escape.

'Name?' demanded Helen in a very authoritative manner.

'Tegan Durand.' Helen was taken back to the day that she learned of the death of her daughter, Tegan. She hadn't heard that name spoken in a very long time, and she had to pause for a while.

'Where are you from?'

'A small town in England called Iver Heath.'

'That's not exactly round the corner is it, so what are you doing chained up in a barn so far away from home?'

'I came here to investigate the illegal trade in those weapons that you found in that barn up there, but I was abducted before I could do anything.' Helen looked at Gareth.

'Abducted! Do we believe that?' she asked him.

'Carry on with your questions Helen. We can decide that when you have finished.'

'When did you arrive in Canada?'

'Last Sunday. The flight got in at about five minutes past ten, Spanish time, five past four Canadian time.'

'Good, we can check that.'

'Where were you staying when you got here?'

'I can't tell you that because I don't know who *you* are, and I might put *my* colleagues in danger. Please take these chains off me. I won't run away.'

'That's a reasonable answer, but I need some sort of proof. Do you have any means of identification with you?'

'No. I was abducted from my hotel room before I had even unpacked. They took my mobile phone, and everything else that I had in my pockets, away from me. They even removed my tracker chip. Look at my ankle.' Helen looked at her ankle and saw a now rather grubby sticking plaster on her heel, just by her ankle.

'Tracker chip?'

'All of my colleagues have one fitted so that we can be found if things turn ugly. My abductors must have known about that so it seems likely that they have infiltrated my organisation. It's imperative that I find my colleagues to tell them about this.' Gareth butted in at this point.

'It also seems likely that we need to get this done quickly because I imagine that someone will be along soon to find out why that alarm has been triggered.' He broke one of the chains from the cuff using the chisel and hammer from his tool kit, but he left the second chain and the cuff in place. 'In case you try to leg it,' he added. They got back in the truck, with Tegan making no attempt to run, and drove further down the mountain

'Have either of you got a mobile phone?' Tegan asked, quite suddenly.

'You can borrow mine,' said Helen, 'provided that we can listen in.'

Tegan dialled the only number that she could remember, and trust, and she hoped that he was awake.

Chapter 14

Earlier that morning, James Jackson Martin, one of Helen's neighbours, had woken up with a headache. It was only 2am, so a long time before he needed to get up, and his wife was fast asleep. Their farmstead stood just a half a mile from Ned's barn and he would drive past it on his weekly trips into town. He was due to do that later today, but not if he couldn't shift this headache and get some sleep.

'I'll have to lay off the booze for a while,' he told himself. His wife was snoring peacefully, so he carefully got out of bed to find some water and an aspirin. He found that in the kitchen, where he sat for a while before dozing off on the kitchen chair. He awoke with a start at about 4.30am, and it took him a while to work out where he was. He was just about to return to bed when he thought he heard a noise, which he was in two minds about whether to investigate. Hoping that his hen house was still intact he decided that he had better venture out, so he went to find his flashlight. After a brief look around he decided that all seemed well with his small holding, but then he heard a truck in the distance. He climbed on top of his porch wall and peered down the mountain. There were lights on down there, near to that barn, and a truck or something similar was driving toward it.

'Now what could be going on down there at this time of night?' He decided to call the local police in Sainte-Agathe-des-Monts. He hoped that it would be his friend Eric who would be on late duty, and he was delighted to find that it was.

'Hey dude, there's something amiss by Ned's barn. Think you should investigate it?'

'Hi Jackson. Yeah, this is the second night in a row I've heard reports of goings on around there. I'll get onto the station and see what they want me to do.'

'Thanks dude. See you Thursday next as usual?'

'Sure thing Jackson. Bye now.'

Eric found the police in the station at Saint-Jérôme to be very helpful but this was mainly because they had already become concerned about what might be going on up there. Their new drone was already prepared and they relished the chance to finally use it. It was despatched within minutes and they knew that it would be over the barn in about twenty minutes more. It was too dark for officers to attend on horseback so a car containing three officers (who had, up until then, been bored witless) followed, expecting to be there in about 40 minutes. The drone, which was fitted with an infra red camera, arrived at the barn just as Helen, Tegan and Gareth were leaving it.

The operator spotted them quickly and he got the drone to follow them. He watched the three of them enter Gareth's truck, and then he got the drone to follow that until it reached the clearing. After a while, fearing that this might be a decoy, the drone returned to the barn where it carried out a tour of the area. The three torches shining up at the security cameras was a concern but, seeing that nothing else seemed to be amiss, the operator decided to send the drone back to look in on the three in Gareth's truck. It was at that moment though that Josh's truck arrived, and so the drone operator changed his mind, and he watched this action instead, and noted that one of the men from the truck had keys to the barn. He saw that, while the key holder went inside the barn, the other could be seen patrolling around outside.

'How long before you reach the barn?' the operator asked when he radioed the driver of the police car.

'About 5 minutes,' came back the reply.

'It looks like the owners of the barn, or the caretakers, are there now. Do a silent entry, see what you can catch them doing.'

'Will do. We'll keep this channel open so that you can update us if needed.'

'Excellent. Currently, one individual is in the barn, one outside patrolling.'

'Got that. We'll stay in touch.'

It was at this point that Akmal's phone rang in Philippe's flat and, though he had left it by his bedside, it failed to wake him. Tegan continued to ring him, hoping that Akmal would eventually answer, but it seemed to be of no use. Fortunately, at about 5am, Philippe had got out of bed to use the bathroom.

'Now why's Akmal's phone ringing?' he thought. When it was still ringing as he returned to his room he thought he had better knock on Akmal's door in case he was dead or something similar. When he got no reply from Akmal's door he went in and answered the phone.

'Allo.' Relieved, Tegan almost shouted down the phone. 'Could you get me Akmal please?'

'Yes, if I can wake him.' Tegan didn't know what time it would be in Paris, and she was confused as to why a man would be next to Akmal while he was asleep.

'Please do try,' she shouted down the phone. Akmal finally woke to Philippe's shaking and now it was Akmal who was confused when Philippe passed him the phone.

'Hello?'

'Akmal, it's Tegan.'

'What?'

'It's Tegan. Your girlfriend remember? The one who promised to buy a plastic replica of you if you were in Paris for too long.'

'Tegan. Is it really you? We were worried sick in case you were dead?'

'Akmal, what are you talking about? Why did you think I was dead and who's "we"?'

'It's a long story Tegan, but I'm so relieved to hear your voice. Where are you?'

'Akmal, you won't believe this, and it's a long story too, but I'm in Canada. You need to contact the British Embassy in Canada to come and rescue me.'

'Exactly where are you? I might be able to come and get you myself.'

'What? Have you any idea how long it'll take you to get here from Paris?'

'Tegan, *I am in a town near to Montreal*. Where exactly are you?'

'What are you doing in Montreal? Never mind,' began Tegan, but then Akmal heard her muffled voice ask where she was.

'You can pick me up as soon as possible in Sainte-Agathe-des-Monts. Please come immediately if you can. Once you get to the town ring me back and we'll arrange a place to meet.' Tegan heard Akmal tell Philippe to wake Camille and Marie. 'And who are Camille and Marie, and Philippe for that matter. Just what are you up to? Don't forget that I know your weak spots so if there's mischief going on there I will hurt you a lot!' After that rather brusque comment, Akmal knew that this *must* be *his* Tegan.

'Tegan, it's so good to hear you, you have no idea how scared we've been. We'll be there with you soon.'

Philippe's house now became a hive of activity, and they decided that Philippe would drive Akmal and Camille to Sainte-Agathe-des-Monts. Once that had been decided it had only taken them ten minutes to get ready, and to programme the sat nav, and they were on their way shortly after that. Akmal rang Tegan back on the number she had used to call him. Helen answered the phone but then put the call on speaker phone.

'Tegan? We'll be in Sainte-Agathe-des-Monts in just over an hour. Where do you want to rendezvous?' Gareth answered that.

'It'll be better if you meet us in Saint-Jérôme because that is halfway between us and you. We don't want to stay and wait for you and then for you to have to pass through Saint-Jérôme to get here. There's a park in Saint-Jérôme called Parc régional de la Rivière-du-Nord. Programme your sat nav for that and we'll see you there in about forty minutes. Ring when you get there.'

'Will do,' replied Akmal. 'Back to Saint-Jérôme then. We'd better keep well away from the hotel though while we're there. We don't want to bump into "Tegan"!' Meanwhile Camille, who was sitting in the back of Philippe's car, had seemed very quiet.

'What's up Camille?'

'I think I'd better ring Marie,' she replied.

'Why?' asked Akmal. Camille didn't reply further but instead removed her phone from her jeans pocket, and dialled Marie's number. Marie answered surprisingly quickly.

'Marie, I've been thinking about the fake Tegan. I think you know that my gun is in the drawer next to my bed.'

'I'm ahead of you Camille. I've unlocked Philippe's gun cabinet so I've got a pistol and my Taser, and I'm already on my way.'

'Excellent Marie, but be very careful and don't take any chances. Ring the hotel on your way and have somebody prepared with either a key to her door or a battering ram.'

'Already on it Camille, it's all arranged. I'll let you know when the job's done.'

'What was that about Camille?' asked Akmal.

'Leave things to us now Akmal. Think about Tegan and what you two want to do when you meet up again.'

Akmal was becoming increasingly agitated in his seat because he had been running everything he had so recently learned through his head, and he was impatient to talk to Tegan. Forty eight hours ago he was looking forward to going home, perhaps going off to Oxford for that romantic weekend that they had originally planned for the previous weekend, and now all this. *All* of it. He wondered whether anything he knew about Tegan had ever been real, and whether she really had fancied him enough to arrange that blind date that he had

115

supposed had been all his friend Paul's doing. He looked at his watch and the sat nav. They would be at the meeting place in about ten minutes, and he hoped that this really was Tegan, that she was OK, and that his many questions might then finally be answered. Somehow, deep down, he felt that that wouldn't be the case, and that nothing would be the same again.

The scene was set and they were soon to become united again, the only fly in the ointment being that two men had finally got out of bed to answer their alarm call. They had estimated that they would be at the barn in twenty minutes or so.

Chapter 15

Light was beginning to appear in the night sky as the truck containing the two alarm company operatives began slowly driving up towards the barn. Neither of the occupants was in the best of moods, having had their sleep disturbed for a second time this week. Driving an old Ford truck, and both wearing white tee shirt and jeans, they looked an unlikely pair. The passenger was about twenty two years old and, with a carefully manicured stubble and a gym fit body, it was clear that he spent a lot of time looking after himself. Despite having been roused from sleep so unceremoniously, he had combed his hair, checked his beard, and applied some face moisturiser. The driver was a little older but heavily overweight, and he had an unkempt face that his mate said could probably shatter glass.

'If it's a fucking cougar or a moose again I'll shoot it's head off.'

'Yeah, I'm tired of this too. It's the second night in a row that we've had to get up at this hour to visit that damned barn. That stupid old woman we saw yesterday was just nosing about I reckon. Now this. If it's her again she'll be a target for shooting too.'

'Yeah, and we drove all the way to her house and the fucker wasn't there. Waste of time that was.'

'Perhaps she fell down the mountain in the dark last night, in that stupid old truck of hers. That will have put paid to the interfering old cow.'

'Funny that we couldn't see anything on the cameras tonight though. Just a sort of fog. If this is a fault in the system, I'll shoot the installers of that lot too.'

'Perhaps we can wake up our guest? Have some fun with her. We can take turns if you like. I'm just in the mood for some play time.'

'Yeah. Nice idea but you are an ugly fucker, and I don't reckon I want to see you play with anybody. Leave her be tonight. There's other ways for me to have *my* fun with her.'

'You want her yourself then do you pretty boy? You think she'll fancy you after you've chained her up?'

'I've never been refused before. Anyway, it wasn't me that chained her up and she'll be mine once I release her, and I don't want her soiled by you.'

'Charming. You really fancy her don't you?'

'Yeah, actually I do, and I wish we had met properly. When I turn into the good captor and let her go free she'll be like putty in my hands. She'll very probably go out with me.'

'What, like go out on a dinner date and stuff? You'll chat her up, take her out for the night and then back to your place? You live in a fairy tale world Jean.'

'I suppose I do but it's worth a go, and I can dream can't I? I will release her in two days time when the cargo's gone, and sod the boss. I'll explain to her that I had no idea what was going on, and let her know that it was me that saved her from a grizzly death. I'll put on my little boy lost act and she'll be all mine.' There was silence for a few minutes as they got closer to the barn. Josh was secretly very jealous of Jean's good looks, and his prowess with women, and he was hatching a plan to get this woman for himself.

'Who would want gorgeous Jean when that pretty smiling face had a scar a mile wide across it?' That thought had gone through his mind while Tegan was speaking on the phone to Akmal, and while he and Jean were just pulling into the area in front of the barn.

'I hope that she's had a good night's sleep,' said Jean, looking dreamy eyed.

'You've really got the hots for her haven't you?'

'Yeah,' replied Jean. 'I've had quite a few hot dreams with her playing the lead role, and I want her looked after, so you keep away from her, do you hear? I don't want her spoiled.'

'You think that you're the only good looking man in the world, don't you. What if it's me that she fancies then Jean?'

'You'll be dead before you get close to her.'

'You're really serious aren't you.'

'*Deadly* serious,' grunted Jean.

They were silent as they got out of the truck. Josh sent Jean to see what the problem was with the cameras while he went to look at the barn doors.

'There's a torch shining up at all three of these!' shouted Jean.

'The barn doors are still locked though,' shouted Josh. 'I'll just check inside.' After a few minutes Josh shouted for Jean.

'Jean, get in here. You have to see this. Quickly, just to the left of the crates.' Jean stopped collecting up the torches and ran into the barn, but he didn't see the metal bar that Josh had poked into one of the crates, just above ankle height, or the knife that was sticking out from a pole attached to the wall.

119

He caught the bar, just as Josh had hoped, but he missed the knife that was meant to slash his face. He had been running so fast though that he landed headfirst on the concrete floor of the barn. Howling with laughter, Josh ran to his aid. With his script learnt he knew what he was about to say. Unfortunately, Jean seemed unconscious when he reached him.

'Shit. I'll have to wait for him to come round now.' But then he saw the blood, the blood that was slowly oozing out from his nose, then appearing from his mouth, and then from between his eyelids.

'Jean, Jean, wake up!' Josh shook him, but Jean wasn't waking up, nor was he responding to being prodded. Then, after a gasp, he shuddered slightly, and then he was no longer breathing. Josh realised with horror that Jean was dead. 'Fuck, fuck, fuck. That wasn't the plan at all. You were supposed to get your face slashed by my knife, not die! What the hell do I do now?'

Now in a panic, Josh ran outside to think.

'I'll get that Tegan woman and put her in the truck. I can say that we disturbed an intruder. *That will work.* I'll say that he tried to run past me and that I tripped the intruder up, but he knocked Jean down as he fell. The intruder wasn't harmed because he fell on Jean, but Jean had hit his head on the concrete floor. *Yes, that will work too.* The intruder escaped after knocking me down before I realised just how hard he was running at me. Jean was dead when I reached him. Then I'll say that when I went to check on the woman she was gone. *Yes, that's definitely what I will do.* Then I will keep her as my woman. She can have my kids. Yes, that's the best way out of this, *and I get to keep the woman*. I'd better go and get her now.'

After those rather cartoon like thoughts, Josh headed for the curtained area of the barn. Once there, and despite his great weight, you could have knocked him down with a feather when he found that Tegan had gone, that she actually really had escaped. He had killed Jean to get that woman to be his "fuck buddy" and now he couldn't have her either.

'Now what? Could this day get any worse?'

It had actually just become substantially worse for Josh; he hadn't heard the police car arrive while he was still in the barn, and he stiffened when he saw them as he left. But once he *had* seen them, and he had realised that somebody must have telephoned the police and given them the whereabouts of the crates of weapons, he began to panic. The police must have acted very swiftly indeed. Now, Jean was dead, *he* would soon be arrested, and the weapons would be impounded. The owner of those weapons, he realised, would be very displeased. Whatever the owner's plans were, they would now have to change and he, Josh, would have to have a very convincing story for him, and for the police. He decided to try to make a run for his truck, but the police car had glided into his path, just as he was emerging. He began to run but his bulk held him back, and he was quickly apprehended by two of the officers. One of the officers handcuffed him to a downpipe on the barn wall before helping his colleagues explore the barn, the other remaining outside to look around.

The outside of the barn had seemed perfectly normal, a bit clean for an old barn perhaps but nothing to worry about.

Inside it though was a completely different matter. Between the three officers the finds included lots of crates of weapons, the remains of what looked like a bed that had been used recently because it was warm inside, and a dead body, also still warm.

'What the hell do you reckon's been going on here then?' asked officer Lee as the three officers assembled to the rear of the barn.

'God knows, but whatever it was it's happened recently, and we've got that dude in the yard. He must know something about it,' replied officer Storey. 'Maybe get the drone operator to look around and see whether anything comes to light.

'Good idea. I'll contact him now. You two help our friend from outside to get into the car. I'll get onto Montreal and order a truck to collect these crates. We'd better look after them until their owner can be found. We can't just leave coffee crates that contain weapons in a barn in the middle of nowhere, can we? Williams, will you be OK to wait for the collection vehicle?'

'Should be. I'll also check out that truck over there in case I need a getaway vehicle in a hurry! I'll order an ambulance for the dead dude.'

Officer Storey approached the apprehended man, asked his name and address etc, removed his phone and demanded the keys to his truck. Josh hadn't been very forthcoming with his personal details.

'Well then "No Comment", when you left your home in "No Comment" this morning, were you alone?'

'Yes.'

'That's better. So did you arrive here with a man, the one who is now dead in that barn? Maybe you collected him from his home, and brought him here with you?'

'No comment.'

'OK, well I actually know the answer to part of that question because this truck is registered to you, and we have video footage of you arriving with somebody else, a man that looked rather like the dead man in the barn, and that means that we will have to assume that you killed him, so I will ask you again, did you collect that man from his home and bring him here with you.'

'Alright, yes I did.'

'And what brought you both up here in the middle of the night?'

'We've been employed by the alarm company to come out to investigate alarm soundings. This one rang this morning.'

'What time?'

'It will be in the log. About 4.15am I think. Look, can I sit down somewhere? I'm shaking because I'm cold and my mate's dead. Have a heart.'

'OK. We'll pause at this point, and you can continue this interview down at the station.'

Within minutes of that conversation, Josh and officer Storey were in the car and ready to leave. It turned out that a weapons truck would take a while to get to the barn so it was decided that both officers Williams and Lee would wait for the ambulance, and then remain and wait for the weapons truck. Officer Storey and Josh though were soon on their way to the station, at about the same time that Helen and her party were arriving in Saint-Jérôme.

123

Officers Williams and Lee paced around for about 15 minutes and spent a while studying the area around the barn. The structure itself was surrounded by trees and the remains of a wooden fence. There were two access roads, if you could call those dirt covered tracks roads, and the nearest house was just a spot in the distance. 'Ned's' house had been demolished after his death, mainly because it had begun to fall down and was deemed a hazard. The two officers decided that this was a desolate place, especially in the slightly eerie early light of that May morning. They eventually settled into Josh's truck to wait for the weapons vehicle and the ambulance.

Chapter 16

While still at Philippe's house, Marie studied the pistol and the Taser that she had unpacked, and, after some thought, she decided that Angus would have to be called in. He was the nearest backup now that Akmal and Tegan weren't around. Upon reflection, she had decided against calling the hotel before their arrival, and instead only called Angus.

'Hi Angus, it's Marie.'

'Hi Marie, when and where do you want me? I assume that this is an emergency or you wouldn't have called at this hour.' Marie gave Angus the name and address of the hotel and the room number where he would find her. He replied that he would be there in forty five to fifty minutes. Marie thought that she would be there before him, and she set off in Camille's hired Prius.

She arrived at the hotel at about 6am. She didn't call at reception, instead she marched straight up to Tegan's room, but as she rounded the landing at the top of the stairs she could see Tegan's door and she could see that it was open. "Tegan", it appeared, was just leaving with a large holdall, so Marie pulled out her pistol.

'Stop right there.' "Tegan" was startled by this but she managed to keep her cool.

'You aren't stopping me, I'm off.'

'I'm afraid that you're not "off", at least not yet. Back in!'
Reluctantly, "Tegan" re entered her room. Marie followed her
and sat on the bed. She used the pistol to gesture to "Tegan"
that she was to sit on the chair by the window. She kept the
pistol in her hand as she began to speak.

'So, exactly who are you really "Tegan"?'

'My name is Tegan Durand, just like it says in the signing
in book downstairs.'

'No it isn't. Show me your ankle.' "Tegan" showed Marie
both ankles and there were no signs of a scar or new wound
on either.

'So where's your tracker chip "Tegan"?'

'You know where it is.'

'I know where it should be and I know that you have
Tegan's about you somewhere, so where is it?' There was no
reply. Marie was becoming impatient and her voice moved
up a gear. 'My colleague will be here soon, and he will delight
in being able to strip search you, *so where is it?*' "Tegan" sighed
and showed her left hip to Marie. A new but healing wound
was there, suggested that that was indeed where the tracker
chip had been inserted.

'Open the holdall.'

'No, you open it.'

'I'm tried of this game now "Tegan". I will happily wait for
my colleague to do this and he really isn't very nice. So open
the damned holdall.' "Tegan" eventually obliged, and Marie
could see that all of Tegan's electronics kit was in there,
alongside some of Tegan's clothes. She had no idea which
"Tegan" was the real owner of the clothes so she ignored
those.

'Take the electronic devices out of the bag then do it back up please.' "Tegan" obliged with very little enthusiasm and, just as she finished, there came a knock at the door.

'Come in Angus.' Angus obliged.

'Tegan?'

'No,' said Marie. 'A Tegan clone. Have you got your police ID with you?'

'I do.'

'We'll be off then.' "Tegan" walked very slowly out of the hotel, in the manner of a naughty schoolgirl who had been caught steeling sweets. Marie followed her very closely and occasionally whispered 'Don't forget that there are two guns trained on you.'

Eventually "Tegan" behaved herself and walked out of the hotel in a nonchalant manner and, probably because of the two weapons that were trained on her, she had made no attempt to alert the reception staff to her evacuation. It was Angus who drove them to the police station because the officers there knew him, and his car, so access would be easier in that than in the Prius. It wasn't far to the "Poste de Police" in Saint-Jérôme and, after business had been concluded, he and Marie went out for breakfast, and a long catch up session.

Helen, Gareth and Tegan had said very little during their journey and it was a little after five thirty when they drove into the car park of the Parc régional de la Rivière-du-Nord. They had arrived before Akmal's little group and it was Helen that broke the silence.

'I know Iver Heath. Is there still a small, curved parade of shops near there, and is there still the film studios?'

127

'Yes to both of those,' replied Tegan. 'Pinewood studios is still there. We visited the place last summer and we could see the remains of the latest James Bond film sets. They let you in sometimes for a tour. I went with Akmal, the man who should soon be here. The parade of shops is still there but it's no longer greengrocers and stuff. I have seen pictures of it from the 1970s and it was much nicer then.'

'I was last there in the 1980s and we used to sometimes go shopping in Slough. Can you still get good shopping there?'

'You can, but Slough is now so full of offices that it's difficult to drive into. I spent 55 minutes getting there last week and it's only about 2 miles away.'

'So what businesses *are* in that little parade of shops near Iver?'

'As I said, the parade is still there but it's mainly hairdressers now. People in England don't shop any more, they just order online. Why do you know Iver Heath so well?'

'I worked at Pinewood once and was an extra in a "Carry On" film.'

'Wow. That must have been really cool to meet film stars and stuff. I've seen some of those films though and I didn't like them much.'

'Neither did I!' laughed Helen, 'though the early black and white ones were quite good.' Just then, Philippe pulled into the car park in his Range Rover and parked immediately behind Gareth's Ford. Akmal flew out of the passenger side and Tegan leapt out of the Ford. They looked at each other for a few moments.

'Tegan.'

'Akmal.'

'We have things to talk about,' said Akmal.

'Indeed we do,' said Tegan. Then they embraced, for quite a while.

'You smell,' said Akmal.

'So do you,' said Tegan.

'We need a shower,' they said in unison, and tearful laughter spilled from both of them.

Introductions having been made and embraces temporarily over, Akmal suggested that all six of them should have breakfast somewhere. A quick internet search revealed that Saint-Jérôme had one cafe that opened at 6am. They decided to leave the vehicles where they were and to walk to the cafe. After locking them they strolled along in three groups, Tegan with Akmal, Camille with Helen, and Philippe with Gareth. They found that they got along quite nicely, and by the time they had ordered breakfasts, they had the appearance of a gang of cafe regulars.

After finishing his breakfast and after having heard Tegan's entire tale about her abduction (the abductors had indeed already been in position in her hotel room when she had arrived on Sunday night, hidden in those drab but large cupboards, leaving suspicion both with the organisation *and* the hotel), Akmal suggested that it was time to decide what to do next.

'Well Tegan. You are the boss, so what do we do now.'

'What do you mean by "you are the boss" Akmal?'

'I know everything Tegan. *Everything.* From the prearranged blind date that you set up via my lying friend Paul, to your abilities in combat situations. I suppose that I should be upset about the blind date thing, but it fades into insignificance compared with the revelations about

129

everything else. I suppose I could just say that it all fascinates me, and it just goes to prove that nobody knows everything about their partner. But then I kept you in the dark about my involvement with the organisation so I shouldn't complain that you kept your part from me, except that you already knew about me before we even met, formally at least, so the secrecy from the organisation's point of view shouldn't have been necessary. So, since you do have the upper hand at the moment then you must decide what we do from this point on. I know what I would want to do, but now I must leave you to tell me.'

'Wow. That was quite a speech Akmal. I don't know whether to be impressed, upset or annoyed.'

'I feel the same myself,' interjected Akmal. Tegan looked slightly stunned for a while.

'I suppose that I need to stay here to help bring my abductors to justice, but I will need to find somewhere to stay. I will also need some money.' Akmal noted the continued use of "I", rather than "we", and this was despite her apparently knowing what a good agent Akmal has always been. He was about to respond but before he could begin his reply Camille approached them both and sat down with them.

'You two are going home to England.' The pair of them adopted expressions that Camille realised meant that they were about to argue. 'No discussion, no debate. I assume that you have read the organisation's rules the pair of you? Section 64, subsection 7a part (ii). "Should any agent be compromised in any way, or their life put in danger, then they must immediately cease any further involvement in their current job and return to their normal existence, and their own home.". So you see, you have no choice. I will arrange the flights, and there will be NO argument. You must find accommodation for tonight if I can't get you onto an afternoon flight. You must erase all details about Gareth or Helen that you have on your phone Akmal. They must not be put in any more danger.'

'What do we do while you are organising the flights? Do we need to keep out of sight or can we go into Montreal and sightsee before we leave?'

'Keep out of sight Akmal. I'm sure that Tegan would like to freshen up so maybe book into somewhere and wait to hear from me.' Camille then added 'Perhaps you shouldn't even stay in here for too long. You never know who might come in!'

'Then I must go and say goodbye to Helen and Gareth,' said Tegan. 'If it weren't for them I might still be stuck in that awful barn.'

'Good idea Tegan. Explain to them that they must remove all traces of us from their phones for their own safety. Actually Tegan, do that job for them will you, and make sure that they can't restore any thing from a backup.'

'Will do.' Tegan went over to the unlikely pair of heroes and gave each of them a hug. They were reluctant to hand over their phones but they complied in the end.

'I wish that we could keep in touch,' said Helen. 'It's been lovely having a young woman around for a change.'

'Once this is all over we will contact you again, at some time in the future. Maybe holiday here and look you two up.'

'I just live in...' began Gareth.

'No Gareth,' said Tegan, firmly but calmly. 'You must not tell anybody here your address. Nobody. Is that clear?'

'Yes,' they said in unison.

'And you mustn't stay here now in case you are seen. It's time you left the town to be honest. Thanks again for all of your help, but for your own safety you must go now.'

Reluctantly the pair of them obliged. They did as instructed but they perused a few shops, then the park itself, before returning to Gareth's Ford. It had been an astonishing day, and they were back at Gareth's place by tea time. They both had a long nap before attempting to prepare dinner. It had been a short night, but a very long day.

Chapter 17

Josh and Officer Storey arrived at the "Poste de Police" in Saint-Jérôme at about 6am that same morning, and Josh was given pride of place in a comfortable cell. He was held on suspicion of murder, and there he stayed while Officer Storey filled in the necessary forms, and then had her breakfast. She dealt with some other pressing matters next, but her mind was firmly on the events of the morning, and what she would say to Josh during the interview scheduled for later in the day. She had a twelve hour shift to enjoy today and she had started at 4am. She was already very tired, but she felt that it was nothing that some proper French coffee wouldn't cure.

At about 12.30pm, she and Inspector Roberts met in the interview room to discuss the morning finds, Josh was then brought in, and the interview began. The recorder was switched on and it was Officer Storey who began.

'Interview with a man arrested during a call to "Ned's Barn", Sainte-Agathe-des-Monts, this morning, May 24th. The arrested man has refused to give his name at the scene.'

'Good morning,' said the inspector. 'For the tape, would you please provide your name and address?'

'I want an attorney.'

'Do you have anybody in mind that we can call or are you happy to have our resident solicitor present?'

'There's nobody that I know, so yes, I'll have the resident solicitor.' After a twenty minute break, the interview resumed in the presence of the solicitor, who had already had ten minutes in private with Josh. After hearing what Josh had to say, the solicitor had spoken sternly to him.

'I advise you Josh to cooperate, and to stop saying "no comment" because this is a real situation that might become very serious, it is *not* a TV show.'

'But I don't want to go to prison,' wailed Josh.

'The truth please Josh!' Josh blurted out the entire morning's events, the solicitor said nothing in reply, and he then called for inspector Roberts to resume the interview.

'For the tape, this is a resumption of an interview with the man arrested during a call to "Ned's Barn", Sainte-Agathe-des-Monts, this morning, May 23rd. Sir, would you please tell us your name and address?'

'Josh Howard. Rue Principale, Saint-Sauveur.'

'Thank-you. And who was your colleague, the man that we found dead in the barn this morning. He was your colleague wasn't he?'

'We worked together yes. He was Jean Belanger.'

'And his address?'

'Four doors down from me.'

'Why did you go up to the barn this morning?'

'We've been employed to monitor a burglar alarm attached to that barn and it rang this morning at about 4.25am, I think.'

'Did you go straight there?'

'It took a while to get Jean out of bed, lazy bastard, but then we went straight there.'

'In your truck?'

'Yes.'

'Who employs you to do this Josh?' asked officer Storey.

'I don't know.'

'What do you mean, you don't know?' asked the inspector.

'I mean just that. I work for "Paddy's alarms" in Saint-Jérôme, and one day I got a phone call, out of the blue, telling me that I had been "hand picked" for a special alarm job. I thought it was a scam so I asked for $100 up front. They said that they would deliver that to my workplace within two hours. When I got back to the office after work that night it was there waiting for me, in an envelope. Next day they called me back. I asked whether Jean could help me and they said yes, but that I would have to share the $180 a day with him. Seemed a good deal.'

'And when was that?' asked the inspector.

'Ten days ago.'

'And were you paid?'

'Yes. An envelope arrived every day. I once saw a young kid put it through the letterbox.'

'Could you describe the kid?'

'No. Just a kid. They all look alike.'

'So you've no idea who was paying you?'

'No.'

'Did you know what was in the barn?'

'Not before I accepted the job, but we did look around on our first security visit. There are lots of coffee crates.'

'Did you open those?'

'No. Can't stand coffee.'

'Anything or anybody else there?' asked officer Storey. Josh now became hesitant.

'There was a, err, woman. She was in a room at the back of the barn.'

'A woman? There was no woman there when we arrived.'

'She must have escaped. She wasn't there today.'

'Was she there for the whole ten days?'

'No, she was there Monday night when we went to check the place. We used to drive up there every night after work. Just to check round and to be seen on the cameras so the boss knew we were doing our job.'

'What was she doing there?'

'I don't know. She was chained to a wall plate. We always saw food and drink in there so she wasn't starved and she was free to move, except for being chained to the wall by her leg. She was clean and all, but chained up.'

'Did you speak to her?'

'Yes. Jean fancied the pants off her, and wanted to free her and run away with her, but I said we shouldn't because our boss wouldn't be pleased.'

'So you spoke to her?'

'Yes. She always pleaded with us to let her go, but we couldn't, and it tied our stomachs in knots to leave her there, but we had no choice.'

'So you spoke with her when you inspected the barn?' asked officer Storey.

'Yes. She was nice, English I think, but she spoke our language very well.'

'Did she give you a name?'

'Yes. Tegan Durand she said. She asked us to tell the police she was there, but we couldn't. The boss might well have killed us.'

'And she was gone when you got there this morning?' asked the inspector.

'Yes. Jean unlocked the barn and let me in, but then he went and checked around outside to see why the alarm was ringing. I checked inside, the coffee crates were still there but I found her gone.'

'And Jean followed you into the barn?'

'What makes you think that he followed me into the barn?'

'We had a drone watching you.'

'So that's how you saw us up there this morning you bastards! So you don't need to ask me all these questions do you?'

'Please just answer the question.' The duty solicitor nodded to Josh.

'Yes, I shouted for Jean to come inside quick, and it wasn't long before he ran into the barn. I was looking around the woman's prison room, in case she was hiding, when I head Jean scream. I went out and found him next to a crate, dying. He died in my arms. He had tripped over a pole and landed on his head. There was blood coming out of his.....' He broke down then but recovered after a few moments. 'She must have left a trap for us before she escaped. I had come the other way around the crates so that must be why I missed her trap.'

'Alright. I think that we had better leave things there for now. Officer Storey will escort you back to your cell and, once the paperwork is done, you will be released without charge, provided that you don't leave the area, and that you promise to contact us immediately if your employer rings you. We expect your full cooperation. Is that clear?'

'Yes inspector. Thank-you.'

'And don't think that we won't be watching you!' Josh said something rude about a state where you can't even have a shit without being watched but all around him ignored it. They were used to much worse.

'Do you believe all of that Carole?' the inspector asked officer Storey after Josh had been escorted out.

'I think he's holding something back,' replied the officer, but before she could add any more she heard her phone ring. 'Shall I get this ma'am?

'Go ahead. We'll talk again later.' Officer Storey had been called because there was trouble in one of the cells.

'There's a woman in cell 3 that's creating mayhem, and she keeps demanding to see the officer in charge. She keeps shouting that she needs to speak to some organisation or other.'

'Well that sounds intriguing, so go along and see what she has to say. Keep me informed.' Carole Storey walked along to cell 3 after leaving ten minutes for the prisoner to wear herself out somewhat. After the interview, which she had conducted through the bars of the cell, she returned to see inspector Roberts. Storey knocked on the inspector's door and Roberts seemed pleased to see her.

'I've been thinking about that Josh character and I thought I'd like to speak to him again. Is he still here?' asked the inspector.

'Yes, he is, but before you do that you need to hear this,' replied Carole.

'Sounds intriguing. OK, carry on then!'

'There's a character in cell 3 who was brought in by a Marie Bernard of the "Organisation for the Investigation of Worldwide Corporate Fraud", based in the Netherlands. She was actually driven here by Angus, remember him?'

'I do, *Angus*, well well well.'

'Marie provided some identification papers that we are looking into now. The *documents* were scanned into our database, but no match has been found for those yet. Further checks have been made though, and there *is* such an organisation (the OIWCF), and we are trying to get information about this Marie woman from them. She claims to be French, but at the moment we can't find such a person either here or in France. There are many Marie Bernards, but none fit her description. The really interesting thing though is that the woman she brought in *claims to be Tegan Durand*, the same name as the woman who apparently escaped from that this morning. But the Marie that brought her in said that this woman was an imposter, that she was *impersonating* Tegan Durand, and that the real one had been abducted. Now that would fit in well with Josh's story. The real one has escaped from her captors and this Marie character has brought in the imposter. But the woman in our cell, who also claims to be with the OIWCF, is demanding to speak to the OIWCF, and for us to do the same. She wouldn't do that if she were an imposter would she?' The inspector had to think for a while as she absorbed all that information.

'Well, you wouldn't think so would you? Does the Tegan in our cells seem genuine?'

'It's hard to tell, because at the moment she is really upset. Perhaps we should try to locate the one that the drone saw leaving the barn today.'

'I think that the chances of finding our early morning escapee are quite slim because she was clearly helped by comrades or whatever. Did the drone identify the getaway vehicle?'

139

'Yes, but the registration couldn't be seen. It's a Ford truck but there are literally thousands of those in the area, and in the dim light we can't even tell what colour it was.'

'What about the direction of travel?'

'All that we know is that it was coming down towards here, but it could be anywhere now. One of the accomplices appeared to be an old woman, but that might have been a disguise.'

'I agree.' She thought for a while. 'Perhaps I know the very person to discuss this with, someone with a vast experience of some of the weirder people of the world and who might be able to advise us!'

'I'll bet I know who you mean!'

'Yes, and you'd be right. I think I will visit my old dad tonight. He's seventy two now, but I bet you in return that he remembers a case or two like this from when he was an inspector back in England. I'll pick his brains I think. It'll be an excuse to let mum make my dinner anyway, and Henri can make his own tea tonight!'

'I don't suppose that I could join you could I?' Officer Storey had heard about Mrs. Roberts' cooking.

'No, they'd know that I want to discuss work and mum does her best to keep dad's mind off his old job.'

'OK. Have a nice evening then, and think of me with my baked beans while you enjoy some lavish haute cuisine!'

Chapter 18

Inspector Roberts arrived at her mum and dad's house at about 6.30pm that Friday night. It was her mother that greeted her at the door, and many hugs later they entered the living room, where her dad was smoking a pipe.

'Very Sherlock Holmes,' said the inspector as she entered the room. 'Is that brother of mine out again?'

'Janice! It's lovely to see you. Robbie is out trying to patch up his relationship with his girlfriend, as usual. How are you? How's work?'

'Both very well thanks dad. And you?'

'Mustn't grumble,' he replied. 'How's Henri?'

'A picture of health as usual. He thinks more about his abs and biceps than he does about me I think.'

'You wouldn't want him flabby and overweight now would you?' asked Mrs Roberts.

'What are you having for dinner mum?'

'It's shepherd's pie with carrots, greens and mash, now answer my question.'

'I think that you have just answered it for me! Can I stay for dinner?'

'Perhaps I see what you mean about Henri. Does steamed fish with rice get a bit boring then? '

'Just a bit!'

After a very filling dinner, which had included a steamed pudding dessert, Janice offered to help her dad with the washing up.

'Time you had a dishwasher dad.'

'No thanks. This is my contribution to the work that your mother does. I can't cook like she does, and I could never have done my job back in Basingrove without her looking after me the way she did. Anyway, what's the case that you want to talk to me about?'

'Nothing gets past you does it dad?' said Janice.

'Years of practice,' came the reply, and while the inspector's dad listened very carefully to his daughter's description of the day's events, they had no idea that at this point, Akmal and Tegan were on a plane bound for the UK, via Toronto Pearson International Airport.

'Well, now there's a tangle. So you have one Tegan Durand in custody, screaming because she says she isn't the imposter that you were told she is, and another Tegan Durand who is an escapee from abduction, and who has allegedly been sprung by accomplices after murdering a chap called Jean Belanger. This Jean Belanger worked with a Josh Howard for an alarm company but, as a pair, they were "moonlighting" to earn extra cash without knowing who they worked for. Does this stack up with their legitimate employers?'

'Yes, they do indeed work for "Paddy's alarms" in Saint-Jérôme and "Paddy" was devastated to hear of the death of Jean. It seems that Jean was very popular with female clients, and their alarms seemed to be much less reliable than those owned by men! "Paddy" had made a lot of extra cash out of Jean, especially when Jean attended these ladies by himself. It seems that "Paddy" turns a blind eye to his staff making extra money because he knows that he doesn't pay them well.'

'And what of this organisation that the Tegans are supposed to work for? Have you had any reaction from them?'

'Dad, though we have had contact and information *from* them in the past, it took our IT team ages to find a way to contact the "OIWCF" and they had to get into the dark web to find them. The IT guys were actually surprised that they responded to our communication at all, and even more surprised that they acknowledged the existence of a Tegan Durand on their books. They confirmed that she is working in Montreal and staying in Saint-Jérôme which, considering that they are supposed to be a secret organisation, amazed us all. They refused to say which they thought was the real Tegan though and wished us good luck. I'm glad that I don't work for them.'

'Organisations such as their's make huge sums of money Janice. They won't care two hoots about their staff. There is also the chance that this "swap", if it really did take place, was orchestrated from within the organisation itself, so they will be being careful.

And what do we know about the people that managed to find the "real" Tegan Durand, rescue her, set a trap to kill this obviously fit and healthy Jean bloke, and then escape without the CCTV being able to identify them?'

'Despite having a drone watching their escape, we know nothing. A man dressed in black, a woman, presumably Tegan, and what looked like a grey haired old lady were seen leaving the scene. The drone later caught sight of a Ford truck but they are extremely common around here, and in the dark the drone couldn't even determine its colour. The registration plate had been covered over. The drone was sent back to the barn when Josh and Jean turned up, so we don't even know where the truck went.'

'So do you know anything about this Tegan Durand, or the woman that brought her in?'

'The woman that brought her in showed us documents with apparently secret codes that the "OIWCF" confirmed are genuine. Her whereabouts are now unknown, but she was driven to the station by a man called Angus, who is known to us and is reliable. The Tegan that we have in custody told us that she was born in Scotland to Swiss parents and then moved to England with her partner. Her accent sounded English.'

'Janice, if your cover had been blown and you could play no further part in an operation, what do you think the organisation would have you do?'

'Go back home I suppose.'

'Absolutely right Janice.' Her dad was then quiet for a while. Janice could see that he was thinking up some scheme or other, and after about ten minutes sucking on a pipe that was now quite cold, he shouted for his wife Wendy. Wendy came in from the library.

'Yes dear?'

'Remember that trip back to England we have been talking about for a while? The one that we thought might help get rid of our feelings of homesickness even though we've been here for over ten years? Well I think that you, me and Janice should leave for Basingrove as soon as possible, maybe the day after tomorrow!'

'Do you think I can drop everything for a jaunt back to England with only two day's notice?'

'We've done it before.'

'Of course we have, when you were working.' Wendy stood thinking for a while. 'It'll be spring time now in England, with the cherry blossom and everything. Yes of course we will go back, it'll be lovely. Why the rush though?'

'Inspector Roberts here needs to find a missing Englishwoman, and I think that she will need to be in England to do that. I'm sure that she'd like some company so why not use us, and my contacts, to help her?'

'You never change,' said Wendy with a smile.

'Actually mum, I know dad so well that I expected him to suggest a trip back home, and my lovely employers at the Poste de Police have booked all three of us onto a flight tomorrow.' Janice waited for a storm to brew but none came.

'Have they booked us hotels then?' asked her mother.

'The flight takes us to Heathrow, so we are booked into the "Swan Hotel" which is just outside of Slough. We can change that after the first night if we want to. So we get a free trip back to England and Robert can look after the house while you are gone.'

'How did you get them to pay for your mother to come with us?'

'I told them that your sterling work as a detective chief inspector had left you needing mum's support. They became especially keen on the trip once I had told them that you were a detective inspector before you were thirty five. They said it must have been made possible by the presence of a good woman, so they agreed.'

'But, now that I am clearly to be in my dotage, if any police are at the airport, do I need to cling onto your mother for support?'

'That's about it dad!'

'I'm glad to see that you take after your mother!'

'Bloody cheek!' said Wendy.

'Have you checked the flight logs for departures from Montreal airport today Janice?'

'Yes dad. No Tegan Durand was booked onto any flight today, but a wider search revealed over a hundred Tegan's were flying out today. We've been really busy but we finally had time this afternoon to re interview the Tegan we have in the cells. She suggested that the 'other' Tegan might be using a false name, which makes our task almost impossible. However, she did tell us that Tegan lives with an Akmal, and operatives usually use their real first names.'

'So, you need to search the English electoral roll for a Tegan that lives with an Akmal.'

'We are already on it dad. I really ought to be going now though because I need to tell my husband that he will be looking after himself for the next week or so!'

'And we had better get packing!' said Wendy.

Tegan and Akmal eventually arrived at Heathrow just before 7am the next day, UK time. That took some getting used to because their watches said 2am, as did their brains! Ideally, they would have gone to pick up the Range Rover and gone straight home but, since it would only be approaching 3am Canada time by the time they had cleared customs, and they were both tired, they decided to find somewhere for coffee and maybe some food. They eventually

146

found a coffee shop open at that hour and, once woken up by the caffeine, they collected the car and were back at home by 11am, UK time.

'What a week that has been,' thought Akmal. 'And to make things worse I am now unsure where I stand with Tegan.' He realised that he had lied to her about where he was going when he went off on his missions, but it was a secret organisation after all, and the members were forbidden to tell anybody what they were up to. Tegan, on the other hand, knew that they were both members of the same organisation, so she could have mentioned something at least. And she had seen him in action, according to Marie. This definitely seemed a bit one sided, in Tegan's favour. 'She knew what I was doing, and she has lied to me. What other lies has she told me I wonder? Does she really love me or is she playing with me, like a real toy.' He watched her drinking her coffee. 'I do love *her*, so I'll try to take things as they come, and maybe not think about it too much. I have Tegan back, and I'm going home! Once there, I'll start by taking Tegan to Gatwick to retrieve *her* car!'

Chapter 19

The Roberts family left for England at about 9am the next day, about the same time that a very smart black limousine was driving into Helen Morgan's front yard. Two men got out of the car, one ventured around to the yard at the back while the second rang the front door bell.

Helen had been enjoying a leisurely breakfast in Gareth's kitchen as they approached her house. That was a late hour for her to breakfast, but it was Saturday, and the week had been very eventful. Gareth was still in bed. She was deep in thought and chewing some toast when she heard her phone beep. After rescuing it from her bag she opened it to see a sharp image of a tall, moustachioed man at the door. She clicked the button to get the door push to say 'not at home' and resumed her breakfast.

That, it turned out, hadn't been a good idea because, within minutes, he had sprayed paint over the doorbell camera, and then both men had gained entry to the house. They ransacked the place, making as much mess as possible.

'Stupid old woman. That'll teach her to nose into things that aren't her business.' The taller man then stood and urinated onto her hallway carpet while the other looked for, and finally found, what he was after. He put Helen's address book in his pocket, they had a final look round, and then they were gone. After driving for a while they dumped the shiny black car and got back into their truck.

'Now let's see where her family are,' said the taller one. 'We'll see what *they* think of the old woman's messing in our business.' They decided to visit Tom first. Tom didn't live far from Helen so it was just about an hour later that he received a visit from the two men. He had been enjoying a late breakfast before beginning his hospital shift, which was due to start at noon, when he heard the doorbell. He opened the front door to find two men, one carrying a tablet PC.

'Hi,' said the taller one. 'We are from the Astron heating oil company and wondered whether you might invite us in.' Before Tom could say anything both men had barged in and closed, and locked, the door behind them. They drew their guns.

'Get everybody in the house down here, NOW.'

'There's only me here at the moment,' said Tom, trying desperately to work out what to do. He thought he was about to be burgled, or worse.

'Get your phone, now. You go with him Lanky.' Tom lead Lanky into the dining room, and they returned after a few minutes, Tom now carrying his phone.

'Ring your grandmother.'

'My grandmother's dead.' There was a loud cracking sound as the taller one shot Tom in his right foot. Tom fell to the ground in agony.

'Don't lie to me. It'll be your balls next time, now ring your grandmother!' At that point Pierre, Tom's husband, came running downstairs and knelt by Tom.

'You bastards!'

149

'Look at that Lanky, he must be the husband. You, faggot boy, get his phone and ring his gran for him, or you'll both be singing in the church boys choir!'

'His phone's locked and I don't know how to unlock it. And I need to bandage his foot. The *bullet*'s in the floor but *he*'s bleeding.'

'If you don't phone her now he's dead anyway, followed by you.'

'Don't ring her Pierre. If he shoots us both he won't be able to contact gran. You know how well locked that phone is.'

'But I've got your gran's address book, I'll just have to go see your sister Helen if you two don't play ball.' The tall man laughed at this since he would potentially remove four of them before the day was out if the young men didn't "behave".

'At least let me bandage Tom's foot first.'

'Alright! What a fuss. You have two minutes. Fucking sadboys, always so screwed up.' He smiled again at what might also have been innuendo.

Pierre ran upstairs and sent a quick text asking their daughter's Saturday school to ring his mother to collect their daughter today. He didn't give a reason. He then sent a text asking his mother to collect her, and to look after her for a few days, also without a reason.

He ran back to Tom with a bandage and quickly wrapped it around the injured foot.

'You have fifteen seconds left.' The tall one raised his gun again.

'*Alright*! I will do it now.'

'Pierre, no.'

'Think about the younger ones Tom.' With that he unlocked Tom's phone and made the call. The tall one took the phone from him, and waited for Helen to answer.

'I thought you'd know how to unlock his phone. No secrets eh?' He laughed with a high pitched shriek trying to mimic Pierre. Helen answered quickly.

'Hi. Tom. To what do I owe the pleasure of this unexpected call?' said Helen, joyfully. The tall man spoke.

'If you want to see your grandson and his bum boy again you will deliver Tegan Durand to me within forty eight hours.'

'What? Is this a joke? Who are you?'

'Listen old woman.' He pressed on Tom's foot. The scream Helen heard would have curdled milk.

'Tom. Is that you?'

'Helen,' shouted Pierre. 'This man has a gun and he's not playing games. He's already shot Tom.'

'Hear that Helen? You have forty eight hours. I will ring you this time tomorrow with more arrangements. Meanwhile your pretty boys will be with me. Got that? And if I see so much as a hint of the Rozzers they're both dead. Remember that.' He hung up.

'You two, in the truck, now.' Pierre helped Tom into the truck while both abductors stood and watched. The tall man locked them into the truck and then proceeded to have a look around their house. Finding nothing of use, but noting that there was what seemed to be a child's room, he went into what appeared to be Tom and Pierre's room and left a little "message" in their bed.

'That should be beautifully ripe by the time they get back!'

151

Helen had almost fainted after what she had just heard. What was she to do? 'Wasn't it Tegan Durand that they rescued on Friday morning?' She ran upstairs and into Gareth's room. She found him sitting up in bed, listening to the radio. He had been enjoying a lie in after the events of the day before.

'Helen, whatever's the matter?' It took a while for Helen to recover from the exertion of the stairs, but then she blurted out the whole conversation she had just had, and burst into tears.

'He's going to kill them Gareth. Whatever are we to do?'

'We must call the police.'

'He said not to Gareth.'

'Helen, I know that we have solved mysteries between us before, but this is different and we *must* tell the police.' He thought for a moment. 'They must have got Tom's address from somewhere. Has your doorbell picked anything up?'

'Yes.' She told him about the call she had had.

'So you told him you were out?'

'Yes.'

'He must have broken in and found your address book. This Tegan Durand must be very important to them. I'll get dressed and go straight to the police station. Those villains don't seem to know where you are now or they wouldn't have gone after Tom. If I can get the police to come back here we can work out a plan.'

'Should I ring that young man, Akmal wasn't it? Tell him what's happened?'

'But how will you do that? He erased his number from your phone.'

152

'Tom has put a little app on my phone that backs up my numbers to "the cloud". He set it so that if any of my numbers are deleted from my phone they stay in the back up. I still have his number!'

'Wait until we have spoken to the police Helen.'

'Do you want some breakfast? You must be starving!'

'I'll eat one of those cereal bars on the way,' said Gareth.

'Can you not just ring the police?'

'By the time I have listened to that music they play, then been passed around all the stations and departments, it will be quicker to go. They'll see I mean business if I arrive in person.'

'Alright. What can I do while you're gone?'

'Sit in silence with a pad and pencil. Write down everything you remember that Tegan Durand told us. That memory of yours is slower than it used to be, but it's just as thorough.'

Gareth had been dressing as they spoke so he was already heading for the door when Helen went back downstairs to the kitchen to think.

Chapter 20

On returning to their home in Iver Heath, Tegan and Akmal had retired to bed, and managed about three hours sleep. Akmal had woken and got out of bed first, and he headed for the shower, at about the same time that Helen was eating breakfast back in Canada. He spent longer than usual in the shower because his mind was still all over the place. The issue with Tegan was still there, but then so were the events in Canada. He couldn't forget those two courageous people that had rescued Tegan, and he realised that the pair of them were something of a mystery. He also didn't feel that they had been adequately rewarded. They wouldn't even get a Christmas card! He chatted to himself as the warm water of the shower fell gently over him.

'Who were (are) they? Why were they up at that barn in the early hours? Have they been left in danger? They were quite old, especially Helen, so will somebody be searching for them?' Then it occurred to him that the perpetrators of the weapons fraud hadn't actually been found, at least not to his knowledge, so they would most likely be regrouping after the loss of that haul. Then there was the dead man. Akmal had heard the story of the finding of a body in "Ned's barn" from the news that was playing in the taxi on the way to the airport. 'Who was he and had he been a member of the gang?' He began to worry for the safety of Helen and Gareth.

Just then, Tegan joined him in the shower and broke his thought patterns.

'I'll just get dried,' said Akmal as he got out of the shower.

'Not joining me today?' asked Tegan, provocatively.

'No, not today.'

'Are you well Akmal? In all of our three years together you've never denied me fun in the shower. Have you eaten something?' she asked, but then added 'or screwed someone else?' with some venom.

'I'll see you downstairs,' was all that Tegan got in reply.

A short while later, Tegan joined Akmal at the breakfast table, where he was eating toast and marmalade, and drinking coffee. He had really fancied maple syrup but there was none to have. He was in a dream like state when Tegan sat down.

'Earth to Akmal!' she said, quite loudly. 'You're not with me today are you?'

'No, I'm not,' agreed Akmal. He poured out the thoughts that he had had during his shower to Tegan.

'Well, there's a lot to take in! I have been doing this job for a long time Akmal, and I can assure you that it has to be treated as a job. When we finish we finish. We can't dwell on what we have left behind, this time or any time. We have been told to leave Canada and we have done just that. We can do no more.'

'But those people rescued you, and you know that there was CCTV up there, you told me so. They might be in danger. Then there's the thought that you, or we, might not be safe from the organisation itself. This isn't over Tegan. Back in Canada, I was so relieved to have found you that it never occurred to me to find out the answers to any of these questions.'

'Akmal, it's done, it's over. Let's go to Oxford, just as we had planned to do last Saturday.'

'Was that really just seven days ago?' Akmal paused for a while. 'Perhaps you are right. Have your breakfast, we'll get your car from Gatwick and then we'll make the arrangements.'

'That's more like it. It's good to be home isn't it?'

'Yes,' said Akmal, without much conviction, and he left her to her breakfast. He rejoined her a few minutes later.

'We had better get you a new mobile phone and sim card on the way to collect your car, then you'll need to tell everybody your new number. The sooner we get the new one the better.'

'Akmal, I don't need to. The phone I take with me on operations isn't my normal phone. It is setup by the organisation and I just add any numbers from my own contacts list that I might need while on a mission. Anybody that rings me will go to voicemail while I'm on operations, and I listen to those regularly.' She took her phone from her dressing gown pocket and showed it to Akmal. 'This is my phone. All that the imposter has is my "work" phone, and the only people that it will ring, is organisation members. I assume that the Canadian police have that now, and the organisation will have deactivated it anyway.'

'But I telephoned your number in Canada and I heard fake Tegan's phone ring, so that didn't go to voicemail!'

156

'Akmal, you are an organisation member so you would get through to me.'

'Yes, I was forgetting that you knew that all along. Why didn't I have such a phone? All I have is a cloaking app.'

'Had you been sent on a more dangerous mission you would have got one!'

'Do I want to know any details about your dangerous exploits then Tegan?'

'Akmal, I think it's best if you don't,' laughed Tegan.

Akmal drove Tegan to Gatwick later that afternoon and there was very little chat between them.

'Shall I rebook for Oxford then?' asked Tegan.

'What?'

'Oxford, shall I rebook?'

'Sorry Tegan, I was miles away. Yes, please do. I'm not expected back at work next week so we can go then if you like.' Silence returned. As they approached Gatwick Akmal re-joined the land of the living ('good thing that his car has semi autonomous driving activated,' kept going through Tegan's mind) and he asked her which car park to head for.

'South Terminal Akmal. I flew on British Airways.' Akmal drove into the car park and followed Tegan's instructions to find her spot. He was troubled though to find that he couldn't drive into that entire area because it had been cordoned off. So he parked his range Rover and they set off together to find out what was going on.

In the parking office, they were told that there had been an explosion the previous night and that three cars had been totally destroyed, with damage to others. After Tegan had given details of her, and her car's, identity it turned out that

Tegan's car had been in the centre of the three. The manager of the parking company, who had been summoned upon Tegan's arrival, expressed his sincere apologies and advised Tegan that the police would be in touch with her in due course. He added that they would need her mobile number to do that. They had tried to contact her after the explosion but all that they had got was voicemail.

A very pale and thoughtful Akmal accompanied Tegan to his car and they set off back home. Nothing was said until Tegan broke the silence.

'That was a warning Akmal. Looks like you were right, I don't think that we have left *anything* back in Canada.'

Chapter 21

The plane carrying inspector Roberts and her family touched down at Heathrow airport at just after 7pm Canadian time, midnight in the UK!

'Well this is weird,' said Mrs Roberts. 'It's midnight, it's dark and it's warm! It's nice to be back in England.'

'Indeed,' said Mr. Roberts.

'While you two are reliving your dim and distant past, I am going to read my emails!'

'Sorry love,' said her mother. 'It is odd being wide wake at midnight though isn't it.'

'Yes mum. Meet me in the lounge in ten minutes?'

'Yes,' was all she got in reply. Mr and Mrs Roberts attended to the baggage issues while inspector Roberts read some very interesting things in her inbox. The UK police had a Tegan registered as the owner of a car that had mysteriously blown up at Gatwick airport last night. They had provided the details of the owner and, following a request from the Canadian police, Janice had been invited to go and interview her. 'Marvellous, she thought. I'll call in on them first thing tomorrow. It's not far from Slough to Iver Heath.

Back in Gareth's kitchen, Helen had sat for over an hour with a pencil and a writing pad. She had said goodbye to

159

Gareth as he left for the police station and had then begun her task of remembering, remembering the events of an early morning adventure that now threatened her grandson, his husband and, potentially, their daughter. Her first memories though were those of *her* own Tegan. Her beautiful daughter who had died so tragically when she was still a young woman, her beautiful grandchildren who were so dear to her, and the threat that was now hanging over all of them. And Helen! Pregnant Helen. What if the villains went after Helen? They had that address book, the one that she had so meticulously maintained, but Helen and her husband had moved recently. Had she updated that part of her address book? After all, she kept things on her cell phone now so maybe she hadn't.

Helen looked at the clock. It was almost 12 noon. That meant that Helen junior would be about to have her lunch break. Helen waited a very angst ridden five minutes then telephoned her granddaughter.

'Hi Mam-gu. Lovely to hear from you, but you don't usually ring me at work; I hope that this isn't bad news, are you OK?'

'Yes darling I am, but I want you to sit down and listen to me carefully.'

'You are scaring me, what's going on?'

'Helen, I've been a silly old woman and poked my nose into something I shouldn't. To cut a long story short we, me and Gareth that is, rescued a young woman from a barn and now the people who locked her up are after me. They don't know where I am, but they've got my address book, and they are threatening to harm my family. You must tell your husband and go to stay with your in-laws. You must try to get time off and do it now.'

'Mam-gu, slow down. Are you telling me that some villains have got hold of your address book, and that anybody in there is at risk? What about Tom and all of our in-laws. Aren't they in there too?' Helen decided against telling her heavily pregnant granddaughter about Tom's experiences.

'Tom is aware already and I never put your extended families into my address book, so don't worry about them. Tom told me it was better to put them "in the cloud" so that's where they are. You'll be safer at your in-laws so please organise that. I'm sorry Helen.'

'So why are these people after you? Do they want to harm you and want us to give you up?'

'No love, they want me to give Tegan, the woman that we rescued, back to them.'

'And can you do that?'

'We've no idea where she is. It's all complicated but you two must move out and soon.'

'I'd better ring Alfie now then, get him to sort something out. He's at home at the moment because he's taken a few day's holiday to get some painting done. Please be very careful. Shall I ring Tom for you?'

'No thanks, I have done that already and they know all about this.'

'And you've called the police yes?'

'Yes, or rather Gareth has gone to see them. He should be back soon. I'm so sorry Helen.'

'Don't worry nannie, we'll be fine.'

Helen senior hung up the call and looked at her sheet of paper. She hadn't much written down, but there was one thing she was sure of: the perpetrators of the weapons fraud weren't planning to stay long in that barn or the doors would have been properly reinforced, and a more permanent electricity supply laid. They hadn't even repaired the roof, and some of those crates had become pretty wet from recent rain. Then she also realised that whoever was behind this must be some way away from the barn because she had tripped that alarm twice, and both times she had been there for over fifteen minutes. If they had been nearby they'd have come running and she'd likely be dead. *Gareth was right, this wasn't like TV and real harm was being done. If only she could turn back the clock and leave that barn alone.*

Gareth and the police arrived at about 3pm, just as Helen was preparing a rather late lunch. It was taking her longer than usual because her mind wasn't on her work, but she knew that Gareth would need something substantial when he got back. Helen greeted Gareth with a hug and said hello to officer Storey. She invited them to eat, an offer which they both accepted, and they talked while eating.

'Helen,' began officer Storey, 'talk me through your conversation with the man who has abducted your grandson.' Helen went through the whole morning's events in great detail and officer Storey made copious notes.

'Are you sure that it was Tom's voice that you heard?'

'It was Pierre I heard first, that's Tom's husband, but yes, I'm sure that they have Tom.'

'It was an audio only call was it?'

'Yes,' said Helen. 'I couldn't see anything.'

'But you did see a man on your doorbell app?'

'Yes.'

'Does your app record these things?'

'Yes, it does.' Helen handed the phone to Officer Storey who used Bluetooth to download the images onto her phone.'

'We'll get that to the tech guys who will remove the false stuff and do an eyes search because it's very difficult to disguise the eyes and they are quite unique to individuals. Let's hope that he's in our database. I'd like to organise some protection for you Helen.'

'No thanks officer, nobody knows that I am here. I see that it was Gareth that brought you here officer Storey.'

'Yes. Just in case anybody was looking for you and chasing police cars. A police car driving into here might have alerted somebody.'

'What shall we do now officer?'

'Nothing. You two sit tight while we do our jobs. In the meantime, don't leave this house, but do tell us immediately when one of the captors ring tomorrow. We want to know everything that he says.'

'Helen has an excellent memory,' said Gareth. 'Something will come to her to help us out of this mess.' He and officer Storey left and Helen sat before her writing pad for the second time.

'There must be something that we can do,' she thought to herself.

Gareth returned just over an hour later. Helen was still sitting in front of her writing pad.

'Hi Helen. How are you doing? I don't know about you but I need a drink.' Helen didn't answer. 'Helen?'

'Gareth! I'm so sorry. I was deep in thought.'

'So would you like a drink?'

163

'I'll have a small sherry please.' Gareth sat next to Helen and handed her the sherry.

'You must be feeling terrible. There's not much written on that pad though Helen, let's have a look.' On the sheet Helen had written just one sentence. 'This is my mess and I must get us out of it.'

'Helen, what does that mean?'

'Just what it says,' said Helen, her thoughts apparently miles away.

'What do you mean Helen? We have to leave this to the police.'

'Gareth. Thanks for all of your help, and for letting me stay here, but if you could just leave me alone for a while?' She said that very gently, and she had seemed to be in a dream like state as she said it.

'Certainly Helen. Just shout when you need me.'

'Dinner's ready,' shouted Helen. It was now 7.30pm and neither had spoken since 5pm. Gareth came into the kitchen.

'You've made dinner!'

'Yes. I'll bring it through to the dining room. You go and wait in there.'

'Helen, are you OK?'

'Yes. We'll eat, then I'll tell you what I want to do.' Gareth did as he was told and they ate dinner in relative silence. Once they had finished Gareth could wait no longer, and he demanded that Helen explain her thoughts.

'I'm going back up to the barn. Will you get my truck out of your garage please Gareth?' She seemed to be still rather distant.

'Helen, that's dangerous. You might be hurt, or even killed. One person is already dead. The police said to leave it to them.'

'I am going up there Gareth.'

'Then I will drive you.'

'No Gareth, not this time. At the moment, they don't know who you are and it must stay like that for your safety, and for that of your family. I must go in my truck and I must go alone.'

'And do what when you get there?'

'I have this all planned and you mustn't know the details. Please Gareth, leave this to me.' Gareth knew that it was pointless arguing with her when her mind was made up.

'When are you going?'

'I think I need to sleep before I do this so I'll set an alarm for 4am.'

Chapter 22

Helen was already awake when her alarm sounded at 4am. She quickly dressed and headed for the kitchen. She had often told Gareth that the kitchen was a stupid place to keep his pistol, but that didn't worry her now because she was going to need it, and today she didn't care where he kept it. She picked up one of Gareth's many torches, donned her black coat and hat, and left by the back door.

Gareth had been good to his word and had left her Toyota outside for her so that she wouldn't need to tangle with the mechanism of the garage door in the dark. Within minutes she was on her way. She didn't need a map, just turn right and carry on upwards.

Helen had driven steadily, but it had still only taken twelve minutes to get close to the barn. As before, she approached the barn with her headlamps on their dim setting, and was pleased to see that the lights that had originally brought the barn to her attention were switched on. She parked just outside the entrance to the clearing in front of the barn and walked up the last part while keeping in the shadows. She kept looking around to make sure that she missed nothing, but she wasn't entirely successful. She certainly hadn't noticed a now slightly dizzy Gareth emerge from under a cover on the back of her truck.

Helen approached the barn with Gareth some way behind. She noted that the poles bearing the security cameras were now gone, and she didn't see the tell-tale red leds of alarm sensors. With astonishing speed and lightness, she slipped into the barn. It was empty. The lights were on, but the barn was completely empty. Everything had gone, the crates, the curtained area where they had found Tegan, the pipework that had been installed, all of it was gone. She stood still and listened. Silence. The battery-based electricity supply must still be here and active, so what was happening here now? Why were the lights still on?

It had never occurred to Helen that this might be a trap, at least not until now. But then, that might be a good thing. She would go with them if they released Tom. Fair swap perhaps. She continued to search the barn. Nothing. Not even a candy bar wrapper. So where was the electrical installation? It must be somewhere, and it wouldn't be outside. Remembering cartoons from her childhood days she began tapping walls to see whether anything sounded hollow. It didn't. 'Now what?'

She sat in a corner to think and to wait, but she didn't have to wait long because the sound of an approaching vehicle pulled her from her trance like state. Gareth, who had positioned himself in a dark corner outside, saw it first.

'I hope that this isn't Gareth coming to rescue me,' thought Helen. Gareth had had considerably less pleasant thoughts, but he stayed put. Helen hid in the corner next to the barn doors which were, as they had been when she arrived, wide open. They wouldn't be able to see her in that dark corner, or so she hoped.

After what seemed like ages two women came into the barn and headed straight for the area where Tegan had been

167

held. One of them unscrewed the metal plate that had held Tegan's chain so securely, and extracted what looked like a mobile phone. They read something from it, returned it, and then sat down for a while.

'Going according to plan?'

'Yes', replied the other. They laughed loudly and Helen took the opportunity to escape the barn. She wasn't yet ready for home though, and she walked slowly around the outside of the barn looking for anything that might lead to Tom's abductors.

'Psst.' Helen froze.

'Psst.'Helen thought for a while then realised who it probably was.

'Gareth?' she whispered.

'Yes. What are you up to Helen? Aren't we in enough trouble already?'

'How did you get here Gareth? Isn't it risky bringing your truck up here?'

'I hid in the back of your Toyota Helen. Can we go now, while those two women are still in the barn?'

'They're not still in there Gareth, look:' Sure enough, the two women were now leaving the barn, still chattering loudly and still, apparently, in high spirits. Helen and Gareth stood for a while in the shadows, just watching the two women. After what seemed like ages the women got back into their car, an old blue Nissan, and drove off. Helen and Gareth waited until the sound of the engine had disappeared before speaking again.

'Gareth, have you got a screwdriver with you?'

'I put a tool roll in the back of your Toyota, just in case you were locked in somewhere. I don't know what further mischief you are planning but I'll get it anyway.' Once Gareth had retrieved his tools Helen persuaded him to follow her back into the barn. 'Helen, this is becoming dangerous.'

'We, or rather I, have passed that point now Gareth. You don't need to stay here, but I need to get Tom and Pierre out of the trouble that I have caused them. So I am going back into that barn.'

'OK. But not without me.'

'Alright.' They crept back into the barn and into the space where Tegan had been imprisoned. Helen asked Gareth to unscrew the plate that the women had removed earlier, and he obliged. He handed the phone like device to Helen.

'Now, what on earth is this?' She found the on button and the screen lit up. On it was a message that simply read "Gotcha!"

'Morning!' came a voice from near the barn doors. The two women were back. 'Pixie, you get *him*, I'll deal with *her*.' Quick as a flash, Gareth had been knocked to the floor and his arms and legs bound with cable ties. Trixie simply stood before Helen and spoke, quietly, but with enough menace to make Helen realise that it was time to get on with her plan. 'Where's Tegan?' asked Trixie.

'I don't know. Please let my friend go.'

'Pixie!' Pixie, who now had Gareth pinned to the ground, began to twist his foot around, slowly but powerfully, until he cried out in agony.

'Stop, please stop,' wailed Helen. Pixie twisted Gareth's foot around further.

'Stop. Until you stop I'm doing nothing.'

'Enough now Pixie.'

'What *can* you do for me then Helen?'

169

'You know my name!'

'We do, and we've got your address book! Now get on with it.'

'I really don't know where Tegan is, but I might be able to phone her boyfriend, but I'm not doing that until my friend is released.'

'I'll just take your phone then.'

'The numbers aren't in my phone, they're in the cloud, and you won't get the password out of me. I'm an old woman and I'll die first.'

'What, like you have a suicide pill or something?'

'You've got it,' said Helen.

'Show me.' Helen revealed a capsule that was in her mouth. It was now between her teeth. She pushed it back into her mouth before speaking.

'Release Gareth or you will fail in your "mission" and I hope your leaders end your weak and feeble lives as a result.' Trixie nodded to Pixie.

Pixie undid Gareth and told him to go, but not before she had removed his mobile phone. Helen told him to leave in her Toyota and said that she wouldn't begin helping these two until she heard him drive away. After protesting to Helen, and after he had recovered enough normality in his leg, he left Helen to it. But then he came back.

'Return my mobile phone.'

'No.'

'No mobile phone, no Helen. Helen, you still got that suicide pill?' Helen now had the capsule between her teeth again.

'Pixie!' Gareth's phone was returned to him.

'Now go, and not a word to anybody.'

'Now Helen, your turn.'

'Let Tom and Pierre go first.'

'We can't do that.'

'Until I speak to Tom, and hear that they are free, I'm doing nothing. You've got *me* now, you don't need Tom anymore.' After a pause, Trixie handed her weapon to Pixie, and she left the barn. She made a call and was back fifteen minutes later. She handed the phone to Helen.

'Nannie, we are in a taxi, and we've been told that we are going home. My foot isn't too bad. Whatever you did to get us free, thanks.'

'You sure that you are OK Tom?'

'Yes. The taxi driver won't tell us where we are, and it's pitch-black outside, but he says we'll be dropped off near our home in twenty-five minutes.'

'Tom, just ask the driver to pull over and let Pierre leave the car.' Tom did that and after five minutes he confirmed that the driver had done that very thing, and that they were now back together and heading toward town.

'I'll ring off now Tom, but find somewhere else to stay for a while will you? Don't go home yet.'

'Will do as you ask,' said Tom.

Chapter 23

Janice, with her dad in tow for company, knocked at Tegan and Akmal's door at precisely 10am on Sunday morning. Akmal opened the door and didn't seem at all surprised to see a woman with Canadian Police ID at the door. He invited them in and offered them coffee.

'I'd love some,' said Janice. 'Me too,' said her dad. As he was now a civilian, Janice's dad would have to remain silent while his daughter spoke to Akmal, and then to Tegan, but he would be able to read their body language and pass comments back to Janice later.

Akmal shouted for Tegan and proceeded to make the coffee. A very sleepy Tegan arrived and sat in her dressing gown. Janice began.

'Good morning, my name is...'

'I know who you are Inspector Roberts,' said Tegan.

'Thank-you, that saves me some time. We know about the organisation for which you work, and we know that you returned to the UK yesterday.'

'That's correct.'

'We also know that your car has been involved in an explosion at Gatwick airport on Friday night, before you returned to the UK.'

'That's also correct.'

'Could you confirm for me your name please, your *birth* name, if you don't mind.' Tegan thought for a while before answering. 'Lives are in danger here Tegan. I want no aliases or deceit please.'

At that point Akmal entered with the coffee.

'I am Tegan Jane Hauser. I was born in Scotland but both of my parents are Swiss. I have my birth certificate if you need it.'

'We will do in time, but not at the moment. So Tegan Durand is the name you used as cover, while in Canada. Do you always use the same name when on operations?'

'No. I choose one that would be appropriate to the place where I will work. Last time I was Tegan Romero and was married to an Italian yachtsman. You get the picture?'

'Indeed I do. What is the make and model of your car Tegan?'

'It's a 2019 Mercedes C class.'

'Not noted for their explosive nature, are they?' Tegan shook her head.

'When was it last serviced?'

'It would be four months ago. It will be in the records.'

'So, a fully serviced, fairly new Mercedes Benz blows up in a car park. We are awaiting forensic information, but I'd like your thoughts please Tegan as to why it went up in flames, endangering life and property. Before you answer that, remember that we have a "Tegan Durand" in custody who was, allegedly, pretending to be you in Saint-Jérôme, that is until she was brought into the "Poste de Police" by a woman who is also a member of your organisation. I need to advise you that our Tegan Durand has made numerous allegations

about you, so the absolute truth please, if you don't mind.'
Tegan noted the edge in the inspector's question.

'I have no idea why anybody should blow up my car, but I
accept that it was either tampered with or booby trapped. I'm
just glad I wasn't in it and that nobody was hurt.'

'So, you can't shed any light on this event at all?'

'No. I am sorry, but I can't.'

'No "intel from above"?'

'I know what you are getting at, but I can't have any
contact with the organisation at the moment. Their rules, to
protect them, and me, and us, prevent any contact for quite a
while after a mission.'

'Is that why you killed Jean Belanger?' Tegan's casual
mood suddenly changed and Akmal almost choked on his
coffee.

'What? Who the hell is Jean Belanger and why would I kill
him?'

'You know who he was. Think back Tegan. The truth
please?'

'He used to be one of two men that checked on me when I
was chained up in that barn.'

'Describe him.' Mr. Roberts was really impressed with his
daughter's technique and he noticed a look between Tegan
and Akmal.

'He was tall, very good looking, always wore tight jeans
and a smart shirt, and he always smelt nice.'

'A ladies man then.'

'Yes.'

'Did he "come on to you"?'

'He did seem keen. I could feel his body language and he kept telling me how much he fancied me. He often asked me whether I fancied him.'

'And your answer?'

Tegan looked at Akmal.

'The truth Tegan!'

'I said yes. I did fancy him. Any woman would have fancied him.'

'So why did you kill him? Did he get physical with you, try to touch you, molest you, have sex with you, rape you?'

'No. No, No.' Tegan was becoming surprisingly upset. 'He was obviously attractive, and there was a chemistry developing between us, but he didn't do anything to offend or to hurt me. He seemed really sweet underneath and he clearly wasn't part of the gang that abducted me. So, I was hoping that if he fell for me, he might help me escape. I had thought that that was working, so why would I kill him?'

'You tell me Tegan. His colleague found him dead in the barn and you were gone. Who else could it have been?' Tegan was now visibly upset and flustered. Akmal had never seen her like this. He got up to comfort her but Mr. Roberts gestured to him to sit down.

'Tegan, I have two people who allege that you killed Jean Belanger. The evidence seems to suggest....' At that point Akmal's phone rang and he went into the kitchen to answer it.

'Seems to suggest that I killed Jean? There were two men that used to check on the barn, and on me. He wouldn't be there on his own. Are you suggesting that I overpowered two men and killed one of them?'

175

'I will read to you what Josh Howard alleges happened the day that Jean was found dead. "I shouted for Jean to come inside quick and it wasn't long before he ran into the barn. I was looking around the woman's prison room in case she was hiding when I head Jean scream. I went out and found him next to a crate, dying. He died in my arms. He had tripped over a pole and landed on his head. There was blood coming out of his..... She must have left a trap for us before she escaped. I came the other way around the crates so that must be why I missed her trap." Now Tegan, that sounds plausible to me and why would he lie? He seemed to be genuinely upset when he told me that and it sounds a perfectly feasible scenario to me.'

'I don't know why he would lie like that. I was rescued from that barn in the early hours of the morning, and at that time neither Jean nor his mate were there. He must have been killed after we left. You need to be looking for somebody else.'

'Can you provide any evidence to support what you have just said? What about those two people that rescued you. Could they vouch for you?'

A now very upset Tegan was about to reply when Akmal came back from the kitchen, looking very concerned because the call was from Helen Morgan who was still in Ned's barn. Helen had told Pixie that she was now ready to fulfil her part of the bargain, so she had accessed her cloud account and dialled Akmal's number. Once Akmal had replied, she explained to him all that had happened to her, making sure that the women heard every word. Akmal's reply was to ask Helen to wait a moment while he spoke to Tegan.

'Stop you two and listen to this, nobody but Tegan speak.' Akmal turned his phone from "mute" back to "online".

'Helen are you still there?'

'Yes'

'You are on speaker phone now and Tegan is here. Can you say all of that again please?'

A very upset Helen shouted 'Hello Tegan, I hope that you are well?'

'I am fine Helen. What's wrong?' Helen spoke first to to her captors.

'He wants to put me on speaker phone and repeat what I just said so that Tegan can hear it.'

'Say yes, and put yours on speaker too.' Helen obliged and Akmal's phone broadcast the repeat performance. Inspector Roberts, Tegan and Mr. Roberts sat is silence, listening. Tegan spoke first.

'Helen, I'm not in Canada now. It will take ages for me to get back there. Will you tell the women that?'

'We heard,' piped up Pixie.

'Indeed we did,' added Trixie.

'What exactly do you want me to do?' asked Tegan.

'Arrange for your flight back to Canada. I will ring you on this number in twelve hours' time. I expect you to be on a plane by then. You can tell me where you intend to land, and we'll meet you off that plane. No police, no hangers on, just you. We have business to do. We'll keep Helen as our little playmate until we see you. That's all.' Trixie then told Helen to hang up, but before she did so Helen had another question.

'Tegan, will you be OK coming back to Canada? My friend is OK and there's only me in danger. Don't swap your young life for an old one like mine.'

'Helen, I'll do as they ask. This isn't your mess, and you don't deserve any of it. I'll be there as soon as possible. If you are still listening you two miserable women, be warned that if you harm Helen at all you will seriously regret it.' Both women laughed heartily.

'Is that a threat? Tell you what we think of that, we'll ring in eleven hours instead! Be on a plane when we ring or she's dead.' Pixie hung up. The two women escorted Helen to their car, the lights around the barn were extinguished, and they were soon on their way. Gareth had already left in Helen's truck and, once back at his house, he changed his clothes and went again to visit the police in Saint-Jérôme.

Chapter 24

After that call, inspector Roberts had a chat with her dad in the garden, away from Akmal and Tegan. Akmal and Tegan also had a chat.

'What do we do?' asked Akmal.

'*You* do nothing. Akmal, you must stay here and just go about your daily business. This is my mess, and I must sort it out.'

'But Tegan...'

'No Akmal. There are things about this case that I can't tell you, and that I won't tell you. If you go back with me, they will kill you, without a shadow of a doubt, and you won't be able to help me in Canada so stay here. I must speak to inspector Roberts when she comes back in from the garden, but Akmal, if necessary, I will burn your passport. Do NOT follow me to Canada.'

Something in Tegan's voice made Akmal realise that she was deadly serious, and that he would have to do as she asked. He also realised at that point that he really didn't know her at all. He loved her and wanted to protect her, but this time he decided that she was right. He had lost the Tegan that he thought he knew, and whatever had happened to their relationship, he couldn't be of any help to her now. So he agreed to stay in England. He gave her an enormous hug and

179

then went upstairs to think. He considered burning *her* passport and then he wouldn't lose her, but there was Helen and her family. If he did do that, he might lose both of them.

'Well dad, what do *you* make of what you have just heard?'

'First, that was a great job in there, you are good at what you do and I'm sure you've got a handle on the case already. But Janice, it's complex isn't it. We have a Tegan who was sent to investigate fraudulent weapons sales and production, and another Tegan sent to stop that from happening. The second is in custody, but it's the first one that the fraudsters want returned. That seems the wrong way around to me.'

'Yes, you're right, you would expect then to want *their* Tegan back. Now that just about sums up the immediate problem, but then there's this organisation that Tegan and Akmal are members of. There seems to be a problem there too.'

'Yes Janice. What do we know about them?'

'The "Organisation for the Investigation of Worldwide Corporate Fraud" is a real organisation and we have worked with them in the past. Akmal found and helped apprehend the other half of the weapons fraudsters just last week. This business with the Tegan replacement is perplexing though, and it looks like somebody within the organisation must be interfering with the attempt to catch the weapons fraudsters.' She outlined the RUMP audio story to her dad and explained that the audio and weapons companies were both owned by the same woman.

'So the "RUMP" organisation makes audio equipment *and* weapons and, presumably, the profits from both parts of the company go to the woman that owns it. But the fake audio scam and fake weapons scam are run by entirely different groups?'

'It would seem that way dad. Why is that important?'

'Well, for one thing, there's unlikely to anything untoward in the actual "RUMP" company because if there was, that individual would likely organise both scams. As it is they seem to be organised separately, and there seems to be a branch of one of them here in the UK. Now, I need something to justify my remaining in England at your expense, so why don't I stay here and try to get information from Akmal, and maybe from some ex CID colleagues, while you go back with Tegan. You *will* have to go back to Canada with her won't you?'

'Yes dad, I will. I will have to assume that those who want Tegan back don't know that I was listening in to that call, so I can fly back incognito and watch what goes on at Montreal airport.'

'Shall we go back in and do some persuading?'

'Definitely!'

They returned to Tegan and Akmal, and found them looking up flight times. The inspector spoke first. 'I think it best if you stay here Akmal, but I must return to Canada and Tegan must come with me. I came here today to interview her about the death of Jean Belanger, but I now believe that we have insufficient evidence to ask for the extradition of Tegan to Canada. On the other hand, I expect Tegan to leave for Canada at the earliest opportunity to help apprehend the captors of Helen Morgan and, hopefully, to help get to the bottom of the weapons fraud.' Janice was astonished when Akmal and Tegan agreed to this without argument.

'There is a British Airways flight due to leave Heathrow today at 5.40pm UK time and it is due into Montreal-Trudeau International Airport at 7.50pm Montreal time. We could try to get seats on that,' said Tegan. Using their phones, the Inspector was able to reserve one of the last two seats and Tegan managed to secure the second.

That had organised the evening ahead, but it was now just after midday so it was agreed that Akmal and Tegan should spend what might be their last afternoon together, without extra company, and that inspector Roberts would later accompany Tegan, and only Tegan, to Heathrow. A car would pick her up at 4.30pm. Akmal acknowledged that that was the best plan and so Inspector Roberts advised Tegan as to what would happen if she wasn't at the house at 4.30pm, ready to leave. The inspector and her dad then left Tegan and Akmal to themselves.

Janice and her parents spent a very pleasant afternoon in Windsor, exploring Windsor Great Park and the Castle itself. Wendy Roberts had arranged a visit to her home town of Basingrove for Monday, and she expected her husband to accompany her. He, on the other hand, had really wanted to spend the day with Akmal, but he agreed that by the side of his wife might be more important on this occasion. He thought that young Akmal would probably need time to himself tomorrow anyway.

Inspector Roberts and her dad arrived, in their hire car, at Tegan and Akmal's at exactly 4.30pm. Tegan appeared as if by magic and got into the car. Mr. Roberts was driving so Tegan and Janice sat in the back.

'I have been out this afternoon and bought what you over there call a "burner" phone. When Akmal gets a call from Helen's captors he will give them this new number so that we can talk directly. Akmal will then send a group message to all of his contacts to advise them of his new mobile number, then destroy his old sim card so that they won't be able to contact him again.'

'That's very wise Tegan. Have you briefed your organisation on current developments?'

'Since I suspect interference from within the organisation I thought it wisest not to.'

'If there is interference from within the OIWCF, why didn't that person just tell Helen's captors where you would likely be? They know where you live and they have blown up your car after all, so why not just come and get you?'

'I was wondering that too,' replied Tegan. 'Akmal and I have put some "feelers" out to try to get some clues.

'Is Akmal in danger do you think?' asked the inspector.

'Now that is something I hadn't thought about, and now I'm the worried one. It's usually Akmal that worries about me.'

'Dad, how about some company for you and mum tomorrow?'

'I was just thinking the same thing. I'll pick him up on the way back to Slough, and he can stay with us.'

'Excellent dad. Tegan, please don't mention that to Akmal if he rings to say goodbye, just in case somebody is eavesdropping, or he decides to run away!'

Tegan was dropped off in a lay-by about a mile short of Heathrow. From there, a taxi picked her up and took her the rest of the way to the airport because they had to make sure that nobody would see Tegan and the inspector together at this point.

* * *

Exactly as promised, Trixie telephoned Akmal eleven hours after she had previously hung up. Akmal confirmed that Tegan was now on a plane bound for Montreal, that he wasn't with her and that she had bought a new phone. He gave Trixie the number of that phone and then hung up.

'Good lad,' said mister Roberts.

'If we are to spend time together, can I call you by your first name?'

'Wendy calls me Jim. It's not my name but it will do.'

'Thanks Jim'. Akmal, now in a hotel in Slough, went back to trying to read his book, "At Bertram's Hotel", by Agatha Christie.

* * *

The flight back to Montreal was fairly uneventful, apart from a little turbulence as the plane flew across the Canadian coast. Tegan disembarked first but it was Inspector Roberts who got through customs, and collected her bags, first. They had obtained the last two seats for that flight, which meant that they had sat some distance apart, which was exactly how the inspector had wanted it to be. Once out and free, the inspector went to make a phone call, while using that cover to watch Tegan pass through the gate. Once through, she saw a man approach Tegan holding up a sign that read "Taxi for Durand". Tegan followed the man and Inspector Roberts followed her. She watched Tegan get into what looked exactly like a taxi and found an empty cab herself.

'Follow that taxi!' She had waited years for an excuse to say that, and now was her chance. She instructed the driver not to get too close to Tegan's taxi, and sat back and waited.

Chapter 25

After only a few minutes, the taxi containing Tegan pulled into a side street and stopped. Curious to see what was going on, but also not wanting to make herself known, Inspector Roberts instructed her driver to drive straight past, but to park up out of sight a little further up the road. It turned out that *Tegan's* driver had pulled over because he had an envelope to post.

'Mobile phone please Tegan.' Tegan handed over her phone, the driver checked that it was switched on and had a good amount of charge, he then placed it in the padded envelope he had brought with him, and then popped the whole lot into the post box. Tegan watched this from inside the locked taxi. She had wondered how her abductor would deal with the GPS signal from that. Once back in the taxi the driver invited Tegan to produce any other electronic gadgets that she might have with her. He assured her that a strip search wouldn't be very pleasant, and also quite intrusive. She assured *him* that she had no more devices with her. The driver scanned the taxi with a microwave detector, just to be sure, but he found nothing.

The journey turned out to be quite lengthy, all the way to a hotel in Saint-Jérôme in fact, but Inspector Roberts' taxi driver had managed to keep sight of Tegan's taxi, and they felt sure that they hadn't been seen. After checking that they hadn't got near to any security cameras, and after watching Tegan disembark from her taxi and walk freely alongside the driver into the hotel, the inspector asked her driver to take her home.

She was more than ready for home and her husband would be astonished to see her back so soon; she hadn't forewarned him and she wondered what her reception would be like. She also wondered whether her suspicions were correct and that she would find him in bed with a fit member of his gym, or some other slender young thing. Someone that would be more in awe of his tight musculature and fat free diet perhaps. Of late, Henri hadn't been as attentive to her as he had been previously been during their fifteen years of marriage. As a serving police officer, she was aware that this is often the first sign of infidelity within a marriage. She felt anxious as she approached her home.

Janice unlocked their front door, listened carefully and smelled the air. The house smelled as it always did, a mix of camphor and menthol, no foreign perfume! She listened again, and could hear grunting coming from upstairs.

'Now, what's going on up there I wonder?'

She silently climbed the stairs and approached the room where the grunting came from. It was their bedroom! She noticed that the door was slightly ajar so she peered in noiselessly. What she saw was Henri on an obviously brand new exercise machine. The machine made no sound, unlike Henri who was dripping sweat, and grunting heavily.

'Henri! Bonjour!' Henri, who had been shaken from his trance like state by Janice's words, reached for his towel. He looked very very sheepish.

'Henri, why are you naked? And what's that machine that you are on?'

'Janice. You are back early, I wasn't expecting you home just yet.'

'Clearly. What's all this, and why aren't you wearing anything?' She looked around for a camera, a hidden woman, or something else to explain something as kinky as exercising naked.

'Sorry Janice, I knew that you would object to my buying this machine because it was expensive, but I thought that, once you saw the improvements to my gluteus minimus, you might approve.'

'So why are you naked?' she asked, still looking around for somebody else in the room.

'I can use the mirror to watch that muscle tighten if I'm naked, so I can tone up without doing any damage. I know that you like a tight bum and that mine isn't particularly taut, so I thought I would surprise you when you got back. Try to make you love me again.' Janice's heart melted.

'Henri you idiot, I don't care about your bum! Come here.'

'But you've been a bit cold towards me recently so I thought I would take the opportunity to tidy myself up while you were away.'

'Janice realised that with work commitments it might actually have been her that had seemed to lose interest in their marriage.' She gave him a tight hug, Henri hugged her back, and the towel that he had used to hide his modesty slipped to the floor. He offered Janice an opportunity to examine his newly tightened gluteus minimus in more detail, which she did, and the machine was then forgotten. It was an hour or so before they emerged for dinner.

Tegan wasn't surprised to find that she was back in the hotel that she had booked into on the previous Sunday. With not much else to do on the plane, she had been making a few connections between some of the events of the previous week. It was clear that "they", whoever "they" were, wanted her alive, so they obviously needed her for something important. This hotel had been a part of the arrangements to abduct her the previous Sunday, so the management here must be connected to them somehow. Then there was that barn. The weapons that were stored there had been removed by the local authorities, and nothing she would do could get them back, but the barn is where *she* had been imprisoned, and where Jean had been murdered.

'Why is that barn so important? Why do they want me back here in this hotel when the weapons are already impounded and the fake Tegan has been arrested? What can I do about any of that? Who *is* the fake Tegan? And how are the organisation involved with this?' She really hoped that she could unravel the whole thing and then get back home very swiftly.

The taxi driver that had collected her from the airport escorted her into the hotel. There was no booking in and the porter appeared as if from nowhere to carry her bags for her, and to let them both into her room. The porter gave Tegan the keys and then left them both to it.

'We'll wait for refreshments. Please freshen up if you need to.'

The taxi driver was a tall man of about thirty five. He looked to be of Spanish extraction and wore a moustache, which Tegan thought looked fake. He was expensively dressed in a business suit and tie and looked, to all the world, like a reputable salesman, or something similar.

'Actually,' said Tegan, I'll just check the cupboards first!' which she proceeded to do. This time there was nobody in there, but the clothes that she had brought with her last Sunday *were* there, as was her laptop and the other equipment that she had brought for her work there.

'I wasn't expecting those to still be here.'

'We want you to be comfortable while you are here. I must apologise for all of this by the way. None of this was part of our plan in the first instance.'

'What was your plan then?' asked Tegan.

'After we have eaten. I am starving.' Tegan realised that she was too.

'What do I call you?'

'My name isn't important, but you can call me Ilef.'

'Ilef? Is that Norwegian?'

'No, its actually an acronym.'

'Will you tell me what it stands for?'

'No.' At that point a very tempting mixture of finger foods arrived, along with various drinks, including alcohol. Tegan looked at Ilef in astonishment. 'We thought we'd do it differently this time,' he replied.

They ate and drank in relative silence. Tegan was surprised by how comfortable she felt with Ilef, and they both seemed very relaxed. Tegan was struck by how normal this all felt, but after eating she decided that some business needed to be attended to.

'What have you done with Helen? She's not being kept the same way that I was surely?'

'Helen is being detained at one of our establishments. She isn't chained up but she is locked in. Despite her age she is very feisty, and it was necessary to be quite strict with her. Do you know anything about her?'

'No, to my shame. She and her friend rescued me from that barn, but I didn't get to know her at all. What do *you* know about her?'

'She is well known in her locality as a bit of an adventurer. She is an extraordinarily inquisitive woman and this has lead to her being regarded as a bit of an amateur sleuth. She hasn't solved murder cases or anything, but she has managed to find lost dogs and cats and that sort of stuff. She has a friend called Gareth who seems to be Watson to her Holmes. He is younger than her but you wouldn't think so. My two young ladies had to spar with him, but he turned out to be easier to get around than Helen.'

'And what about Helen's family. She said that you had abducted her grandson. Is he still in captivity?'

'No, we released him and his husband once we had Helen. It's a shame about his foot, but it will mend we think.'

'His foot?'

'Yes. One of my hired operatives fired his gun to put the fear of God into him, but instead put a bullet through his foot. Fortunately the bullet passed straight through and it's healing nicely, or so I'm told. The floor isn't doing quite as well.'

'Then there's my car. Why did you blow that up?'

'We needed you to take notice. I don't think that you'd have taken us quite as seriously without that. One of my English operatives set that up for me. They really need to improve security at that car park because it was all far too easy to do.'

'And will you pay for a new one?'

'No. It will have to go through your insurance sadly.'

'And what about my family. Are they safe from your thuggery?' asked Tegan, the first signs of real anxiety now entering her voice.

'The organisation for whom you work haven't been very obliging about you at all. We don't know where you live for example, and we don't have any clue about your relatives, except for the rather beautiful Akmal of course. He was booked in here did you know, just downstairs in fact. There was an arrangement made so that you would eat at different times and so that you wouldn't bump into each other, which is rather sweet don't you think?'

'Very,' replied Tegan in a less than enthusiastic manner.

'And the woman that I came here with?'

'Ah. The also beautiful member of your organisation, the one who was calling herself Camille? She has disappeared, and we have no idea where she has gone. She hasn't actually checked out of here so she may be back, but she is of no interest to us at all anyway.'

'So who is of interest to you then?'

'At the moment, just you, and until you have carried out our wishes poor Helen will be interesting too. Otherwise, we have no interest in anybody else.'

Tegan's mood now darkened further.

'How many people in the organisation are in on this?'

'My dear young lady, your organisation is as tight as a drum. We don't, despite our best efforts, have anybody working within the organisation at all. We have just been lucky that some of it's members have secrets that they'd rather not have divulged to the wider world!'

'You mean Gustav!' said Tegan.

'I can't comment Tegan.' Tegan was annoyed by this answer.

'So, what happens next?'

'I will come to see you tomorrow morning, hopefully with a colleague. I think that you will like her, but until then I must bid you goodnight. Just ring for room service if you need anything. They will send up a couple of burly men with anything you desire, have one of them if you want. They are very accommodating and very attractive. But don't think you will escape. Not worth trying, you might just get hurt and we don't want that.' He left immediately after that speech and Tegan heard the key turn in the lock outside. Once he had left she thought she'd try the keys that she had been given, but was disappointed that there wasn't actually a keyhole! On further investigation she found that the keys fitted the door to the en-suite bathroom. She laughed, she couldn't help it and it seemed wrong, but she just had to laugh. If this was on the stage, it would be an old English farce! But at least she had a lot of the answers that she wanted.

'Damn!' she suddenly thought. 'I should have asked him about Jean Belanger. I really would like to find the man that killed him.' It was then that she realised that she had truly been smitten with Jean, and that she really could have happily run away with him.

At eight o'clock the following morning a very well-dressed man arrived at the "Poste de Police" in Saint-Jérôme and asked to see the detective in charge. On being advised that she had not arrived for work he demanded to be told on what charges Tegan Durand was being held. He was advised that the charges were of impersonating another individual, with intent to allow that other person to be imprisoned against her will. The solicitor then insisted on being allowed to see his client while the inspector was being contacted. He advised the desk sergeant that it was his view that she had already been in custody for too long, and that he would be demanding her immediate release.

Back in England, Mr. and Mrs. Roberts, along with Akmal, left their hotel in Slough first thing on Monday morning. They set off, in their hire car, for a town called Basingrove, where Mr. Roberts had been Detective Inspector Roberts, and from where they had emigrated fifteen years previously. Wendy Roberts was looking forward to seeing the town and some old friends again, Mr. Roberts was going to look up some ex-colleagues, and Akmal was driving the car. The journey would take an hour or so.

'Where are we staying tonight Wendy?' asked Akmal, suddenly aware that the last-minute decision to persuade him to drive meant that he wasn't sure exactly where he was going.

'Sorry Akmal, I should have told you.' Wendy, who was looking forward to having "a handsome and hunky young man" as an escort for the next few days, advised him that they would be staying in a rented cottage just outside of the town, and provided him with the postcode and house number. Akmal asked her to punch that into the sat nav, which Wendy was happy to do. Sitting in the front with Akmal she was able to look around at the scenery, and she sat reminiscing about the times she had spent around there as a youngster, but she also had to look in horror at some of the buildings that were either new and hideous, or at ones that had become old, decayed or shabby. She was also appalled by the speed of the traffic. Compared with fifteen years ago, everywhere was now so congested that they had been crawling along at times, especially when they had first set off from Slough. Akmal's driving though had been superb, and Wendy praised him for it.

'Unlike Jim's,' she said to him, then added 'his driving was described by his colleagues as "mental" when he was at work.'

'Your driving isn't much better!' added Jim from the back seat. Wendy also had a reputation for fast and furious driving; it had been after racing each other along the M4 that they had first met, at a service station!

They arrived at their cottage just before noon and Wendy set about preparing something for them to eat.

'I'll do that,' said Akmal, but Wendy insisted that he should join Jim, who she said had things to talk to him about.

'I've had a message from Janice,' began Mr. Roberts. 'Tegan was met at the airport by a taxi driver who put her into a taxi and drove them both to Saint-Jérôme, where they both walked into a hotel. The hotel was the Hotel du Lac, and Janice has asked officers to patrol the area at regular intervals.

'Jim, that's the hotel where we stayed, all four of us. To carry out our mission, I was accompanied by a French operative and we shared a room there, and, though I didn't know it at the time, Tegan had a room on the floor above. She was accompanied by a French woman who now lives in Canada, and she stayed in a room a few doors away from Tegan.'

'The same hotel. Now that's interesting because you said that Tegan was abducted and replaced in the hotel. So that swap, which must have been prearranged, took place where Tegan is staying now. That can't be a coincidence.'

Akmal was quiet for a while before suddenly asking Jim whether he had read "At Bertram's hotel", by Agatha Christie. Jim replied that he hadn't.

Akmal outlined the plot of the book to the inspector.

'So you think that this "Hotel du Lac" is complicit in the attempt to foil your efforts to locate the fake weapons perpetrators?'

'It might even be more,' replied Akmal. The pair of them were deep in thought when Wendy brought in a tray of food.

'Let me get that,' said Akmal.

'I'm alright with this one but you can bring in the tea and cups from the kitchen.' Akmal obliged and, while he was doing that, Jim and Wendy exchanged a number of nods. They were smiling when Akmal returned.

'Have I missed something funny?' asked Akmal when he returned.

'No son,' said Jim. 'Pour the tea will you please?' Akmal obliged.

After enjoying quite a filling lunch Wendy asked Akmal a few questions. She had left him to himself on Sunday but now, since he was to be her companion and chauffeur for a few days, she wanted to know a bit more about him.

'Do you have any family in England Akmal? You never mention any.'

'My parents were quite old when I was born, especially my dad. He died when I was sixteen. My mum is still alive but she has returned to Africa where she has five other children.

196

They will look after her much better than I could. I have an older brother, but he lives in Northern Ireland so I don't see him much. We never really got on anyway. He is a boxer and always thought that I was a bit of a wimp.' Wendy looked at Akmal's muscular bulk and wondered what the brother must look like if Akmal was considered to be wimp.

'So you and Tegan aren't married. Have you plans to marry? You do seem very well suited.'

'Tegan won't marry anybody, or so she says. She doesn't agree with any form of personal ownership, but I was considering asking her, at least I was while I was in Canada. That was before I knew that she hadn't chosen to tell me about her relationship with the organisation.'

'But had you told her that *you* were a member? asked Jim.

'No, but she, it turns out, already knew that I was working for them before we met.' He told them the story that Marie had told him about their prearranged blind date.

'Slightly awkward for you then,' said Wendy.

'And this woman whose room you shared in Canada? Wouldn't Tegan be concerned about that?' Akmal felt some warmth enter his face as he recalled some of the embarrassing times he had had with Marie.

'We had single beds on opposite sides of the room. We were posing as a warring married couple so we had to be in one room. She's married anyway, to a beautiful French woman, so I don't think Tegan has anything to worry about.'

'Such a complicated world that you young people live in,' said Wendy.

'I don't agree,' added Jim. 'I think that young people have straightened out lots of problems that we oldies left for them!' Wendy smiled and announced the plans for the afternoon.

'Akmal, you are to accompany me while I do some shopping. I will enjoy showing off my new toy boy, and Jim, you are going to meet up with an old flame. That's right isn't it?'

'She's an ex colleague Wendy, and I expect a lift there from Akmal before you waste the afternoon shopping.'

Akmal hadn't heard much of this. His mind had wandered as soon as Wendy had said "toy boy".

Chapter 26

Inspector Roberts arrived for work, at the "Poste de Police" in Saint-Jérôme, at just after ten am that Monday morning. This was late for her, but she had felt that recovering slightly from jet lag *before* going in to work might not be a bad idea today. Officer Storey had already telephoned to tell her about the solicitor's visit, and to update her on some of the other goings on while she had been away. The inspector's response had been to get Storey to ask the solicitor to return at 10.30am, and also to arrange for Helen's friend Gareth to be brought into the station at 2pm this afternoon, in an unmarked car. As she entered the building she was met by "Tegan"'s solicitor.

'Good morning inspector. I am here to speak to you about my client and I....' Janice stopped him in his tracks.

'I am well aware that there is a need to re-interview "Tegan Durand" and I have arranged for that interview to take place at 11am. Until that time you are free to wait here and refreshments will be provided, or you can return in time for the interview. In the meantime I have a number of issues to which I must attend and, if you don't mind, I will get on with those now.' With that she left the now slightly taken aback solicitor to consider his next move.

The interview with "Tegan" began precisely on time, those present being Detective Inspector Roberts, Officer Storey, Jerry Withnal (solicitor) and "Tegan Durand". The inspector made the usual pre interview announcements, and she began by asking "Tegan" for her full name. Her solicitor was about to speak but the inspector raised her voice and asked the question again. This time she added a little extra.

'Following extensive enquiries, I am satisfied that the woman here present is *not* Tegan Durand and, until we have her true identity, this interview cannot proceed, and therefore I will not be able to arrange for any bail terms or for any other form of release.' Jerry Withnal nodded to "Tegan".

'My name is Olivia Martin, and I live at "Rue des Bordes", Spencerville.'

'That's better,' replied the inspector. 'I believe that you have been masquerading as "Tegan Durand" for the last eight days. Do you wish to comment?'

'It is true, I have been employed to take on the persona of Tegan Durand.'

'Had you any previous knowledge of Tegan Durand, or had you met her before last Sunday?'

'No.'

'Yet it seems that you were able to perform a very passable impression of Tegan Durand.'

'I am an actor by profession, and I was approached by an agency to carry out a two week job. The pay was really good and I was told that I already bore a striking resemblance to Tegan. I had no idea that what I was doing was illegal.'

At that point the solicitor intervened and the inspector allowed the intervention this time. She was hoping that he would be predictable.

'As I understand the current legal position, it is an offence to impersonate another individual if that impersonation causes harm or financial gain. None of my client's actions have caused either harm or financial gain, or anything even approaching that, and I wonder whether the inspector has any evidence to the contrary?' That is exactly what Janice wanted to hear and she turned back to Olivia.

'What, *exactly*, were you employed to do Ms Martin?'

'I was told that I was to relieve the real Tegan because she hadn't wanted to carry out a job for somebody called "The organisation". I was given a thick booklet of stuff to learn, including how to work some very sophisticated gadgets. I was to work with a woman called Camille, and she hadn't to know that I was acting a part. I was told that Tegan lived in a place in England, and that she lived with a black man called Akmal. I had to do whatever Camille told me to do. That's it really.'

'And what did Camille tell you to do?'

'I had to be trying to find some people that were making and selling fake weapons. I had lots of sheets of information about that and I had to keep looking at those to keep up with what I was doing. That was hard, but every other part of the job was easy.'

'Did you find any of the fake weapons dealers?'

'I have no idea. I just used that gadget thing and it gave me thousands of hits. I followed the instructions to send most of them back to that "organisation" and then I pretended to investigate some local ones. It was fun at times, and scary at others.'

'Why did you kill Jean Belanger?' That question came out of the blue and Olivia's mood now changed. She became visibly upset.

'I have no idea what you are talking about.'

'Inspector, I really must protest. I am aware of the mysterious death of Jean Belanger, and I understand that it occurred in a barn about fifty minutes drive from here. I also, from reading the newspaper, know that his death occurred shortly before my client was brought into here. You cannot possibly have any reason to suspect my client of involvement in that!' The inspector ignored that interruption and turned back to Olivia.

'Did you know, or know of, Jean Belanger?'

'No, I never heard of him. They never told me anything about killings or I wouldn't have gone near the job. I was just acting a part. Oh why did I get involved in this?'

'Why did you?'

'Because I needed the money. And, being honest, I was attracted to the mystery of the thing. I never hurt anybody though, and I didn't steal anything either. I really was just acting a part.'

'Who actually employed you Olivia?'

'I don't know, really I don't. I was approached during my last acting job by a woman who said she liked my stuff, and would I like a job. She came to my house with all those instructions, and gave me a lot of money as deposit. I couldn't resist it.'

'And you have no idea who it was?'

'She gave me a card with a name on but I have lost it. I have never broken any laws, honestly.'

'Inspector, do you actually have any evidence to suggest that her acting role had caused anybody or anything any real harm? If not, then I ask that you release her.'

'And who is paying *you*, mister Withnal?'

'Inspector, you know better than to ask me that.'

At that point the inspector ended the interview and asked officer Storey to escort Olivia back to her cell. She asked Mr. Withnal to accompany her to her office. Back in her office she turned to speak to him.

'Mister Withnal, this whole thing stinks. It stinks of deceit, of corruption and the worst form of wrongdoing. I do not believe that everything I have heard today has been the truth, but I do believe that Olivia is guilty of nothing more than poor judgement, and a desire for excitement. You are correct that I have no evidence to suggest that she has caused any harm towards, or personal gain against, the real Tegan, and so I will release her. You may either wait while my officers carry out the necessary form filling, or return in about thirty minutes. As usual, I will need a place of residence where she, and you, can be contacted, and I will expect Olivia to be made available at any time should any new information come to light. Is that absolutely clear?'

'It is indeed. I have already told her that she will have to stay nearby for a while and she has booked into a hotel for a few nights.'

'At whose expense?'

'Inspector, again, you know better than that.'

'All contact details must be left with my officers today.'

'Agreed.'

Thirty minutes later, Olivia and her solicitor exited into the bright sunshine of that late morning, and headed for the Hotel du Lac.

Chapter 27

By 2pm that same day, Gareth had been collected from his home, given refreshments, and asked to wait for the inspector. He was only expecting to talk about Helen Morgan, so he was more than a little surprised to be lead into the interview room, where inspector Roberts and Officer McNeil were waiting.

'Please sit down Mr. Jones. The tape will be running for this interview, but you are not under arrest. Do you understand and are you happy to proceed? We will switch off the recorder if you aren't comfortable with being recorded.' Gareth noted the "Mr. Jones" and said that he was fine to continue.

'May I call you Gareth Mr. Jones?' asked the inspector.

'Yes of course,' he replied, now sounding slightly nervous. He had an idea as to why he would need to be interviewed, but he hadn't been expecting anything quite so formal.

'Mister Jones, would you confirm for me that we have your correct home address?'

'Yes, the address that you just picked me up from is my permanent address. Is this about Helen?' The inspector ignored the question.

'Gareth, please talk me through the events of the early morning on Friday last, when you disabled CCTV cameras around, and then forced entry into, the property commonly known as Ned's barn?' Gareth wasn't expecting quite such a formal and direct question, and he could see how this officer had risen so quickly to become inspector. There was something about her manner that made him feel forced to comply with what she asked, even though he hadn't seen his jaunt with Helen in quite the way the inspector had just phrased her question!

'Helen Morgan, my near neighbour, had been to see me the previous day, she had seen some lights on up at old Ned's barn, and asked me to go up there with her to see what was happening.'

'At four o'clock in the morning, wearing dark clothes, and armed with a number of high powered flash-lights and a pistol?' Gareth was taken aback.

'It wasn't like that.'

'So you didn't go up to there with criminal intent, to disable security cameras, and to break into that barn?' Gareth didn't know what to say. 'And you had no intention of freeing the woman known as Tegan Durand?' The inspector paused. 'And then of murdering Jean Belanger?' She paused again. 'Doesn't look good this does it?' 'Long prison sentence...'

'Stop, please. It wasn't like that, and I don't know a Jean Belanger though I have read about his death in the paper. Helen had been up there the previous night, and while she was visiting me she had a call from somebody that frightened her. So we went up to take another look, that's all.'

'And calling the police wasn't an option you thought? You were both *so scared* after Helen's first visit *that you decided to go up there again*? How old are you, 65? and Helen's what, 75?

This isn't a fairy story, so I will ask you again, why did you go up there and how did you know Tegan Durand?' Gareth closed his eyes. How had he got into this? After a while he began again.

'Helen and I have done amateur stuff before, found some lost dogs and cats and even some missing silver. We were intrigued to know who now owned Ned's barn, and doing it in the dark seemed more exciting. Helen also pointed out that if we had called the police and said there was a light on around the barn that they would have laughed at us. Tell us that it's the twenty first century and electricity has been invented now. That sort of thing.'

'Then talk me through exactly what happened when you went up to that barn, and exactly how you came across Tegan Durand.'

Gareth told the inspector the full story of that morning, as far he could remember it.

'So you heard Tegan, rather than saw her?'

'Yes.'

'Then, *exactly*, how did you exit with Tegan?'

'I broke the chains using the tools I took with me.'

'"Going equipped" is the expression they use in the UK for taking tools with you to a burglary. Go on.'

'I left the shackle on her ankle in case she turned out to be a baddie of some sort, and then we left the barn. I did put the hasp back on the barn door and we didn't take anything.' The inspector smiled at Gareth's use of the word baddie.

'Now Gareth, this is important, did you walk between the packing crates and the barn wall to get out of there?'

'Yes.'

'Right side or left, as you leave the barn?' Gareth thought for a while.

'We must have walked to the right of the crates because the barn wall was against my right arm. I am sure of it.'

'Was there any impediment to your exit, any rods or bars that you had to step over?'

'No. The aisles were very clear, as though they had used them to push machinery along there, or left them clear for manoeuvring the crates.'

'Then, once you had left the barn, you closed the doors and relocked them?'

'Yes.'

'So Tegan Durand just stood patiently waiting while you re attached the hasp to the barn door?'

'Yes, she did. I think that she was just delighted to be free from her prison.'

'And did you see anybody else up there, anybody at all?'

'No. We saw a truck pass us but we were well clear of the barn at that point. We assumed that the alarm had finally attracted some attention.'

'Did you see who was in the truck?'

'It was dark inspector.'

'And then you just happened to meet up with Tegan's friends I suppose?' Gareth told her about the last part of their journey, and how they were now sworn to secrecy about everything. The inspector gave a long sigh.

'Can you possibly describe the truck?'

'My lights just caught it. It was a scruffy red flatbed thing. Looked like a farm truck to be honest.' The inspector sat and tapped her pen against the side of the table.

'I think that that will do for now. Officer McNeil will escort you out and arrange for a lift home for you.'

'Will there be any charges?'

'You are lucky Mr. Jones. Nobody has brought any charges against you for breaking and entering. I could charge you with "going equipped" but I won't this time. But I must warn you against any more amateur detective stuff. I won't be so lenient next time. Is that clear?'

'Yes inspector. Crystal. I still haven't heard from Helen.'

'We'll advise you if there are any developments with your friend. Thank-you for coming in.'

'My pleasure,' he responded, now sounding less sure of himself.

Officer McNeil offered refreshments before he took him home. Gareth refused, but decided that he would have some whisky (Welsh of course) when he got back!

The inspector found officer Storey once Gareth was gone. 'Could you please contact Josh Howard. Ask him to drive down and see me this afternoon at 5.30pm. Tell him to drive here by himself.'

'Will do Ma'am.'

That afternoon, Akmal had dropped Jim off at Basingrove police station while he and Wendy headed off to Basingrove's shopping and cafe areas. Jim stood and looked at the police station for a while, then strolled with mixed feelings into the building he once called work. While memories flooded through him, he noted that the building was now covered in a modern grey cladding material that hid the rather scruffy brickwork that had been the image projected by the building in his day. On entry, now through electric double doors, into the still familiar "air lock" ante room, he saw a large sign inviting him to use the "self-check in" screen if he had an appointment, or to ring the bell for emergencies. He entered his details onto the screen, cleaned his fingers with sanitiser, and then sat and waited. After a while a young PC, who looked to Jim to be about twelve, lead him to a door which bore a brass plate bearing the name "Detective Chief Inspector Bradley". The young officer invited him to sit and wait and said that she was sure that he wouldn't have to wait long. Jim was impressed by the calm politeness of the officer. He looked around again. Gone were the vending machines and the huge notice boards of his days here. The place now looked rather bare, but smelled of fresh coffee and air freshener, rather than the disinfectant odour that used to exist there.

After a while, a rather elderly but sprightly woman opened the door. 'Inspector, how lovely to see you again It's been years since I saw you. You look well.'

'For an old man you mean? Remember that I haven't been an inspector for twenty years now, so please call me Jim. Everybody does.'

'How is retirement suiting you? I've got five months left and then "They" want me gone. I've filled in the forms and it's all planned, but I'm not sure that I am keen. Did you hear that I lost Paul?'

'No I didn't. I'm sorry. How long were you married?'

'Nearly thirty eight years, but we'd been together for nearly forty. It comes to us all in the end though. There's nobody left here now that worked with you, except me. Happy days perhaps?'

'Sometimes,' said the inspector. He noted the lack of a computer on her desk. There was a large tablet PC in front of her, and he realised that technology was still changing the look of an inspector's desk.

'Now, you had something you wanted to discuss with me, a case perhaps?' Jim eyed the rather expensive looking coffee machine that stood behind her desk.

'Sorry sir, would you like some coffee?'

'Yes please, milk no sugar.'

'Do you mean a latte?'

'Probably. I'll let you know when I drink it.' The machine made it's range of noises, from grinding to steaming and then dispensing. Jim drank some and approved, and then he began. He told the inspector just enough about Akmal, Tegan and the organisation to gain her interest, and then asked whether her area still included Gatwick.

'It does. What would you like to me to do?' He told her about the explosion in Tegan's car.

'So you want me to obtain and go through the CCTV from the car park, arrange to get hold of the forensic evidence from the blast, and report it all back to you.' Jim was delighted.

'Yes please.'

'You know that I shouldn't.'

'Yes I do.'

'Do you know what Jim, I'm tired of sitting behind this desk. I'll leave the CCTV stuff to one of my sergeants but I'll look into the forensics myself. I'll do any follow up that I think necessary too.

'Thanks WPC Bradley. I knew that you would.' The inspector hadn't been called that in thirty five years, and she was taken back to her first months in the job.

211

'I'd forgotten that we were called WPCs when I first joined the force. Woman Police Constable. Isn't that what it stood for? That should make you lot MPCs or Man Police Constable. Sounds ridiculous now doesn't it.' Jim agreed.

'Time you went now then Jim. I've got work to do.'

'You're starting now?'

'There's lives at stake Jim. Time to get on with it.' Jim noticed a twinkle in her eye and said his farewells. On leaving the station he rang Wendy.

'Shall we meet in Debenhams?' he asked.

'We can't love,' she said. 'It's closed down now. There's a tea shop in the arcade. I'll wait for you there.'

Jim decided that a walk would do him good and he set off at a brisk pace. Wendy and Akmal were chatting happily when he met up with them.

'You two look happy! Had a good afternoon?'

'Not really,' replied Wendy. 'There's only a few of my old shopping haunts left. In fact, a large proportion of the shops are boarded up and there aren't many shoppers either. The "retail therapy" they used to talk about doesn't work any more. Akmal has explained that UK shoppers are the world's most likely to shop online, so shopping has just about died out here. I'm glad we've moved to Canada where it's not so bad. Do you want coffee Jim?'

'I've had some at the station dear.' He tasted Wendy's coffee. 'Actually, the stuff at the station was better than yours.'

'Akmal wants to have a look around the old part of town before we go back to the cottage. Do you want to join us?'

'Why not. Shall we eat out?'

'No. Akmal wants me to cook tonight. I think he likes my food.' Akmal smiled and nodded.

Chapter 28

Josh arrived early for his interview at the station, which pleased the inspector. He was met by officer Storey who asked where he had parked, and whether he wanted to use the station car park. He replied that he had taken the liberty of parking in there anyway, and that he hoped that his truck wouldn't be dragged away to a pound. Officer Storey reassured him that that wouldn't happen, but asked for his registration number anyway, then lead him into the interview room and asked him to wait.

The inspector then popped out the back and found his truck, a rather scruffy red flatbed. That was all that the inspector needed to see, and she prepared herself for what might be a difficult interview.

'Good afternoon Mr. Howard. Please be advised that this interview is being recorded. Is that fine with you?'

'Yes.'

'Do you want to have a solicitor present?' Josh thought back to his previous encounter with the police and decided that he no longer needed one.

'Tell me about Jean Belanger.'

'What do you want to know?'

'Anything.'

'He was my best friend.'

'Your fit, handsome, healthy, womanising, successful and sexual stud, best friend. I've seen him on the slab and even in death he's gorgeous.' Josh was totally thrown by this. It wasn't what he had been expecting at all.

'What?'

'Would you like me to repeat those sentences Josh?'

'No, but I'm confused.'

'Confused, or jealous perhaps? We've heard from your boss that alarm customers asked for Jean rather than you. We also know that he even enjoyed a very personal and sexual relationship with some of the female customers that he would visit. Unlike yourself, eh Josh?' Josh couldn't believe his ears.

'What are you getting at?'

'You had been checking on Tegan Durand, hadn't you?'

'The woman in the barn you mean?'

'Yes, the woman in the barn.'

'We did see to her, yes.'

'See to her is an interesting expression. So, you had to provide her with food and drink, and *stuff*.'

'*Stuff?*'

'She was coming on to Jean wasn't she. She would watch him walk towards her, she would take his hand sometimes, lick her lips, smile maybe, or even remove some clothing for him. He would respond, they would cuddle, maybe she undid his shirt a little to admire the gym work he does, maybe he fondled her breasts a little, maybe she responded and fondled him, you couldn't stand this...'

'It was me that she wanted!' The inspector knew that she had hit a nerve.

'Really! So, it was you that she couldn't keep her hands off. You made the advances, and it was you that she responded to? Maybe Jean said you mustn't let her. You wanted to let her go so she could be your girlfriend. You really had the hots for her didn't you, you couldn't control yourself, Jean tried to get you to stop with Tegan, but you were out of control.'

'No, No. What are you saying?' Josh still couldn't believe what he was hearing, he wasn't prepared for this at all. He had his statement ready in his mind, but this was way off his script and now his head was spinning.

'That you got physical, not just with Tegan, but with Jean, but *not* sexually with Jean. That handsome face, muscled chest, lean physique. You hated him, but you had the upper hand because she loved you, only you, and you would show Jean, perhaps you pushed him away from her as he tried it on, he banged his head and he was stunned, so you knew you had him, you could kill him, Jean would be dead and Tegan would be all yours, yours alone, so you hit out at him again, and again, and again, and down he went'

'STOP. It wasn't like that at all.' Josh was sobbing and the inspector paused.

'What was it like then Josh?' she asked, now sounding tender.

'I just wanted to scar him.' He paused. 'His pretty face. I wanted to spoil his pretty face. Then Tegan would want me. He wasn't supposed to die, he missed the knife. Oh God.' Josh continued to sob quietly, and Janice gave him a while to gather his thoughts.

'Tell me *exactly* what went on that morning please Josh.'

It took inspector Roberts some time to fully deal with the remainder of the interview, and to summon a solicitor prior to her first cautioning, and then arresting Josh. She had decided

216

that the charge would be of homicide, with the expectation that Josh would be tried for manslaughter. Strictly, Josh had intended to inflict grievous bodily harm rather than death, but he had still killed Jean. It would be up to Josh's law team to decide how serious the charge would have to be, indeed if it were proven that Josh had carried out his act on behalf of somebody else, such as the "gang" that were being investigated by the organisation, then Josh would be facing a murder charge. On the other hand, thought Janice, the *actual* evidence that could be brought before the court would be tiny, and the jury would have to rely upon his confession to judge his guilt. She felt that Josh had already been punished anyway. The killing of his friend had turned the previously calm and composed, if rather jealous individual that he had been, into a very unhappy and disturbed man. She couldn't help but feel just a little bit sorry for him.

Back in England, Jim had had a visit from Detective Chief inspector Bradley. After a chat between themselves, Jim asked Akmal to join them.

'Good evening Akmal. It's nice to meet you – you are the nearest to a secret service agent I have ever worked for, and at my great age I have been intrigued enough to get off my arse and do the work myself!' Akmal smiled.

'Jim may have told you that he has asked me to look into the explosion of Tegan's car at Gatwick last week, and I have just been discussing my findings with him. I, or rather my team, haven't yet finished looking through the CCTV from that night, but with modern developments we can scan two whole days in just a few hours, so it won't be long before I can report back fully to you. The forensic findings from the blast are interesting though. Identifying the substance that caused the blast took a while because nothing that is routinely scanned for seemed to be present, except lead, which appears to conflict with later findings.'

'So, her car wasn't blown up by anything that local gangs might usually use?' asked Akmal.

'Indeed not, but I *can* tell you what the substance was. Now I will need to read this carefully to you, so I will just put on my glasses!' Jim and Akmal smiled because the inspector seemed suddenly to have drifted into a scene from an Agatha Christie or J.K. Rowling novel.

'The explosive was a quite modern substance called a tetrazole azasydnone salt, and the confusion comes from the fact that these compounds don't usually contain lead. In fact, they are usually marketed as lead free, so this wasn't bought commercially!'

'Does that narrow down who the perpetrators might have been?'

'It does, but we need more information before searching our databases. You, Akmal, can help with some preliminary questions. Firstly, apart from you and, presumably, your neighbours, who would know what car Tegan drives?'

'Tegan is an accountant, and she often wines and dines clients, which is why she drives, or drove, a well-respected car. Loads of people would know it.'

'And how many of those would also know that she flew from Gatwick last Saturday?'

'Presumably none of them. So I suppose that it would have to be somebody that worked for, or knew the operations of, the organisation.'

'Does she have a contact with that organisation?'

'You'd need to ask Tegan that.'

'Would Tegan have told anybody that she was leaving for Gatwick Airport that Saturday?'

'I doubt it. Her liaison was supposed to be a secret and if our neighbours watched us leave they would assume that we were off to Oxford, which is where we had told them that we would be going before her liaison, [which became her "liaison (unexpectedly) dangereuse"], had got in the way!'

'And, presumably, your liaison had the same effect!' Akmal now looked a little shame faced.

'Yes, I suppose so.'

'Had Tegan introduced you to any new friends of late Akmal?'

'No, nobody.' At that point, the inspector's phone beeped.

'Ah, the CCTV footage has been scanned and my team have sent me some images to watch. Is there a TV here that I can "Screen Mirror" to?'

Between them they hooked up the phone to the TV and they watched three video clips. The first showed a car, that was very similar to Tegan's, enter the car park. The driver picked up his entry ticket, parked the car, and then two individuals got out. One was carrying a holdall. The video stopped and the second clip began. The man with the holdall was then seen walking, alone, past Tegan's car in one direction and then returned slightly afterwards. He stopped to tie his shoelace but then didn't pick up his holdall. Within seconds of leaving the bag there his partner walked by and kicked the bag under the car. A third clip showed the pair driving out of the car park, paying as they left. A final photograph showed a full-frontal picture of the car as it left the car park. Only the driver was now present.

'When did that happen?' asked Akmal.

'Just five minutes before the explosion. They timed it well. I do recognise the driver though,' said the inspector. She now used her phone to ring the station and asked for somebody to pick up Sam Spencer, or Swindler Sam as he was known locally. He was an odd job man that would do almost anything if the price was right.

'Do you know who owned the car that they used?'

'We do, but it had been reported stolen almost a week before this happened. It was found yesterday in a very dark street by a woman walking her dog. She reported it because it had been left in the middle of the lane with its engine running. I doubt whether anything will be found in it. There's no CCTV around there and we often find abandoned cars in that area.'

'So, are we any nearer to finding out who blew up Tegan's car?'

'I think that depends on you as much as on the inspector here. You must have somebody in your organisation that might help with this,' said Jim.

'It's going to be my ex-organisation soon. I've had enough of it now and I may even quit my proper job, move north perhaps, get some fresh air.'

'What about Tegan?'

'That will be entirely up to her. I do have one person I can contact before I quit though, and I will go and do that now.' Akmal left Jim and the inspector and sat a while in his room before making a cloaked call to Marie.

Downstairs, Jim had invited the inspector to join him and Wendy in a drink. She thanked him but declined, saying that she wanted to go home and put her feet up. 'Make some arrangements for my retirement,' she added.

Chapter 29

Tegan felt as though she were going to go mad. She had woken with a start at just after 11am and had had to remind herself of where she was. 'Back in that hotel room', she thought. 'Damn, and with no means of escape. If I get out of this alive I'm going to leave the organisation for good this time. I've had enough. And I will stay clear of hotels, probably forever.'

She thought back to two years ago. She was at that time living comfortably with her new man Akmal, and she was actually enjoying her life for the first time ever. It was certainly the most relaxed that she had ever been, and the organisation was, at that time, starting to become too much of a memory of her former, madcap life. But when she approached the organisation with her intention to quit, she had been persuaded that she should stay, and that they would only contact her when she was on her own, or she could contact them instead. She was certainly on her own now, and she was fed up, anxious and worried. Worried about herself, about Akmal but, more pressingly at the moment, she was worried about Helen Morgan, and she felt powerless to do anything to help her. This was the emotion that Tegan feared most. She hated not being in control and now this was all really getting to her. She decided to freshen up and dress, and then to call room service. She wandered into the bathroom, but she didn't enjoy her shower. Memories of Akmal kept coming back to her and this added tremendously to her feeling of melancholy. 'Pull yourself together,' she thought to herself. 'Have breakfast and then plan your day!'

After dressing she rang room service and ordered a standard breakfast and some "company". This duly arrived but, since it was 11.45, it had become more like an early lunch. As Ilef had promised, it was delivered by a well-dressed, approachable looking man of about thirty-five. He knocked and waited to be invited in, which Tegan thought was, at least, a good start.

'Breakfast for Tegan,' the guard said simply as the man entered the room. Tegan noticed that he didn't lock the door. Quick as a flash she made a run for it, reaching the door in double quick time, opened it and made a dash for freedom.

'Morning Tegan.' The man outside the door had a very nasty looking pistol in his hand. 'Go back in please Tegan. If you leave now it will result in two deaths. Better go back in, have breakfast, enjoy Jock's company and consider Helen Morgan.'

'It was worth a try,' said Tegan, nonchalantly, and she walked very slowly back into her room. The guard introduced the man who had brought breakfast as "Jock".

Jock remained silent while Tegan ate.

'Join me in some food?' asked Tegan. Jock shook his head.

Tegan ate her breakfast, which she had to admit had been very good.

'You sure you won;'t have some?' Jock shook his head.

223

'Can you get me some books to read?' Jock gestured towards a large bookcase filled with a range of books.

'Ah, not very observant am I?' Jock smiled.

'How about a TV?' Jock gesture toward a cupboard. Tegan opened twin doors and a TV emerged on a sort of pedestal arrangement. There were instructions on how to receive a range of cable services.

'Thanks,' she said.

'If I tell you to leave will you go?' Jock nodded, and stood up.

'No, don't go yet. Is there anything that I asked you to do that you would refuse?' Jock shook his head.

'Let me out then, now.'

'Jock stood up and opened the door. He pointed at the man outside. He re-closed the door. Tegan spent a while thinking of the most outlandish things she could get Jock to do, including some very kinky stuff. She realised that he might actually do any or all of those kinky things, but she wasn't in the mood today, and she decided that she would keep such mischief in mind for if she became thoroughly bored.

'Jock, shoot yourself.' Jock stood up and patted all of of his pockets. He opened his arms and wore the standard expression for "I can't".

'No gun eh.'

'Tell me that I am beautiful.'

'You are beautiful.'

'So you *can* speak.' Jock nodded. Tegan was surprised that this rather wiry blonde haired, blue eyed man had such a deep, dark brown voice.

'So why aren't you speaking?' Jock made some gestures that indicated to Tegan that he did not want to. 'Go now

224

please.' Jock bowed slightly and then complied with that, and Tegan was alone again.

'So, what's the game here. Why send somebody up to me to who is instructed to do anything I ask, but he won't *speak* unless instructed to by me? Must be an attempt to drive me onto some sort of submission. Well, it isn't working is it, not *yet* anyway.' She spent a while reading a book that turned out to be quite good. She watched a little TV and then, at about 4pm, she ordered high tea, restaurant's choice. Jock was again the bringer of the food, and she ate that with relish.

'I must recommend this place to friends,' she thought, then laughed. She hadn't spent much time talking to Jock but, before he left, she decided to have some fun with him. She mischievously gave Jock another order: 'You must bring up my dinner when it's dinner time, but wear swim shorts, which my boyfriend loves to wear, even around the house, and blue socks, the only colour socks that he hates'. He nodded, she smiled, he smiled, and then she asked him to leave.

She felt curiously troubled after this instruction and her mind wandered back to her life at home. She thought about some of Akmal's odd ways and wondered just how upset he really was with her. Yes, she had arranged the 'blind date' that allowed her to meet him, but so what? They had a mutual attraction so did it really matter that she hadn't told him about it afterwards? She thought back to the many times that her friends would call round and Akmal would be just wearing his swim shorts and she would make him put on a dressing gown. She thought about his simple grooming, about how she would enjoy trimming his hair for him sometimes, and she suddenly yearned to be back home. But

225

then her mood darkened, and she decided that Akmal just needed to grow up. 'He can do his own grooming and wander about the house any way he likes now because he is there by himself. He'll get used to it, and then be glad to have me back.'

She had ordered that dinner for 6pm and Jock arrived at about 6.15pm. He was wearing a black suit, tie and dark brown shoes. After giving him time to serve the food she spoke to him.

'I told you to wear swim shorts and blue socks, but you are wearing a suit. Won't you be in trouble for not doing as you are told?' Jock pulled up his trouser legs and showed her the blue socks. 'I suppose that you have the swim shorts on under your trousers?' Jock nodded. 'And if I tell you that I expected you to bring dinner wearing *only* blue socks and swim shorts, would you remove everything else?' Jock nodded.

Tegan was warming to Jock, and she was beginning to genuinely enjoy his company, and his offbeat sense of humour. He had a happy face and he smiled again when she had asked him that last question. She decided not to ask him to remove the suit, and that she wouldn't embarrass him further, not today anyway, and she chatted to him while eating. He continued to respond only with gestures, which Tegan found to be really cute for some reason. She had been sufficiently naughty to suggest that *he* wear very little for *her* benefit, so she thought it time to do something for him.

'What would you do if it was me that was just wearing very skimpy swimwear when you came in with my food?' She was really feeling mischievous now, but Jock responded by performing a brilliant impression of a man fainting, as he

226

wiped non-existent sweat from his brow. That broad smile returned to his face, and this time Tegan smiled back but, just as she was finishing her dessert, there came a knock at the door. Jock opened it and saw Ilef, and a woman, standing outside.

'May we come in?' asked Ilef.

'Can I stop you?' asked Tegan

'No.' Jock stood aside to allow them in. He then left immediately, closing the door behind him. 'How are you getting along with Jock?' asked Ilef.

'Fine,' was all that Tegan replied. 'To what do I owe the pleasure of this visit?' she asked.

'Tegan, I want to introduce you to Olivia Martin, who is an actor of my acquaintance. She will be staying in the room next door to you.' Tegan looked Olivia up and down.

'You are the woman who impersonated me aren't you?'

'She is,' replied Ilef.

'I was asking Olivia, not you. So I will ask the question again.'

'Yes. I was acting as you for a few days, and it's really nice to meet you in person.'

'Likewise,' said Tegan, with very little enthusiasm. 'You don't look much like me though.' In response, Olivia stood a while, and Tegan watched as she tensed muscles in her face, one at a time it seemed.

'How's this?' she asked.

'Wow,' said Tegan.

'She's good isn't she? I have offered employment to Olivia for a little longer than I had originally intended, and she has graciously accepted my offer.'

'It was generous,' said Olivia.

227

'Olivia is going to resume the role of Tegan Durand. She will be your eyes, ears and general gofer. You see Tegan, I want you to unmask those sons of bitches who are muscling in on my territory. They are costing me thousands a day in lost sales and I can't have that. So you have everything you need, Olivia here has all of your electronics kit to return to you, and you can have anything else you need, just ask. Once you have found the little darlings I will deal with them, you and Helen will be free, and Olivia here will have something to add to her resume.'

'This is classic,' said Tegan, 'You are defrauding the "RUMP" organisation by producing copies of their weapons which you then sell on illegally, thereby reducing their profit margin, and making yourself lots of money. But another organisation has muscled in and is doing exactly the same to you. So you consider that you are in the same position as the "RUMP" organisation and you want me to find them for you?'

'That's about it,' said Ilef.

'Well there's a twist. Two fraudsters for the RUMP organisation, and now one is pitched against the other. And Olivia is allowed out but I'm not.'

'Correct. She is still wearing your transmitter beacon meaning that we can trace her, so she isn't really much more free than you are. The sooner that you are successful the better.'

'So Olivia will be locked in her room too, until I need her?'

'Pretty much. Her door won't be locked but she'll have the same room service as you, so you will both be spoilt rotten.' Tegan felt an odd pang of jealousy and she couldn't work out why.

'When do we start?'

'I will come by tomorrow morning at ten,' said Olivia. 'I'll bring the last of your kit back to you then.'

'Thanks,' said Tegan, moodily. Ilef and Olivia left and Tegan spent quite a while in deep thought.

Olivia had been quite pleased with this booking; being waited on hand and foot in a hotel room while acting a role that she had already played was like money for old rope. She moved into next door and felt really carefree. Tegan was, obviously, less happy, and she made a few notes for the inspector. She would make contact tomorrow, when she had all of her equipment back.

At just before 10pm that night, Tegan rang down to room service, asking them to send Jock with a bottle of whisky. She had had enough for one day, and she needed something to help her wind down. After a lengthy wait, which had begun to annoy Tegan, there came a knock on the door.

'May I come in?' It was Jock's voice.

'Yes. Open the damn door,' Tegan shouted, with some annoyance, but that faded very quickly. There, in front of her, was Jock, wearing just white swim shorts and bright blue socks, and holding a small tray containing a bottle of whisky and two glasses. He wasn't even wearing shoes. She realised that he had been a while because he was getting changed, and he had remembered what she had said her boyfriend liked. She could make trouble for him because she hadn't specifically ordered him to do it, but this man was really growing on her, and his appearance just then softened her mood massively. She ordered him to come in and to pour two glasses of whisky, which she then ordered him to share with her.

They chatted, or rather mimed, for a while and they found lots of nonsense to chat about. Tegan didn't drink too much; she wasn't about to lose control here, no matter what Jock had been ordered to do, and he didn't drink any more than she did.

'Time you left,' said Tegan. Jock picked up the bottle and the glasses and put them back on the tray. As he was heading for the door, and she was obviously more inebriated than she realised, she asked Jock whether he would remove the swim shorts if she ordered him to. Jock shook his head. 'But you are under orders to obey me. Ilef said that you would do *anything* I asked. So take off your swim shorts.' Jock gave Tegan a very winning smile, but shook his head again. He mouthed the words 'Not yet,' and left.

Tegan had never met anybody like him, he wasn't her type at all, and she didn't generally go for older men, but, when she was asleep, she dreamt that she had dreamed the whole day.

Chapter 30

The next morning, Inspector Roberts was at her desk at her usual start time of 9am. 'Any messages for me?' she asked. The response was negative.

'Nothing from a Tegan, a Helen, a Gareth, my dad?' The response was still negative.

'Any unusual activity at the Hotel du Lac?' Again, a negative response. After the excitement of the last few days, she felt rather disappointed.

'Anything new out of Josh Howard?' Negative response yet again.

At about the same time as Inspector Roberts was beginning that work, Tegan had just ordered breakfast. It was brought up to her by a woman called Serena. 'Where's Jock today?'

'He's not working today.'

'At least this one speaks,' thought Tegan. She was about to ask when he would be back but thought better of it. 'Stay and talk to me?' Serena nodded. Tegan ate her breakfast but said very little to Serena. She realised that the two things on her mind this morning were Olivia and Jock, so she dismissed Serena and studied the list she had prepared for Inspector Roberts. Just then there was a knock at the door and Olivia was allowed in.

'Morning Tegan.'

'Morning Olivia.' Tegan was reminded, with a shudder, of school assemblies that started that way.

'I have your kit with me. Do you want it now?'

'Of course, put it down over there.' Olivia obliged and sat down facing Tegan. Olivia's first thought was to see how Tegan felt about her, and the role that she had been given. She began to talk to her about it, but Tegan's response was brief. 'Let's just get on with it shall we?' Olivia looked disappointed but Tegan gave her a nod, and then picked up a piece of equipment. She plugged it into the mains to allow it to charge up and then made some notes on it which she gestured Olivia to read.

'Olivia, read this but make no comment. You and I are in a very dangerous situation. Don't respond, they can hear us, they might even be able to see us. You need to do everything that I tell you, but first, answer some questions. Nod if this is clear so far.'

Olivia nodded. Tegan and she swapped a few more verbal pleasantries, including 'why didn't you charge this bloody thing?' while Tegan continued to silently type.

'Answer these questions by gesture only. Are you alone here?' appeared on the screen. Olivia nodded.

'Do you have a car?' Olivia nodded.

'Is it yours?' Olivia nodded.

'When you get back in it, check it for anything unusual before you drive it. Are you really an actor and are you really not connected with Ilef in any other way?' Olivia nodded again.

'You will never be free of this bunch now so can I trust you to help me get rid of both of these organisations, at considerable risk to yourself?' After a pause this time, Olivia nodded again.

'Are you in a relationship with anybody at the moment?' Olivia shook her head. Aloud, Tegan said 'Do you have a boyfriend?' Aloud, Olivia explained that she had recently divorced, and she was travelling as a jobbing actor to find somebody new.

'Please ask to leave in about ten minutes. Tell me that you need some women's things and that you will be back in half an hour. Ask the man outside to get coffee sent up in thirty minutes.' Olivia nodded.

Once Olivia had gone, Tegan connected to the 5G network (in case the hotel's wifi was bugged or monitored) and she accessed her cloud account. From there she downloaded her contacts list, her recent software updates, and the emergency contacts list from the organisation. With that done, she parcelled up the sheet of information that she had made out for Inspector Roberts, encrypted it, and then sent it directly to the inspector via the internal police network. She had previously e-mailed the inspector with instructions on how to open this file, and she hoped that she would get a response quite quickly. That done, she applied her updates to her device and sat and waited for Olivia to return.

Olivia and the coffee arrived at the same time. They then both dismissed Serena at the same time, which made them laugh, and prompted Serena to ask whether they were twins. This made them laugh again but, once Serena was gone, they became serious. While drinking coffee they made plans for the rest of the day.

Back in England, Akmal had overslept and had to spend a while trying to work out where he was. He was really missing

Tegan and he decided to take an early morning walk. He spent about an hour strolling around the lanes and the riverside walks of Basingrove, and got back in time to have a rather late breakfast. He had gone into the kitchen to prepare that, but Wendy had insisted that he was far too thin, and so she would prepare a proper breakfast for him. Not being keen on the modern trend of breakfasting on a cereal bar or a bowl of strawberries, she asked him whether he wanted a full English breakfast. Not sure exactly what that entailed he agreed, and was soon sitting in front of a plate of bacon, eggs, sausage and black pudding. He was then expected to eat toast and marmalade and to drink huge amounts of tea. Afterwards he had to declare that he had enjoyed his breakfast, but that he needed to rest before he could move! He went on to say that, while breakfast had been lovely, he hadn't been keen on the black pudding and then made the mistake of asking what it was made from. Once he had learned that it was made from animal blood, he politely asked not to be given it again.

He was just recovering from that huge meal when Jim's phone rang. Wendy asked who it was, and Jim replied that it was Inspector Bradley.

'They've got Swindler Sam and want us to go and sit in at the interview with him. Shall I say yes?'

'Of course,' said Akmal. Wendy declined the offer to join the two men because she wanted to spend the day catching up with old friends. She was therefore going to use the hire car, so Akmal and Jim walked to the station in the spring sunshine. They strolled along saying very little, Akmal deep in thought and Jim reminiscing about his time as an inspector.

He was surprised that he wasn't really enjoying this trip as much as he had anticipated.

The interview itself began at 11.30am and the usual requisites had been put into place. Inspector Bradley began by asking Sam to confirm his name etc. but then got quickly to the point.

'Putting a bomb under a car isn't your usual business is it Sam, so what, or who, put you up to this?' Sam gave no reply. At that point Akmal stood and towered over Sam.

'That was my girlfriend's car that you destroyed. You might be safer in here than outside with me, so answer the inspector's question.'

'You can't threaten me. Coppers are stuck to rules so I couldn't give a shit how muscular you are, you don't frighten me.'

'He's not a copper Sam, neither am I. We are not bound by any police rules, *and the inspector has a hearing problem,*' said Jim.

The inspector hadn't been expecting that, but she asked the question again, adding that they had CCTV of the whole event.

'Money.'

'Is that the best that you can do Sam? I will still have to arrest you, even if you don't help us, but it might be better for you if you do!'

'Then arrest me. Get it over with. I'll be better off in here than outside with him.'

'I will arrest you, but I'll do it tomorrow, after I have tied up some loose ends,' and she stood up and opened the door for him to leave. Akmal stood up too.

'Alright, alright. I'll help you.'

'I would advise you to have a solicitor present from this point because I will record the interview from now on, and it may end with you being cautioned.'

'OK.' They left Sam alone while the duty solicitor was summoned. Sam asked whether he could make a phone call to his mother.

Back in Canada, Olivia had left Tegan's room and gone to visit *"Sunny's Brick and Mortar supplies, Montreal."* Both she and Tegan knew full well that this organisation had nothing to do with fake weapons, but they wanted Ilef's crew to follow her there. Meanwhile, Tegan had sent further details to inspector Roberts and had suggested a possible route for her enquiries. She had also used one of the lesser-known parts of her device to lock onto the signal of the mobile phone that belonged to the guard outside. The scene was now set, so she relaxed and ordered lunch.

The duty solicitor took about an hour to arrive at Basingrove police station, long enough for Akmal and Jim to visit a local pub for lunch. They found a quiet spot by the window of the "Gaping Chasm" public house and ordered beer and a ploughman's lunch.

'Thanks for backing me up in there Jim. To be honest, I don't know what came over me. I'm not a violent person but I miss Tegan so much that all I wanted to do was to beat the little toad into telling me what was going on.'

'What you did wasn't wise, but once you had dropped yourself in it then we had no choice but to go along with you.'

'We?'

'I would have cautioned you to retract your threat when I was an inspector, and my comment in that room was designed to stop the inspector from doing that to you. She could have arrested you for threatening behaviour you know!'

'Sorry, I wasn't thinking. It worked though didn't it. He will spill the beans soon, won't he?'

'That remains to be seen.'

They ate and drank and then headed back to the police station. It was 1.30pm, and they didn't hurry because they knew that Sam would likely still be talking to his "brief".

The two loud rifle shots that rang out destroyed the peace of that spring afternoon in Basingrove.

'Akmal!'

Akmal's body had closed up like a Swiss Army knife, and he fell to the ground making no sound at all. There were screams and shouts from passers-by and Jim crouched by him, mobile phone in hand. He dialled 999.

'Which service please?'

'Ambulance, a man has been shot.' Jim gave the ambulance service a "What Three Words" position and then sank to the ground himself. By that time two police officers had run from the police station and were now at the scene. Jim had blood on him, but he assured the officer that it was just splashes from Akmal. He told them to look for the gunman and he would tend to Akmal.

Akmal had fallen in the curled-up position that been inflicted on him by the bullets that had gone straight though his abdomen. He was still alive but unconscious and there was a lot of blood. Jim realised that he would have to try to stem that, so he pulled off his shirt and wedged it into

Akmal's stomach to try to do just that. While he waited, he wondered how big this criminal organisation was, and he was struck by the thought that Akmal had come with him and Wendy because they thought he might be safer there than in his home!

The ambulance arrived about ten minutes later, and Akmal was taken quickly for emergency surgery. The ambulance crew described his condition as "critical", and they asked Jim to accompany him.

Helen Morgan was a strong woman, but she wasn't coping well with captivity. She didn't know where she was, which always stressed her, she was developing an increasingly powerful hatred for Pixie and Trixie, and she had been trying to come up with a scheme for escape, but nothing had come to her yet. Unusually for her, she was beginning to feel very depressed, and she was seriously considering it a shame that the suicide pill she had brought with her had been a fake. She couldn't see a way out of this predicament, and she suddenly felt very old. The reality of the situation, Tegan imprisoned, Akmal looking like he may not pull through, and nobody with any idea who the perpetrators of these scams had been, would have increased her malaise even further.

Chapter 31

Camille and Philippe had just made love. Philippe was working late nights this week and he wouldn't be expected home until after 2am, so they were enjoying a little "afternoon delight" in his flat. They were still "holed up" there, but they had decided that they would have to start to make plans for their future. They had already decided to return to Camille's home in Toronto and Philippe had typed out the resignation letter that he would hand in later today. That gave them a month before they would leave, unless the restaurant allowed Philippe to end his contract early, which he was confident they would do since he was owed some holidays. They couldn't wait. They had both resigned from the organisation, but they had been expected to carry out any follow up action after the complex recent events.

'Do you ever wonder about Akmal and Marie? You don't mention them since they left,' said Philippe.

'I don't mention them because it is a necessary part of working for the organisation that we learn to forget every mission. Having said that, I do wonder about them, especially Akmal. It would be nice to know whether he and *his* Tegan are back together and whether they still work for the organisation. But there's no means of contacting them now because all contact numbers will have been changed on our behalf.'

'So those phone calls that we made weren't to their personal numbers then?'

'That's right, they weren't. The only calls made over the last week or so that went via "normal" cell phone signals were between you and me and from Helen Morgan's phone to Akmal's phone.'

'So, if I use the recent calls list to ring Akmal it won't work.'

'Try it,' said Camille. 'Ring him now.' Philippe got out of bed and stood with his phone in his hand. Camille lay back and stared at him, which made him feel suddenly very shy and he grabbed the duvet to hide his modesty. That meant that Camille was now naked on the bed.

'Oh, what the hell!' said Philippe. He put the phone down and went back to Camille. 'I'll try ringing him later. I have something else to do right now,' he said to Camille.

'How much later?' asked Camille.

'Half an hour or so, maybe longer,' he replied.

'Smashing,' said Camille.

Detective Inspector Bradley was now very angry, with the gunman and with herself. *She* had invited Jim and Akmal to sit in on that interview. Surely, she should have realised that it would potentially put them into harm's way? She hoped desperately that Akmal's injuries weren't as severe as they seemed, but she now felt even more determined to get Sam to spill the beans.

'This is an interview between Detective Chief Inspector Bradley and Sam Spencer, which relates to an incident at

Gatwick Airport on the evening of Thursday 26th May. Present are Detective Chief Inspector Bradley, Sergeant Egebe, Sam Spencer and the duty solicitor.

'Right Sam. What were you doing in a car park at Gatwick Airport last Thursday?'

'Nothing.'

'Come on Sam. We have you there on CCTV, and you were acting suspiciously, so why were you there?' The duty solicitor nodded to Sam.

'Alright, I was plane spotting.'

'Plane spotting?'

'Yes, I like to watch aeroplanes.'

'What was in the bag Sam?'

'What bag? There's a man who was just sitting in here this morning who is now critical in hospital, just minutes after you made a phone call, now what was in that bag? I won't ask again, but the evidence from the CCTV is damming so think very carefully before refusing to answer.' The solicitor nodded to Sam.

'It contained my camera equipment.'

'In a carrier bag? Not a very secure way to transport expensive equipment is it?'

'Yes, it was in my carrier bag. I'd gone to look at, and to photograph, some aeroplanes'

'So it didn't contain any bomb equipment?'

'No.'

'When you got out of your car carrying that bag, what did you intend to do with it?'

'The bag?'

'Yes, the bag, and it's contents?'

'I intended to photograph some aeroplanes.'

'So why did you leave it in front of a black Mercedes C Class, and then walk away?'

'I put it down because I was going to tie my shoe lace, but then I saw somebody that I didn't like the look of.'

'And who was that?'

'Never mind.'

'Alright so you bent down to tie you shoelace, you saw the man you didn't like, and then stood up and walked away?'

'Yes.'

'Without your bag?'

'Without my bag, yes.'

'You left a bag containing expensive camera equipment in front of a car?'

'Yes, but I went back for it.'

'We didn't see that on the CCTV!'

'Well I intended to go back as soon as I had realised that I hadn't got it any more.'

'So why did it take you that long to realise that you no longer had it?'

'It was only a few minutes.'

'So why didn't you go back then?'

'Because the fucking thing blew up didn't it!'

'Oh indeed it did, just shortly after your mate kicked it under the car, it being the carrier bag that contained the bomb equipment.'

'I know nothing about that.'

'You sure?'

'Certainly I'm sure. I was terrified. I just went home.'

'Inspector, do you have any evidence at all that my client went to that car park carrying a bomb in a carrier bag, with intent to blow up a car?'

'We have the CCTV footage.'

'And does that show my client placing a bomb under a car?'

'No.'

'Then I suggest to you that you find that evidence, but until such time as that is available, my client and I are leaving.' They both got up and walked out of the room, and Chief Inspector Bradley swore loudly.

While this was going on, Tegan was busy with her work. Olivia was out of the way, she had had a very acceptable late lunch, and there was no Jock to distract her today. She had been very busy with updates and modifications to her "device" and it was almost ready. Once it had indicated its readiness to proceed, she activated program one, and then sat listening. After a few moments she heard the guard outside's phone ring. She glued her ear to the door. He had answered the phone and listened for a while. She then heard him say 'No I don't want a new mattress and if you ring again, I will come to India and shove one down your fucking throat.'

Tegan smiled and she activated program two. Still with her ear to the door she listened out for a beep from his phone. 'Now what?' said the guard. She heard him fumble with his phone then curse again. 'Stupid thing!' Tegan smiled. His phone was indeed a stupid thing because she had just uploaded his maps timeline from it, and she now had a record of everywhere that he had been while carrying his phone. She had all of his history since 2021, and she was pleased that his phone hadn't received the latest security patches.

She then activated program three. This was a tracking program that the organisation didn't know about, at least not yet. It allowed her to find those agents that were online with the organisation *and* those that had logged off. It meant that Marie that could be found, and she was the only one that could help with the next phase of her plans. That would take a while, but once Marie had been found it would send her a lengthy document that Tegan had uploaded. This was a coded dossier of Tegan's predicament, and details of all of that she wanted Marie to carry out on her behalf.

She then activated program four. This redirected all of Gustav's mail to Tegan's phone. She was really looking forward to reading that.

Finally, she activated the program that would find and ring Akmal's phone. She wanted to assure him that she was locked up but fine otherwise. Unfortunately, that had been the only one of the programs that had *failed* to find it's target.

Inspector Bradley and Jim met up at his rented cottage at about 6pm that evening. She found him and Wendy in a very sombre mood, Wendy looked particularly distressed and had red rings around her eyes. She spoke first.

'Why has this happened inspector? I have been married to Jim for nearly fifty years, from when he was a beat constable and all the way up to his being inspector, but I never thought somebody that we knew would end up gunned down in the street, near the police station no less, and now in such a terrible state.'

'I'm sorry Wendy. Do you know how he is?'

'He's on a life support machine and not expected to pull through,' replied Jim.

'He was all alone you know inspector. He obviously has friends but we can't contact any of those, but he had no family. He told me that I was.......'

Wendy had to stop there and Jim sat next to her and provided as much comfort as he could.

'Wendy had grown very fond of Akmal,' he said as Wendy left the room. 'I believe that she was beginning to think of him as the grandson that it looks like we will never have.'

'There is to be an enquiry,' said the inspector.

'I'm not surprised,' said Jim.

'They have handed the Gatwick car bombing over to Evans now. He's a good man and he'll get to the bottom of it.'

'I'm sorry to have involved you in this Bradley. I should have gone through official channels.'

'Don't worry about me, all that will happen to me is that I will retire sooner than I intended. Think about poor Akmal, and Tegan, that's if she ever gets away from Canada.'

'Is Sam Spencer put away then?'

'No. He had a clever brief and I had to release him. He made a phone call after you two left for lunch and he must have ordered that shooting, so he knows a lot about this whole business. What the hell is so important that a young man can be shot by a sniper in our sleepy town?'

'I don't know. From what you've told me about Sam he wouldn't seem likely to be behind all of this, so he's informing somebody who is very powerful. Do you know where he lives, and where he hangs out?'

'I do. I'll jot the address down for you but then I had better go. They will know that I am here.' Jim allowed the inspector a few moments to get in the car and leave, and then he went to find Wendy.

245

'I've got that villain's address Wendy. Are you coming with me?'

Wendy wiped her eyes and stood up from the seat she was using to gaze at the dressing table. 'You're damn right I am. Let's get our coats and see whether we can't get something sorted. Have you got your gun?'

'It's in a drawer by the bed. Have you got yours?'

'Indeed I do.'

Wendy drove their hire car to the address that they had been given and parked up a few doors away. Jim was in the back, hidden by the darkness of the car's tinted windows. They took it in turns to sleep and to watch, and to wait.

Chapter 32

Earlier, back in Canada, Inspector Roberts had finally found time to read the communication that Tegan had sent to her. It had taken her a while to understand the "instructions" that Tegan had previously sent ('why do people who are IT professionals think that the rest of us can understand the very brief instructions that they give us?' she had thought, after her first read through of those,) but she had eventually got the hang of it. Tegan's message contained just about everything that had *happened* to her, and a resume of what she had *learned* so far. She didn't mention Jock, but she did mention the guard outside her room, and the story given to her by Olivia. She ended the message by asking the inspector to keep her officers away from the hotel until she had received Tegan's next communication.

Inspector Roberts carried out those wishes and went home to Henri. He had finally decided that his wife could cook instead of him, and that she could prepare whatever she wanted, at least a few times a week anyway, and she was looking to try out one of her mum's recipes on him. She was looking forward to seeing the panic on his face when he is presented with mashed potatoes instead of rice, and she smiled. 'Finally, a sense of normality,' and then she thought about the early night that she had also planned.

Olivia returned to Tegan at about 5pm and they ordered dinner, which they intended to eat together. Tegan couldn't leave her room so it had to be consumed there anyway, but that was useful, it meant that when Ilef arrived later, as she knew that he would, he would be within communication distance of her devices. She had earlier looked at the guard's timeline but she was disappointed to see that his phone hadn't done a good job of recording his travels, and there were a great many gaps. She decided that he must spend a lot of time in areas where satellite coverage is poor, but she did notice that he had spent quite a bit of time visiting the Hotel du Lac over the previous months. She noted also that he didn't return to what appeared to be his home at a particularly regular time, even though her searches of local electoral details suggested that the address was occupied by a man, a woman and two people under the age of sixteen. She would get Olivia to follow up on those tomorrow.

Tegan and Olivia enjoyed their dinner and then discussed the events of the day. As Tegan had expected, the offices to which Olivia had been sent appeared to be totally legitimate, but it was at this point that Olivia decided to tell Tegan about her and Camille's visit that had culminated in their meeting with Pixie and Trixie. Tegan pondered the significance of that encounter and decided that she would mention their names to Ilef later.

About an hour, Ilef turned up to see Olivia, exactly as Tegan had expected. Her device was already primed and running. Though disappointed that he would need to get Olivia's daily breakdown of events in the presence of Tegan, he nevertheless proceeded as he usually would.

'Good evening Ilef. To what do I owe the pleasure of your company this time?' said Tegan.

'I want to know about your progress Tegan, and you Olivia. I want to know whether my money is being well spent and whether you have made any progress.'

'Tell me about Pixie and Trixie Ilef,' said Tegan.

'Ah, Olivia has told you about her encounter with my best operatives eh?'

'Indeed she has Ilef. Quite the pair of brutes by all accounts.'

'Yes, they are indeed. You wouldn't want to get on the wrong side of them Tegan, and I'm surprised that Olivia dealt with them so well. That woman is full of surprises.' He smiled at Olivia as he said that.

'And they really are running a sex games palace?'

'They don't run it as such, no. They take turns with "Felix" and "Jasmine" to look after the place. They don't much like the work there, but they do a good job. Anyway, what progress?' Tegan filled Ilef in with her data on who and where weapons had been advertised and she said that she had a few jobs for Olivia tomorrow.

'I'm sorry the work is slow Ilef, but I am a bit restricted by these four walls.'

'Yes, but that is necessary. I expect results by the weekend by the way. If nothing is clear by then I will feel the need to dispose of both of you.' He said that in a tone similar to somebody talking to two old vacuum cleaners that were surplus to requirements.

'I'll bear that in mind Ilef, but now we need our beauty sleep, so if you don't mind?'

'I gather from the guard outside that you have been humiliating my friend Jock, making him turn up in skimpy clothing. Is he not to your liking Tegan?'

'I apologise Ilef. I know that he is only doing a job, and that it's not his fault that I am locked up like a caged bird. I have no issues with him at all and if he wants to come back tomorrow, I promise that I won't tease him again.'

'His wife was killed in a car accident two years ago and he hasn't had a girlfriend since then, so you might easily sway his normal judgement. He is a gentle and calm man, but he is also an excellent marksman, and a kick boxer. Don't provoke him; you might be surprised by his reaction.'

'I'll bear that in mind.'

After Ilef had left, Olivia began to ask Tegan what teasing she had done to Jock.

'I'm missing Akmal to be honest Olivia. He hates to be given blue socks and won't wear them. He also has a habit of lounging around the house in swimming shorts. He says it's because his parents couldn't afford clothes for him when he was a child, but of course that's rubbish. I thought that since Jock had been ordered to follow my instructions to the letter that getting him to wear swim shorts and blue socks would be comforting for me, remind me of Akmal. In fact it wasn't comforting for me at all, especially since he had donned actual skimpy swim shorts with the blue socks, and that must have been really embarrassing for him. I'll apologise to him if he comes back tomorrow.'

'Everything is much more serious than you were expecting eh Tegan?'

'You aren't wrong there Olivia. Goodnight Olivia.'

'Goodnight, and don't worry Tegan, it won't be long before you see Akmal again.' With that, she knocked for the guard to let her out, and she was gone.

After Olivia had gone, it was a very sombre and thoughtful Tegan who downloaded Ilef's travel timeline. She hoped that Jock would come back because she realised that she had developed a soft spot for him. Those mouthed words "Not yet" kept coming back to her.

'Jim, wake up! There's movement.' Wendy had managed to stay awake until 12.15 am but Jim struggled to wake when she had tried to rouse him. She turned on the ignition of their car and it silently travelled forward in electric mode. Once he was fully awake, she explained that Sam had got into an old battered Renault and had set off at speed.

'Will you be able to keep up with him Wendy?'

'No, but he's leaving a trail of oily fumes and there's nobody else on the roads. I'll be able to follow without him realising.'

'Excellent Wendy. You haven't lost your ability to tail villains then.'

'We'll see,' replied Wendy.

Wendy drove for a few miles, pulling into the side and stopping from time to time so that Sam wouldn't become suspicious, and after a while she saw him pull over and stop. She continued to drive and passed him by, being careful to not look at him. Jim, not visible through the darkened glass of their hire car, made a note of the address. Once Wendy had driven around a few blocks she pulled into the side and they both got out. They linked arms and Jim sprinkled her with some of the gin that she had brought with her, and she took a sip of the stuff.

Jim had always been impressed by Wendy's impression of a drunken woman, from the very persuasive stagger with her handbag over her wrist, that she actually enjoyed doing, to the slurred voice that sounded so convincing. He hoped that she would still have the ability to do all that, and that she would be safe with the plan she had put together.

They approached the house that Sam had entered and checked for any signs of cameras. Having seen no signs of security Jim hammered on the front door, and Wendy leant against the door jam. He then quickly ran around the corner and waited. After a while the door opened.

'I really need the toilet, or I'll wet myself,' said Wendy in a marvellously authentic drunken manner. 'Please let me use your toilet.'

'Piss off,' said the man at the door. Wendy howled with laughter.

'That's very funny, you are so funny, but I really want to do that in a toilet, if you don't mind,' she said, continuing the drawl.

'Oh for God's sake come in. Can you manage the stairs you stupid old bat? If you fall down them, we won't bother picking you up, so it's up to you.'

Wendy howled with laughter again. She began to ascend the stairs, three up then two down, laughing with each attempt. The man that had let her in was now bored with this spectacle, swore profusely and disappeared, which gave Wendy the chance to look around. There were only two rooms upstairs and a bathroom, so she chose one of the bedrooms and wandered in. She was surprised by how tidy it was and a quick look in each drawer of a chest took very little time. She also investigated two ancient looking wardrobes, but she could see nothing of interest there either. She had begun to repeat this in the second room when she heard somebody on the stairs. She lay down, feigning unconsciousness. A man of about thirty appeared at the stop of the stairs and saw her on the floor.

'What are you up to?' he shouted. Wendy remained still so he dragged her to her feet and asked the same question again. She opened one eye.

'Have I wet myself?' She feigned unconsciousness again.

'You'd better not have you stupid fucking cow. Why the hell did Phil let you in?' He led her to the bathroom and made her go in.

'Be quick.'

'I'll do my best,' Wendy replied in an even slower drawl. After about five minutes she emerged, smiling.

'That's better,' she drawled. 'You've no idea how much better I feel. Help me down, will you?'

'In a minute. Stay there, I need a shit.'

'Ooh, language young man. I'll wait here.' She sank to the floor, but as soon as the man had locked the bathroom door, she went back into that second bedroom. After a quick look around, and again finding nothing, she had to return to the landing when she heard the toilet flush.

'Come on you daft old woman, you are going now.'

'I've just been thank you.' This actually made the man smile and, more gently now, she was led down to the front door.

'I'm hungry now,' said Wendy.

'There's an all-night pub just up the way. Get some crisps or something.'

'Are you playing cards, I love cards.' She giggled and staggered along the passageway to the room from where she could hear laughter.

'Can I join you? I've been now so I won't be any trouble. I love cards.'

'Go home,' said Phil.

'Oh. I see, too old I suppose. If I was young and beautiful you'd let me stay, wouldn't you?'

'Damned right, now clear off.'

'I will. I know when I'm not wanted. You'll be old one day,' she said, a tear running from her eye. As she was leaving, she heard Phil say, 'If that black man isn't dead soon, we won't live long enough to become old.' This was followed by laughter, and they continued their game. Wendy was almost pushed out into the street, she heard the front door slam, and she staggered up the road. Jim, relieved to see her, gave her a few minutes then ran to catch up with her.

'I was beginning to worry back there,' he said when he caught up with her.

'So was I. Let's get away from here now.' It took about ten minutes to reach the car and Jim supported her, to maintain the pretence of her drunkenness, just in case they were being followed. Once back in the car she told Jim all that she had heard, and seen. Jim, while continually looking in his rear view mirror in case they were being tailed, said they should write it all down when they got back to their cottage, and go to see Inspector Bradley in the morning.

Chapter 33

Marie got off the plane at just after 2.15 pm. It was a cold Wednesday afternoon at Heathrow, and she was worried. She had been contacted by Akmal from England, but now she could get no response from him. When she had tried to find his transponder chip she found that it was in a hospital in a town called Basingrove. and that it (his transponder) hadn't moved since yesterday afternoon. That could only mean that Akmal was in a hospital bed, and it was obvious that things in England hadn't gone well. When they had last spoken, Akmal had given her a resume of all that had happened since they both got home and, initially, she had given the standard response expected by the organisation; that the job in Canada had been aborted, and that neither he nor Tegan should return to it unless there was an emergency. It was now clear that this *was* just such a circumstance, and that she had to pay Akmal a visit.

She arrived at the hospital at about teatime. Initially, she was denied access to Akmal, but eventually she was able to persuade the staff that he had no family, and that she was the only visitor he was likely to get. She showed some photos of herself and Akmal together, and this had seemed to be enough evidence to persuade the staff that she wasn't going to be a problem.

She was led into a private room and she had to sit down when she saw him. He was lying flat on a bed wearing a pair of hospital issue pyjama trousers, and his entire middle section was heavily bandaged. It appeared to be very swollen but what upset her most was the tangle of tubes that were there to keep him alive. Eventually she spoke.

'Akmal, can you hear me?'

'That's unlikely,' said the nurse. Marie studied him. His face was set in a grimace, his eyes were closed, and his breathing was being carried out by a machine. A tear appeared in her eye as she thought back to how she had teased him while working with him. She asked how Akmal was. The nurse indicated that they should talk outside.

'He hasn't regained consciousness since he was brought in. All that I can tell you is that the two bullets that hit him went straight through his abdomen. His spine is OK, but there is quite a lot of swelling and damage *around* it. Surgeons have managed to repair the rest of the damage to his internal organs, but he lost a lot of blood after the attack. We don't know how much of him there is left, and his recovery is very touch and go.

'But he will pull through, won't he?' asked Marie. The nurse just gave her a look as a response, and Marie's heart sank even further.

This wasn't what she had expected when she had left France earlier that day and she had no clue about what to do next. She went back into his room and held his hand. It seemed to be the right thing to do. She was just about to leave when a man entered and spoke to her.

'The nurse told me that Akmal has had a visitor and I understand that you are Marie. My name is Roberts, retired

256

Detective Inspector Roberts, father of Detective Inspector Janice Roberts of the Montreal police department. I suspect that you were with Akmal in Canada.' They shook hands and, ever the professional agent, she demanded an account of what had happened to Akmal.

'Let's go and find a quiet spot to chat,' said Jim. 'I know just the place.' They walked together and, while enjoying the chilly spring sunshine, Jim told her everything that had happened since he and his wife had returned to England. The hospital had telephoned Jim when Marie appeared, so he had gone along to meet her there, and walked her to the police station, where detective chief inspector Bradley was already waiting for them.

After the introductions and the commiserations had been concluded, the inspector began. 'Today we have had some lucky breaks relating to the perpetrators of the shooting of Akmal and the blowing up of Tegan's car at Gatwick, and we also have some information gleaned by Jim's wife. It turns out that the owner of the local phone shop has just had CCTV installed to his premises and he was watching through some of the recordings made on its first afternoon of use. He was very impressed with its clarity, so impressed that he showed it to his wife. It was she who noticed a man crouched down in a corner, just opposite their shop. The man can then clearly be seen standing up and firing two shots in the direction of the police station. He rapidly retreated but, since the image quality was so clear, he was soon identified as a well-known local man called Philip Trainor. We, I mean detective inspector Evans and his team, have applied for a search warrant which should come through soon. They have the house he lives in under surveillance in case he decides to leg it, but we know that he is a home bird, and they expect to pick him up tomorrow. We also have Sam's phone records, and it was "our" Philip that he telephoned after being interviewed here.'

'Excellent,' said Marie. 'How can I be involved?'

'I, or rather the Thames Valley Police, would like you to return to Canada. We are hoping that we will find enough evidence to lead us back to the main gang back there, and we would like you and your team to be there as backup to our opposite numbers in Saint-Jérôme, and probably Montreal itself.'

'I will have all of my local team made available to you. Can I request a total media blackout on Akmal's identity?'

'Certainly. That was our intention anyway and it's already done.' The inspector paused a while as the information began to sink in. 'I don't think that Tegan should be told just yet, assuming that she is still alive and that you know where she is.'

'Agreed,' said Marie. 'I will tell her when the time seems right, again assuming that she survives her current predicament.'

Chapter 34

The newspapers and the local Gazette had already reported details about the shooting, and the panic that it had caused, in their Wednesday editions. The headline in the Basingrove Gazette had been "Shooting Outside our Local Police Station", and the full story, as they knew it, was published. The police had obtained an order preventing all publications from identifying who the victim was, but Jim, (as "ex detective inspector Roberts"), had been mentioned as a passer-by who had "bravely gone to the aid of the man when he had heard the shot. He had done all that he could to stem the man's bleeding, but the injuries had been severe". The papers only stated that the victim was a young man who was visiting the area, and that he had travelled to Basingrove from a town in Berkshire. They indicated that the young man's injuries were so severe that the outlook for his recovery wasn't good.

On Thursday they had had to run the story again, but this time the headline was very different, and rather more sombre. It now read "Basingrove Shooting Victim Dies Overnight", and they had had to add "The medical staff at Basingrove University Hospital have done their best, and the victim has fought bravely, but at 3.30am this morning, the young man lost his battle for life, and he has died peacefully. The man was a visitor to our town and our heartfelt sympathies go out to his friends and family. His body will be returned, in due course, to his place of birth for interment. The police are now investigating a case of murder, but they admit that, currently, they have absolutely no leads in the case. They have appealed for any witnesses to come forward."

It was further reported that the local police had appointed an additional detective to help investigate the case, but that no arrests had yet been made. The police had confirmed that the young man hadn't been a member of any gang, and that they weren't treating his shooting as racially motivated. It was felt that he had been mistaken for somebody else. They advised the public to be vigilant as they went about their daily business, but not to be afraid. They had no evidence that the shooter might strike again.

Jim and Wendy had wondered whether, or even how, Tegan should be told about Akmal's death. They decided that she *should* know but, even though they knew where Tegan was being held, they had no means of speaking to her. They decided to telephone Inspector Roberts and give her full details of the incident, and Marie's wishes, and they left their daughter to decide what to do with the news. They added that, as far as they knew, Marie was arranging Akmal's funeral and that she would then be on her way back to Canada.

Oblivious to all of these proceedings, Tegan had spent the morning studying Ilef's timeline, and the one thing about his movements that most struck her was that he went, every day, up to Ned's barn. This was something that surprised her, and felt that she would need to do it tonight. She already knew how she was going to get out of her prison room, and she hoped that Jock would be around today so she could ask him for his help. Now though, she was hungry, and so she ordered breakfast.

Tegan had been pleased when Jock had brought that breakfast up to her. He had asked, by a peculiar set of miming actions, whether she had any requests for his dress today. She had replied to him using the screen of her device, and explained that she wouldn't be teasing him again. She used it to ask him a few more questions, and learned that he was prepared to be her ally, and that he was happy to help her. He stood silently while Tegan ate her breakfast and then she began her questioning.

'Are people listening in to our conversation?' He mimed a yes.

'Can they see us?' He mimed a no.

'Can you get the guard to let Olivia in?' He mimed another yes, and Tegan gestured for him to do that. He hammered on the door, the guard released him, and he returned some while later with Olivia. He stood silently in the corner while Olivia and Tegan chatted, again via her screen. After what seemed like ages, he hammered on the door again, and he and Olivia were released. Olivia returned to her room and Tegan and the guard settled down for another dull morning.

What the guard didn't know was that Olivia and Tegan had swapped places. It had taken lots of practice, but Tegan and Olivia could now both distort their faces so that nobody could tell which of them was which, and now they could be taken for twins, as either Tegan *or* Olivia. Today it was actually Tegan, looking just like Olivia, that was free and, once she was well clear of the hotel, she took the opportunity to contact Marie. She learned that Marie was on a plane, apparently returning from a mission, and that she would be available from that evening onwards.

On learning that Tegan could now walk freely from her room, Marie had sent her some details about Philip Trainor. Those had been provided for her by the British police and included his phone records and his flight details from the last two years. It seemed that he was quite a jet setter, and that he liked nothing better than flying. She advised Tegan that she had already provided inspector Roberts with that information, and that it would be helpful if they could liaise with each other as soon as possible.

Tegan's first task then was to send one of her coded messages to Inspector Roberts by email. Tegan was delighted that it was read promptly and they arranged to rendezvous at the cafe that had provided breakfast after her release from the barn. That meeting turned out to be very interesting.

Back in England, Wendy and Jim had decided that it was time to return to Canada. They had done all they had intended to do on their return to Basingrove, and they now felt that they needed to distance themselves from the very sad events of the last few days. They understood that Marie had arranged a funeral of sorts for Akmal, and that it had been arranged to be in ten days time. They had no wish to stay for that, and they decided that they would stay in their rented accommodation until their departure, which was scheduled for Saturday. They had no desire to even have a final tour of the area, and they had made that booking with a feeling of relief, which left them very saddened. They were unhappy to be leaving nonetheless.

Tegan felt really odd going back to that cafe. She arrived first and ordered a late lunch, but her mind was pulled back to the day that she had been released from that first prison. She thought about Helen and Gareth, but most of all she thought about Akmal, and she now realised that the revelations about her past must have been difficult for him to accept. Now sitting here alone she remembered how chivalrous he always was, and she finally admitted to herself that he must now feel rather foolish. She yearned to be back with him but felt a sudden pang of panic. She couldn't understand that, and she was relieved when the inspector turned up and asked to share her table. Since they were in a spot that Tegan was sure wouldn't be secure, she suggested that they share a table outside. Once eating, the inspector asked Tegan for an update on the situation as she knew it, and then Tegan received information from the inspector, all done via Tegan's device and screen. They laughed occasionally, as though they were sharing funny YouTube videos. After that Akmal was gone from her mind.

Helen Morgan was now making life difficult for her captors. She refused to eat when food was brought for her, and then demanded food some time later. She would demand endless toilet visits and then take ages when she got there. She would turn her back when she was spoken to, and very occasionally she would throw her crockery about. Her captors were particularly annoyed that she kept producing the capsule that she alleged was a suicide pill! They had tried hard to find where she kept it, between her threats to use it, but to no avail. One thing that particularly annoyed them was that she would speak or sing in Welsh. Since none of those charged with caring for her could speak Welsh, they thought that she was likely calling them all manner of things and, while that would be like water off a duck's back if they knew what she was saying, it really *really* annoyed them now. They had threatened to make her swallow that damned suicide pill next time they saw it, but Helen just shrugged and smiled at them.

Marie got off the plane from England during the late evening and she booked into a hotel under another false name. She felt weary but she knew that business must be attended to and she contacted Camille. They met up at Philippe's restaurant, swapped acquired knowledge and discussed tactics.

Ilef arrived to see Tegan earlier than usual that night, but was told by the guard that she was unwell, and had taken to her bed. He opened the door for Ilef and checked that she was indeed asleep in bed. Ilef then asked after Olivia but was told that she hadn't yet returned from her day's investigations.

Chapter 35

Later that evening, Jock drove Tegan up towards the barn and parked some way away from it, just in case there was anybody there that they didn't want to meet. They approached their target on foot, the twilight making the barn seem huge and uninviting. Armed only with torches, a screwdriver and a crowbar, they felt that they had taken enough equipment up there for the task that they wanted to do. Once in the grounds they split up, Jock was tasked with investigating the area around the barn while Tegan decided that she should go inside. She wasn't keen on doing that, memories of her incarceration still fresh in her mind.

'What is it that's so important about this damned place?' thought Tegan. She knew that it had stored fake weapons for a while, but she didn't know which of the two gangs had put them there, she remembered that she had been a prisoner here, and that Jean Belanger had died here, but why did Ilef come up here so often?

Jock scrambled about outside while Tegan approached the barn doors with some trepidation. She saw that they were bolted but, as Helen and Gareth had found, the wood was so rotted that she had no problem removing the hasp with the screwdriver. She entered the barn carefully and left the doors open to allow as much of the fading light as possible to flood in. As she walked about, she thought that the shadow cast by the setting sun left an eerie look to the place. She continued to wander about, she tapped walls, she hit the floor in places, she removed that strange metal plate that was on the wall in her "prison". Nothing.

'So what the hell brings him up here?' She stood back, surveying the floor from the doorway, hoping for some inspiration. Then, out of the blue, she could see it. 'The floor's not level. The floor's not level! This is a compressed earth floor, no concrete here. There's something under that floor!'

'Jock, come here, quickly.' Jock left what he was doing and ran to her aid. 'We need to dig up that part of the floor. Look!' They both studied the area and agreed that there was a shallow mound on the floor, as though it had been dug up and refilled in a hurry.

'I hope it's not a body!' said Jock.

'Only one way to find out,' replied Tegan.

'There's some tools leaning against the barn wall outside. I'll see what I can find.' Jock returned with a very rusty spade and a worse still shovel, and they set about removing the fairly loose earth of the mound. It took quite a while, and many rests, before Tegan declared that this had probably been a waste of time.

'You are probably right,' said Jock, as he sat down for a rest.

'Have you noticed that smell?' asked Tegan, suddenly.

'Yes, it wasn't there before and I think its coming from the hole.' Jock gave Tegan a look. 'There really is something dead under there.'

'I think we'd better fill it in and let the inspector know what we've found.'

'Yes Tegan, I think that you are right.' Fearful of what might be under there, and the detrimental effect that it might have on their health, they began their task.

'Tegan I assume?' The voice that came from the barn doors made them jump, and they both spun around to see Ilef standing as a silhouette against the now quite dim light from outside. He had a gun in his hand.

'Ilef!'

'I assume that you are Tegan and not Olivia?'

'You are correct Ilef.'

'And Jock is with you. Remember that you work for me son! You might not...' Tegan interrupted him.

'You told him to follow my orders and that's what he's been doing. I would have shot him if he hadn't.' She revealed her small pistol to Ilef.

'So, it's gunfight at the O.K. Corall then is it?' said Ilef.

'Doesn't have to be,' said Tegan.

'Jock, fill that hole in, Tegan, you come out here with me.' She obliged without complaint and Jock set about his work. Ilef invited Tegan to sit down on a rock with him. He said it was time to "fill her in". Tegan dutifully sat down, her gun still pointing squarely in Ilef's direction, his still on her.

'What's this about then Ilef? Why have you *really* got me here?'

'That's my fiance who is buried in there. She was beautiful but she was tough, and she was originally my boss. It was she that ran our business, I was her treasurer and we just fell in love. Proper, head over heels, stupid, "Love story" style love. We found this barn, tidied it up and we made our little den here, in that place where we kept you out of the way. We

267

loved it here, watched the sun set from here, made love here and made our plans here. But one night we were disturbed, bothered by three men. We were in the throes when we heard them just barging in. We quickly dressed and peered through the curtains to see them eyeing the place up, describing it as the perfect place for storage. Jennifer just picked up her gun and strolled out through the curtains and into their path. She waved her gun and told them to go. She was so used to being obeyed, and she had such an evil reputation, that she would never have expected what happened next.' He paused.

'What did happen Ilef?'

'They just shot her. Twice, three times, four times, they just kept on, like a firing squad, and after laughing at what they had done they just left. I heard one say that he had killed two birds with one stone. That's all.' Tegan studied him for a while.

'So you buried her.'

'What else could I do? I was no match for them so there was no point in my trying to catch them. God only knows why they didn't come into our den to see whether anybody else was here. I suppose that they had recognised Jennifer and were so pleased to have killed the leader of one of there oppos that they could now leave. They had even found a local storage space for their fake weapons so they could go. Job done I suppose.'

'Ilef, I'm so sorry.'

'Don't be. You can see now why we kept you away from finding those bastards. You would have turned them in to the police, but I wanted to kill them myself. I thought that we could use Olivia to get to them first, with Gustav's help.'

'So you do know Gustav?'

'We go back a long way.' Tegan looked at Ilef for a while.

'You are brothers aren't you.'

'Yes. When our parents split up he stayed in Spain, I came to live here. We are members of very different organisations but we knew what each other did and we had a sort of respect for each other. He helped me plan this whole revenge thing.'

'So it was him that arranged for Akmal to leave that weekend.'

'Yes, but don't be too hard on him. It was a one off arrangement to help me, that's all.'

'He'll have to resign from the organisation.'

'He already has.'

'Ah. And what about Jean Belanger.'

'Not my doing at all. He just worked for an alarm company and we used his services to monitor the alarms.'

'And Helen Morgan?'

'Yeah. Initially she had just got in the way, but then she helped me to get your services back. We don't need her now.' He picked up his phone and dialled. 'Pixie, let Helen go, take her home, or anywhere else she wants to be. It's over, everything's over.'

'Just like that?' said Tegan.

'Just like that. Pixie and Trixie will deliver Helen and then disappear, and you will never find them. There will be a new leader of our bunch now. When he doesn't get my usual call, he will assume that I am out of the loop, or apprehended, and they will up sticks and move on. You'll never find them either.'

'What about the Hotel du Lac? How do they fit in?'

'The owner is my cousin, and the hotel is in debt. He was only helping me for money. He's an honest man. My organisation isn't based there; it's not like "Bertrum's" in the Agatha Christie novel. So, you can leave them alone. The guard outside your room will disappear if he doesn't get my nightly instructions so he'll be gone by morning, and he'll undo the modifications he made to your door lock.'

'Ilef, are you prepared to tell me how I can contact the new leader of your gang?' Ilef didn't reply, and there was a pause.

'I suppose that you will take me in now, so get it over with, I'm tired.'

He put down his gun and Tegan made the call.

'They'll be here in twenty minutes. Why did you come up here tonight? Did you know that *we* were coming up here?'

'No, as I'm sure your electronics must have told you, I come up here every day, just as it's getting dark, to talk to Jennifer. The dim light helps me imagine that she's still here. Just to be clear to you, we run, or rather somebody else now runs, a business that is essentially a smuggling business. We never killed anybody. That wasn't our style. That was Jennifer's mistake. She assumed that other organisations would have the same principles, and that assumption cost her her life. You have found those bastards haven't you?'

'We, as in me and Olivia, and Jock, are in the process of pinning them down. She should be making some arrangements now.' Tegan sat for a while, thinking.

'Ilef, those coffee crates full of weapons that were in this barn when I was prisoner here, whose were they?'

'They were ours. Our oppos haven't yet used this barn as far as we know.'

'So, since you've given me the impression that your "oppos" get the lions share of the weapons, how did you manage to get hold of those ones?'

270

'We have a guy that continually searches the dark web for anything that we can buy that has a ready market. We knew about these weapons, and how profitable they were, and he just managed to snap them up before anybody else did. This sort of stuff appears on a first come first served basis and we were lucky that time. We were unlucky of course that they are now in the hands of the authorities.'

'So you have no idea where they come from?'

'No, we just place the orders and they appear, along with a number of beefy chaps that demand immediate payment. We buy all manner of stuff and we've never seen the same people twice.'

'And none of you are actually Canadian born?'

'That's correct.'

'So why base yourselves in Canada? It's a long way from here to China where most of your stuff is produced.'

'Tegan, it's close to our major market for these weapons. Also, think of where you would most likely find fraudulent import export goods. Does Canada spring to mind?'

'Actually, no it doesn't.' Tegan sat thinking again.

'So why are you not head of your gang now? Surely, as Jennifer's right-hand man you should have been in charge?'

'It doesn't work like that. The new chap was always next in line, and he will be good, you wouldn't be wise to tangle with him. Everything that you currently think you know of our organisation is actually just my work. Jock, whose real name is James Montgomery by the way, the guard, and Pixie and Trixie all work for me, not Jennifer's gang. I am just a small part of that organisation. The two unfortunate men who looked after the alarm for this place were recruited by me, but

271

the weapons that were here were bought by the Jennifer's gang, *not* by me.'

'So, the whole business that I, and Olivia, and indirectly Akmal and his team have been investigating, isn't directly connected with the fraudulent weapons trade at all.'

'That is correct. You have all been recruited to try to get justice for Jennifer. I did though expect you to find the gang that does import them and then we could maybe deal with them too. I never intended any of the harm that happened, and it's time to stop.'

'Ilef, where can I find your new boss?' This time he answered.

'As if I would tell you that.'

'What if it will help you get revenge on Jennifer's killers?'

'How?'

'Don't ask any questions, the police will be here soon, so will you help me?' Ilef got out his phone and sent a document to Tegan.

'It's all in there, I will ring him now if you like.' Just then they heard a police siren.

'They're here already, they must have had a patrol car nearby. It won't be long now,' said Tegan.

'Let's get it over with,' said Ilef.

'By the way, what does Ilef stand for?'

'It's not important, it was given to me by Jennifer as the name to use if ever she was to depart this life and I was to take over. It stands for "I Lead, Everybody Follows". Rubbish isn't it!'

Chapter 36

Tegan had just asked James where he wanted to be dropped off. It was well past midnight by the time that Tegan and James had finished with Ilef and the police, and everybody was really tired. They had given many statements and the police had taken many samples for forensic analysis, including some from the remains under the floor.

'I could do with some company to be honest Tegan. Can I stay with you tonight?' Tegan's pulse began to race and this wasn't what she wanted, at least not now. She wasn't sure exactly whether he just wanted somewhere to stay, or whether he was offering far more. Either way, she couldn't understand her excitement. She felt like a teenager meeting her first boyfriend, and realised that she had unexpectedly fallen in love with this rather weedy, slightly older chap. Despite all of her combat skills and technical knowledge she felt suddenly powerless, a feeling that she had never felt before. She remembered again those mouthed words "Not yet" and her excitement grew even more. She managed to pull herself together and addressed him directly.

'Will my floor do?' James mimed a yes. Tegan had to look away at this point in case he spotted her embarrassment, but they climbed into the Prius and headed back to Olivia in the hotel.

They found her wide awake and sitting in her own, unlocked room. As Ilef had said, Tegan's room was now unlocked, and the plate covering the keyhole on the *inside* of the door had been removed. Tegan's room was the larger of the two so they sat in there, and Tegan ordered some snacks and a bottle of whisky, with three glasses.

'So, it's over,' said Olivia after she had heard the events of the evening.

'I suppose that it is', said Tegan. 'But then it isn't is it. The fraudsters are still selling fake weapons, and Jennifer's death has gone unpunished. If the truth be told I still have two gangs to find, both of them guilty of selling potentially dangerous fake weapons.'

'Well I'm still in if you want,' said Olivia.

'And so am I,' echoed James.

'So you think that we should continue to try to find these characters?'

'They have caused a lot of problems for a lot people now Tegan,' said Olivia. Tegan thought for a while before answering.

'It's late but I am going to make a call. Would you two mind waiting in Olivia's room while I do that?'

'Of course,' said Olivia, and they got up to go.

'And no mischief in there,' shouted Tegan as they were leaving. James responded with a smile and she had to look away again. 'I must control myself,' she thought.

Marie answered Tegan's call quite quickly and, despite the hour, they made some decisions and some plans. Marie insisted though that nothing be done until she had met Tegan privately tomorrow. She suggested that they meet up for breakfast in their now regular cafe haunt. Tegan agreed, hung up, and decided to send Akmal a message before allowing the others to return. She decided to call his number just in case he was up early (it would be 6am in the UK), but his number came up as unavailable. She tried all of his previous numbers but they all came up the same way. Suddenly she was worried, and Olivia and James noticed the change in her mood upon their return. Pulling herself together, she announced that sleeping arrangements had to be made. It was decided that James would take Tegan's floor and Olivia would return to her room. It was further decided that the three of them would rendezvous back there at 11am tomorrow.

Meanwhile, Helen Morgan was wearily walking towards Gareth's house. She had been dropped off by the two women in the blue Nissan but, rather than drive her to the door, she had asked to be deposited about 300 yards from his house. Though it was dark it was also early morning, and she was enjoying the walk, and her freedom, and her first act was to throw away the capsule that she had been using as a threat against her captors. She smiled. It had actually been a sleeping pill, and she hoped that the local wildlife wouldn't get too sleepy once it had dissolved and decayed into the local soil. She was looking forward to greeting Gareth, and hoped that the feeling would be mutual. She approached Gareth's house and knocked on the door but, after quite a long pause, it was Delphine who opened it.

'Helen! How lovely to see you, please, come in, but it's four in the morning, so how come you are out and about now? Up to more mischief? But Gareth has told me all about your tangles with your captors, so I assume that you have your freedom back?'

'I have indeed, my guards dropped me off just a few hundred yards away. Where is Gareth, I hope that all is well?'

'Actually, he has had one of his episodes and he will stay in bed today. He will be delighted to see you though when he recovers.'

'Let me get my shoes and coat off and I will pop up to see him now if you like.'

'Actually, I'd rather that you leave him be for now. Do you want some coffee Helen? You look as though you could do with some. It's dark outside so how did you get here?'

Helen explained that instructions to release her had unexpectedly arrived earlier that night, and that her "guards" were glad to see the back of her. She explained that, though it was quite dark, there was a full moon, so she had managed to see where she was going. Delphine explained to Helen that Gareth had just got to sleep, so she really did want Helen to wait until tomorrow to see him, and anyway *she* wanted to hear all about Helen's exploits first. Helen agreed and she and Delphine sat drinking coffee as the morning light came up over the hills.

'Why didn't you ask your captors to take you home then Helen?' asked Delphine.

'Gareth used my truck to leave the barn that night, and I assumed that he brought it back here, so I asked them to drop me close by so that I could pick it up. I didn't want them to know where your house is, but now I want to go home, and you two won't want to be bothered by me anymore, so, if you like, I'll just collect it and go.'

'Nonsense Helen. You can stay the rest of the night in the room you were in before being taken hostage. We can go up to your house when it's fully light.'

'Do you mean that you will come with me? That's very kind of you Delphine. I wasn't sure what sort of reception I would have from Gareth after our exploits, or from you now that you are back.'

'Well Helen, to be honest, I'd rather that you two stopped playing sleuth together, but I suppose that if you did he would only get himself into some other mischief. I'm glad that you are back, safe and sound, because Gareth has mentioned that he had jokingly offered you the job of live in housekeeper. Well, as it happens, I will be very busy with my new career, so I thought I would redesign the old woodman's cottage in a style that a housekeeper would like, probably something along the lines of a traditional Welsh weaver's cottage. And maybe offer a local Welsh woman the job?' Helen looked startled.

'Well, there's something I hadn't expected. I have always admired that cottage that's in your grounds. I hadn't intended leaving my own home, but I won't say no yet. I'll see what my cottage looks like tomorrow before I make up my mind!'

'Good idea. You get up to bed, your things are still there, and we'll see you later in the morning.'

Marie and Tegan met as planned, at 10am, for breakfast. Tegan noticed that Marie seemed unusually pensive and in a grim mood.

'Shall I order some food for us?' asked Tegan.

'Erm, yes, OK. I'll have what you are having.' Tegan went to place the order and then returned to Marie. They were sitting outside because it was a glorious sunny morning.

'You don't look your usual self Marie. Is everything OK with you?'

'Tegan, I have some bad news for you. I have thought about when and how to tell you, but I think it's time that you knew.'

'It's about Akmal isn't it? Has he left me, found somebody new? He isn't answering his phone.'

'Tegan, Akmal is dead.'

There was silence. Tegan just stared into space and Marie watched, waiting for a reaction. After a full five minutes Tegan finally spoke.

'How? Where? Why?' There were no tears or histrionics. Tegan just sat like an automaton, staring.

'He was shot Tegan. He was with Jim Roberts in a town called Basingrove. Ironically, he had gone with the Roberts because he felt that he might not be safe in your house. He took two shots to the abdomen and was taken to hospital, but he never regained consciousness.'

'When was this?'

'Wednesday afternoon. He made the mistake of threatening a man suspected of bombing your car. It would never have occurred to him that it would place him in danger. I'm so sorry Tegan.'

'I need to go back to arrange things.'

'No Tegan. You might be in danger if you return, and anyway I have arranged for the organisation to put his affairs into place, and his funeral is being taken care of. He had almost no family, but his brother in Northern Ireland will be contacted.'

Tegan's head was now full of things racing around and bashing into each other.

'Have they got the bastard who shot him?'

'Not yet, but things are proceeding. Shall I leave you to think things through and we'll meet up later?'

'No. I want to eat breakfast then get back to why we have met here. I have another reason now to destroy these people.'

The food arrived and Tegan ate and drank like a woman possessed.

Shortly after this bombshell for Tegan, Detective Inspector Roberts began her interview with Ilef. He had declined to have a solicitor present during the questioning.

'Give me your full name please Ilef.'

'My given name is Mateo Reyes. I was born in Badalona; Spain and I moved here in 1998.'

'What is your profession Mateo?'

'I don't have one. I do piecemeal work and get by.'

'Current place of residence?'

'Currently, I am resident at the Hotel du Lac.'

'What do you know about the sale of fake weaponry in Canada, particularly those models made by the RUMP organisation?'

'Nothing.'

'Nothing at all?'

'No.'

'And the dead body in "Ned's Barn"?'

'Which one?'

'The one that was found buried there yesterday evening, the one which we have now exhumed and is currently undergoing pathology investigation for cause of death.'

'That belonged to my girlfriend Jennifer.'

'And her full name and address?'

'I don't know. She never told me where she lived. We were lovers, nothing more.'

'And her connection to you? How did you meet? Do you both belong to the same gang?'

'No comment.'

'Are you sure? You might be arrested for her murder, so the more we know the better.' Mateo gave the inspector the same explanation of Jennifer's death as he had described to Tegan. The inspector didn't seem satisfied.

'So, you regularly met up in a barn for sex, and then one night gang members of an opposing group to Jennifer's came in and shot her dead, but after that you just left, alive, and apparently untouched?'

'Yes, but we didn't just meet up for sex, we were lovers.'

'Look Mateo, if what you say is true then you will want the killers of your girlfriend bought to justice. You must tell me everything that you know if you want us to help you.' Mateo gave no response.

'How does Tegan Durand fit into all of this.'

'I "abducted" Tegan because I knew that she would find the gang responsible for Jennifer's death, but I wanted her to find the perpetrators for *me*, *not* the police, so that I could shoot them myself. I didn't want them arrested because they would likely be out in a few years' time.'

'And Helen Morgan and her grandchildren?'

'Ah, you know about that then.'

280

'Yes, and I know about your connections in England, so spill the beans Mateo.'

'Helen and her relatives were only involved to make sure that Tegan worked for me. They have now been released, and as far as I know they are back in their homes. I have no connections in England, so what you think you know about that is wrong. I do know that the gang that murdered my Jennifer have connections in Europe and the UK, so that's another reason why you need to find and stop those people.'

'You know nothing of the bombing of Tegan's car at Gatwick airport?'

'I did hear about that. It was nothing to do with me.'

'Tegan tells me that you owned up to it.'

'I pretended to to be responsible, but just to pile on the pressure so that Tegan would work for me. I really had nothing to do with it. I suppose it was the same gang that murdered Jennifer.'

'And the shooting of Akmal?'

'Akmal's been shot? Where, how? He had nothing to do with any of this. Gustav only got him on a mission here to release Tegan. Is he alright?'

'He's dead Ilef.'

'Shit. Poor sod. I am truly sorry about that. I never met him, but I know that he was Tegan's partner. So that's why she is now so determined to get these bastards.'

'Tegan doesn't know yet.'

'Ah. She will be devastated.'

'So, you won't help me any further then Mateo?'

'No.'

'Then I have no other option than to charge you with the murder of "Jennifer" and the forced abduction of Tegan

281

Durand, Helen Morgan and her grandson Tom. You will be detained here until I can make the necessary arrangements for formal charges to be brought. Take him away please officer Storey.'

Chapter 37

Tegan spent most of Friday evening walking aimlessly. Her head was buzzing with thoughts, thoughts of anger and regret, revenge even, but mainly she was frustrated. Frustrated because she wasn't sure what to do next. Her private life was now extraordinarily complicated, and she needed to avenge Akmal's death, so she had to think of a way forward. After some peculiarly oblique thinking she came up with a plan. It required James to fall in love with her, which she thought he already had done anyway; she was certainly in love with him though she had tried hard not to be. Then she needed Olivia to be onside, she needed inspector Roberts to play along and, though she would rather not have used them, she needed Philippe and Camille. She would leave Marie out of things this time, she would expect her to go home and leave them to it because the organisation would definitely not approve..

Tegan telephoned Olivia first, then Camille and finally James. They all agreed to meet up in Tegan's hotel room at 10.30pm. She then returned to the hotel in time for dinner and she advised the hotel staff that she would be leaving first thing on Saturday morning. She then advised them that she would be having a party to say goodbye to her friends. She made it clear that they would likely stay with her overnight, and asked for extra sheets and duvets so that they might sleep on her floor. After ordering her dinner she asked that it be brought to her room, and then she waited in the lobby for James.

James arrived in a very smart suit and looked so suave that Tegan almost didn't recognise him. She invited him to join her in her room and they got there just as dinner arrived. They ate and drank and then sat talking, but she did not tell him about Akmal's death. There was then a pause and they both just sat in silence. It was Tegan that broke that silence.

'Make love to me James.'

'Are you sure?' he replied.

'Yes, I am sure. Those words you used while wearing those swim shorts, "Not yet". Can I assume that "yet" has now arrived?'

'Yes, you can, it *absolutely* has.'

Meanwhile, Helen Morgan was dining with Gareth and Delphine. She had enjoyed a lovely day with Delphine but foolishly refused her offer to accompany her to her house. So, after saying her goodbyes to Gareth and Delphine, she had driven up to her house alone. She promised not to return too soon but, unfortunately, that promise wasn't adhered to. Once she had seen the trashed state of her house she had sat and stared at the mess. She thought for a while, like Tegan there were no tears, or histrionics, instead she went round and collected anything that was of value to her. All of the jewellery that she valued was still in the house, so she picked that up, along with a box of photographs and other keepsakes. Nothing else meant much to her now that it had been so soiled. Ever the practical woman, she emptied her fridge and cupboards of food, loaded everything onto the Toyota, and then drove back to see Delphine and Gareth.

'Helen! Back so soon?

'I apologise Delphine,' said Helen, now very upset. She explained all that she had seen at her house. Delphine summoned Gareth and they chatted about what to do next.

'I think that we will need to get that woodsman's cottage restored earlier than I thought.' Helen smiled.

'So, I have a new job then?'

'You certainly do,' replied Delphine.

* * *

Back in England, Wendy Roberts had one last task to complete before she and her husband returned to their home in Canada. That afternoon, Chief inspector Bradley had called to see Jim and Wendy, and told them that a warrant had been issued to enter Traynor's property, and that the search would likely take place that afternoon or evening. Wendy surprised everyone by asking whether she could be involved in that search and, reluctantly, the inspector and Jim agreed to her plan.

At 6.30pm Wendy knocked on Philip Trainor's door and it was answered by the same man that had admitted her on the night that she had been pretending to be drunk.

'Hello again,' she said when the door was opened.

'Who are you?' replied the man.

'The woman who was drunk and asked for your help the other night.'

'Ah, I remember that. You drunk again then or do you just need another piss?'

'Neither. I have brought a thank-you present.' She held out a bottle of expensive gin.

'Thanks. Bye then.' He gestured to accept the bottle but Wendy held it back.

'You get this on condition that you let me share it with you, and you let me play cards with you. Just for a little while. The trouble with being an old lady is that nobody tells you naughty jokes any more, and they certainly don't invite you to play cards either. Please let me in.'

'Alright. That looks like a decent bottle of gin. Be better if it was whisky but Phil likes his gin. Just a half an hour!'

'That'll be enough.' In they went. Though she hadn't recognised him, Sam was there, alongside Philip Trainor. She smiled at them.

'This young man says we can play cards and I will pay you with this bottle of gin.'

'You're brave aren't you?' said Sam. 'What if we just take the bottle from you and throw you out, or just bash you on the head?'

'You wouldn't do that to an old lady now would you?'

'Sam might do that but I won't,' said Trainor. 'Paul, get some glasses and we'll have a game while we wait for instructions. It will be nice to take money from this old dear. What's your name anyway?'

'Dorothy.'

'Right Dorothy. You get the cards ready and we'll get things set up.'

Not sure what they meant by that, Wendy shuffled and dealt the cards and Paul returned with four glasses. The gin was poured, neat over ice, and the game began. Wendy wasn't doing too badly but Phillip Trainor was winning the most, as he had predicted. The gin was going down a treat. They were all beginning to relax when a knock, and shouting, was heard at the door.

'This is the police. Open up.'

'Shit. Paul and Sam. Hide the stuff. I need to make a phone call. Wendy could hear the sound of the police making an entry and this was her moment.

'No you don't. Stay where you are and put the phones down.'

'Or what old lady?'

'Or this.' Wendy magically produced her pistol, and aimed it squarely at Trainor. The police will be in here in seconds. If you don't put your phones down *now*, at least one of you will be in hospital before the night is done.'

'You wouldn't, you couldn't…..' Wendy aimed and shot a hole perfectly through the centre of a wall clock that hung just above Trainor's head.

'Oh yes I would. You don't live with a detective inspector and not pick up some handy skills. Now stand there and be still.' Just then, many police officers arrived and the men were swiftly handcuffed and taken away. Once *they* were out Wendy was escorted outside where Jim and Inspector Bradley were waiting.

'Did they make any calls?' asked the inspector.

'No,' replied Wendy, 'But I need a drink. Tea or coffee I think, no more gin!'

'That's the spirit.' They laughed at the connection.

* * *

287

Tegan's leaving party began at about 11pm. Fortunately, Philippe had the evening off work, and he and Camille arrived first, followed by Olivia, who had vacated her hotel room earlier in the day. Tegan ordered drinks and nibbles and the party began. They did indeed stay with Tegan that night, and nobody was at all surprised that James shared the only bed with Tegan.

Next morning, Tegan checked out from the hotel and told them that Mateo would settle the bill. Plans had been made, and all five were driven to Philippe's house in the Prius. Work had to start almost immediately.

Chapter 38

Tegan was very quiet. It was lunchtime on Saturday, the weather was warm and sunny and birds were singing. Tegan had noticed none of this though, her thoughts were with Helen Morgan, her grandchildren, with James and with Ilef. The events of the past weeks were now over for *them,* and she hoped that Helen and her family would now resume their normal life, and hopefully be unscathed by their experiences. Ilef would most certainly be in jail for a very long time and James, well James was her new lover, as unlikely as having one of those had seemed just a week ago. All that remained for her to do was to find that gang, and avenge Akmal's death.

She had earlier received a message from inspector Roberts. Apart from telling Tegan that her parents would be returning to Canada later today, and describing her mother's heroic actions in preventing Trainor from alerting the Canadian gang that their cover was blown, she provided Tegan with most of the information that the British police had gleaned from their search of Philip's house. They had found some of the fake weapons, some drugs, and some illegal sexual aids, but most important of all they had obtained names and addresses of their contacts in Canada. She further explained that Sam Spencer and Philip Trainor had been very forthcoming during their interrogation, and had buckled when offered a reduced sentence in exchange for information. It was clear from what Sam and Philip Trainor had told them that they were only a small UK division of this Canadian gang, and that they hadn't been on the payroll for long. They hadn't really established themselves yet, and the shooting of Akmal and the bombing of Tegan's car were really their first acts on behalf of the Canadians. Sam had explained that he telephoned the gang after his police interview and he was surprised by the instruction to have Akmal shot, with the intention of killing him. Philip had confirmed that and he said that he hadn't shot anybody before and he was really sorry that the man had died.

Tegan now had some names and contact details of "that blasted gang" and she had the equipment to contact them, but she wasn't yet ready to go and find them. The inspector was in the same predicament. They needed some proof of the activities of it's members and Tegan was working out how best to carry out the plans that they had made last night.

'Penny for them?' Tegan hadn't heard that expression since she was a child.
'Sorry Camille, I was miles away.'
'Thinking about Akmal?'
'Yes, actually I was.'
'You'll soon be back in his arms.' Tegan had to blink back the tears. She hadn't told the rest of her group that Akmal was dead. She thought that it was best that they didn't know. It might encourage them to take too many risks.

'I'll tell you what we are going to do after lunch. I'm hungry.'

They chatted about mundane things while eating but things became serious again when they had finished.

'Philippe, will you be happy as the rich playboy that we discussed last night.'

'Not exactly happy but I will do it.'

'Excellent. I will put feelers out to find weapons suitable for an ambush of the bank, the one that lost you a lot of your money during a failed takeover bid, but you will need to pay out a deposit to secure the weapons from the gang. Is that OK with you?'

'How much might that be?'

'Offer them $1000. That should be enough. Will that harm your finances massively?'

'My accountant won't even notice.'

'And Olivia, how is your acting preparation going, have you got the facial features yet?'

'Very nearly yes.' Olivia pulled her face around again and Tegan showed a photograph to the others.

'Wow, you really are good aren't you. I imagine that with a false beard you could even impersonate me!' said Philippe.

'If it let's me access your bank account then I might do that!' she replied.

'Camille you'll be with me. Is that OK?'

'Indeed it is. Then Philippe and I will be gone from here. We've already sent on most of our stuff.'

'And Olivia, have you put your departure plans into place?'

'Sure have. Flight back to the USA is booked and I haven't a lot of possessions here. Most of them are now in a thrift shop.'

'Excellent again. James, what about you?'

'By your side Tegan. Wherever that takes us.' Tegan actually blushed, something that she just didn't normally do.

'Philippe, you and I have work to do.'

By the time Jim and Wendy Roberts were getting off the plane in Montreal, Philippe, with Tegan's help, had arranged a meet with a contact who would negotiate for the supply of 100 mixed weapons, to include pistols, shotguns, ten rifles and a flame thrower. This was to take place on Sunday afternoon at the Hotel du Lac, this venue having been suggested by the gang's contact. Philippe agreed, inspector Roberts was informed of the plan and the group of five settled down for the night.

Philippe spent an anxious Sunday morning thinking about what was to happen later. He had donned his expensive business suit and dug out his Rolex and his dad's old heavy gold chain. He had printed out a statement of the contents of his bank account, minus some identifying details, and withdrawn $1000 from various teller machines. He had been fully briefed and prepared by Tegan, and Camille drove him to Saint-Jérôme. He walked the last half mile so that Camille would not be seen to be involved. Inspector Roberts had arranged a "shadow" for Philippe, so he wasn't feeling too anxious as he entered the hotel.

'You look very smart today,' said the receptionist as he entered the hotel lobby. 'Not working today then?'

'Not today no,' he replied, hoping that he hadn't yet been seen by his new "associate".

Philippe sat in the hotel bar and ordered a small whiskey. He wasn't keen on whiskey, he preferred Scotch, but he thought that buying American would send out the correct message to his new friend. He hadn't been sitting down long before he spotted a man entered the bar wearing a beige suit and a black tie. This was exactly the attire he had been expecting so Philippe walked up to him, and addressed him as though this were a business meeting.

'Mister DiMarco?'

'Mister Banerjee?'

'I am pleased to meet you mister DiMarco. Please, join me at my table. Would you like a drink?'

'Yes please, Scotch if possible.' Philippe placed the order and the two men sat eyeing each other up for a while.

'You seem nervous mister diMarco. Are you OK?'

'Yes, thank you. I had a heavy night last night.' Philippe commiserated with him and explained that he too had been out partying, with a beautiful woman, who he suspected was only attaching herself to him for his money. "Mister DiMarco" eyed him up and down and noticed the casual manner in which Philippe wore his Rolex, and the gold chain was clearly of quality.

'Are those ornaments real?' he asked.

'Of course,' replied Philippe sounding really offended by the question. 'Are you questioning my ability to pay for these items?'

'Actually, it's part of my brief to confirm that you have the necessary funds for our transaction.'

'Then are you asking for actual proof that I can afford these items?'

'Well, er, yes.' Philippe handed over an envelope containing the deposit and Mr. DiMarco gazed into it to confirm that it was all there.

'We will need substantially more than that to close the deal.'

'You will get the rest when my colleague meets you to collect the consignment.' He showed his bank statement to his new associate.

'You will not collect it yourself?'

'No, my assistant Tegan deals with all of that. She will meet you anywhere you want for the supply of the consignment. She will arrange to have it collected.'

'A woman?'

'So?'

'Nothing. My boss might find that odd.'

'Assuming that you want to finalise this deal I suggest that you remove all prejudice from your contract here or we are done.'

'I have your deposit, so you won't back out.'

'My deposit? That's peanuts. I'll get this contract filled by somebody else.' He rose to leave.

'No, mister Banerjee, do stay. I am happy to fulfil this contract for you, and I would like you to stay while we finalise the details. I was just running a little test for you because our organisation is run by a woman, and she likes to make sure that every transaction runs smoothly.'

'So, you were testing *me*?'

'Yes.' Philippe sat back down. Negotiations began, Philippe asked Mr. Dimarco to confirm that these were genuine

294

weapons from the "RUMP" organisation, various other questions were answered, and the contract was signed. Philippe asked where the transaction was to take place and he was surprised that "Ned's barn" is where they wanted to have the weapons delivered, and then received, by Tegan.

'Do you know where to find "Ned's" barn mister Banerjee?'

'It was mentioned on the news last week, and I'm sure that my colleague will be able to find it. A dead man was found there wasn't he?'

'Indeed. Next Tuesday be OK? 6.30 pm?'

'I will make arrangements.'

After that the two men shook hands and "Mister DiMarco" left. Philippe ordered another drink, whisky this time, and he chatted to the receptionist.

'Are you doing some sort of business now then Philippe? Not enough money in waiting on?'

'Something like that. Please don't tell anybody that I was here. You know what my employer is like.'

'Of course I won't. What if Bill comes in again. Shall I let you know that he is available again?'

'Bill?'

'The man that you were talking to.'

'I was only told that he was a Mister Dimarco. He didn't tell me his first name. I should have asked him I suppose. I'd better improve my skills if I am to make some money out of this venture. Do you like my fake Rolex?'

'It looks almost real, like that chain.'

'The chain's real. It was my dad's.'

'It suits you Philippe. He's not called DiMarco by the way. William McNenemy is what he calls himself down at the market. He often comes in here to chat up ladies.'

'Is he successful?' laughed Philippe.

'No. He's got a phobia of women so he keeps trying to cure it. He told me all about it once. He says it's called gynophobia and it's actually quite common. Shame really because I quite fancy him. Bad luck I suppose.'

'DiMarco sounds Italian. I can't imagine any Italian man being scared of women,' laughed Philippe.

'He's not Italian, he's from Wales.'

'Oh.' Philippe was suddenly struck by just how weird this day was becoming.

After saying goodbye to the receptionist he walked the mile or so to their rendezvous point. Camille, now driving her own old car that she had bought to complete this mission, picked him up and they drove to Montreal. There she handed the car back to the man from whom she bought it, collected her cash and she and Philippe took a taxi to the airport. Within two hours they were in the air, headed for Toronto and, hopefully, leaving all of this behind them. Camille decided that it was time to give up the organisation and, in return, Philippe promised to find a more challenging job, one that would utilise some of the skills he had developed whilst at uni. Though he and Camille both wanted the memories of this last fortnight to fade, they secretly acknowledged that they might not have been brought together without it.

Chapter 39

Tegan was staring at her device. It was Sunday evening and she had just finished reading the information sent to her by Philippe.

'Next Tuesday at 6.30pm,' she said to James. 'You'll never guess where they want to complete the handover of the weapons!'

'Ned's barn?'

'How did you know?'

'Is it really that place again? I honestly only said that because it sounded so ridiculous an idea. Are they really intending to sell their fake weapons to us in such a high profile place? They must be mad.'

'Yes. Mad or very clever. I need to think this one out, decide whether to change our plans. What do you think James?'

'I think that you know best Tegan, but the plans seem to me to be difficult to change without rewriting the whole lot. You've already sent your original plans to Inspector Roberts, so perhaps you should wait to hear from her before deciding.'

'I'll let Inspector Roberts know about Bill McNenemy, if that's his real name, but you are right, we should wait to hear from her before we change anything. I need to get her to confirm that they can wrap up their CSI stuff and remove it's crime scene status before Tuesday. I wonder why the gang want to use that barn?'

'Goodness knows, but remember what Ilef said, he reckoned that his oppos had already decided to use the place, so perhaps they think it will be the safest place now because the authorities would assume it be the last place they would return to.'

'Good thoughts James.' She gave him a hug.

'It's a lovely evening Tegan. Why don't we go out somewhere?'

'How about your house?' replied Tegan, suddenly aware that she really knew very little about him.'

'If you are sure? The weapons fakers might know about my association with Ilef and be watching the place.'

'They might, but I doubt whether they will know who I am, I'll just be your girlfriend. Either way, I need to get away for a little while and maybe we could stay there for a few nights. Be nice to have a look at your world.'

'Yes, why not. Will you drive us there?'

'If you tell me where it is!'

'Of course, you don't know do you. I feel as though we have been together for years so it seemed like you would have already been there.'

Tegan smiled.

'I hope that that is meant in a positive way!'

'Of course it is.'

They picked up a few things and Tegan began the drive to Mile-End, a small suburb of Montreal. Tegan was aware of a Mile End in East London that seemed to be famous only for its large underground station, so she wasn't sure what to expect. She was delighted though to find herself driving down some very leafy streets and James got her to pull up outside a three-storey terraced house of some age, and with huge amounts of old-world character. She smiled at James.

'Is this your house?' she asked, in case he really lived in a shed at the rear.

'It is. What do you think?'

'It's lovely James. Very old world and it seems already to be relaxing.'

They got out of the car and Tegan insisted on a tour of the outside. The garden was rather overgrown, and it hadn't been prepared for the summer ahead, but it seemed characterful nonetheless.

'Looks really charming. It has three floors, so do you have servants?' James laughed heartily.

'Shall we go in?' he asked.

'I thought you'd never ask,' she replied.

As they entered the house Tegan felt as though she were walking back in time. The hallway was actually painted, painted to look like as though they were still outside. Above the wainscotting the walls were a sky blue, and an artist had painted clouds and flocks of gulls. The artwork was clearly very old and, though she wouldn't have ordered such a paint job for her own house, she found it utterly charming. James noticed that her mouth was open.

'This was painted in 1932, twenty years after the house was built. It was paid for by an eccentric man in his sixties, and nobody knows who the artist was. It doesn't continue past the hallway in case you are wondering. Come on into the kitchen, I'll make us some coffee.'

'Wow.'

299

'You like the place?'

'James, this house is amazing.'

Once out of the hallway, James' house was extraordinarily modern and the contrast between the art deco entrance hall and the rest of the house couldn't have been more stark. Everywhere the walls were adorned with posters, some in frames, others just fastened to the wall with pins. In the kitchen though, which was so white and shiny that Tegan felt she needed sunglasses, she spotted two photographs in very white picture frames. Both contained a picture of a woman with very black hair, and a little boy. Tegan wondered who they were and couldn't decide whether to mention them to James.

'I see that you have spotted my wife and son.'

'I wondered whether that's who they are. What happened to them James?'

James poured the coffee and sat down next to Tegan.

'Natalia and I were married 14 years ago and Santiago will now be just over ten. Natalia died in a car crash two years ago. I was very upset and I had a breakdown, so Santiago was taken into care. He now lives with his aunt in Spain and I haven't seen him since the crash. We do write to each other, actual real writing, and we send photos and stuff. We don't Facetime or anything like that because it would be too distressing for both of us. He is very happy where he is and he has two older "brothers" who keep him busy. We have reached a sort of equilibrium where we live our own lives. I intend to go to see him when he reaches 16, and hopefully we can become friends. It would be unkind to him to try to do that now. Do you think me a weak and terrible dad Tegan?'

Tegan listened to this and she could see the anguish that those events had caused him, but she also acknowledged the calm and controlled way that he was managing it.

'James, I can't make any comment on anything that I don't understand. Akmal is dead, and I don't know how I will react when all this is over and I have time to fully appreciate that he is gone forever. I might just react exactly as you did when you lost your wife. I don't have any children and it sounds as though you have done what is best for him.'

They sat in silence for a while.

'Are you OK being here James? Would it be better if we found somewhere else to stay?'

'No Tegan. I love this house, but it's now just that, a house. Natalia's character is all over it, and I love it for that, but now that I am longer tied to Ilef I will sell it at some stage, and move on.' Tegan wondered whether that moving on might include her.

'What did you do for a living before Ilef took you on?'

'Have you seen posters about the place? Can you not guess?'

'Erm, no James. Actually I can't.'

'Tegan, I was, or I suppose that I still am, a mime artist!'

'Of course! How could I be so stupid. So it wasn't Ilef that put you up to all that miming stuff.'

'No Tegan. I haven't done any mime since Natalia died, but it just seemed appropriate while talking to you. Goodness knows why!'

'Come here James.' She gave James a hug, they drank their coffee and Tegan continued her tour of the house.

Monday morning dawned dull and rainy and Tegan, who had woken first, gave James a shake.

'You need an alarm clock James.' James woke and, still bleary eyed, looked at his watch.

'Ten thirty. Wow, that's a lie in! I'm usually up at 7!'

'What shall we do today? There's nothing we can do to prepare for tomorrow, so what do you suggest?'

'I've still got those blue socks and white swim shorts!' Tegan felt mortified with embarrassment.

'James, I'm so sorry about that. I wanted to embarrass and annoy you then because you were part of my internment. I was missing Akmal, and I thought you could be my toy for the night. Please, throw those things away and promise me that you won't ever wear white swim shorts and blue socks again. Not in my presence anyway.'

'Didn't you like them then Tegan. I thought that I was meant to do that to excite you?'

'Please James, just get rid of them. We both need to start a new life with a new outlook.'

'Are you proposing to me Tegan?' Tegan hit him with a pillow.

'Get up and make me some coffee!' she demanded.

'I can't because we have run out. Shall I *run out* and get some more?' She hit him with a pillow again. They went out for breakfast and didn't return until late evening, a very pleasant day of sightseeing and shopping having filled their time.

That night in bed, Tegan asked James whether he would return to England with her after their task was completed on Tuesday. She was disappointed that his response wasn't what she wanted to hear. Though it had been non-committal, she was very used to men saying yes to her. It was then that she realised that life for her couldn't continue as it had done just two weeks ago.

Chapter 40

Tegan, James and Olivia spent Tuesday together. They finalised their plans and they then developed a written a script that they would later follow, as far as was possible. This was designed as a play that would, hopefully, provide enough evidence to put the weapons gang behind bars for a very long time, and then allow everyone to go home. All that anybody knew about the gang was the information provided by Ilef, who had, fortunately, vividly remembered their appearance when they shot his girlfriend Jennifer, and the little provided by Trainor in England, who was the gang's contact over there. So to work on, all *they* had was a description of the three that had murdered Jennifer, and another of the men who called himself DiMarco.

For her part of the plan, Inspector Roberts had briefed her team, and most of them were to spend part of the afternoon hidden near to the barn, Roberts being available if needed. They would watch the events as they unfolded, but not become involved until they had heard from Tegan or a member of her team.

Anxious but excited, Tegan, Olivia and James drove up to the barn at about 5pm. The inspector had been good to her word and the police tape had been removed, and the doors to the barn had been left locked. Everything looked exactly as an old abandoned barn should look. Tegan stood gazing around for a while and declared that this was such a beautiful spot that it really shouldn't be used for the purpose that they were proposing. Olivia agreed, but James pointed out that at least two people had died here in the last few weeks, and that he for one would be glad to leave and never return. Tegan sighed, told James that he was absolutely right, and they set about their preparations.

Olivia unscrewed the hasp from the door, and they entered.

'Look, the floor has been flattened down so there's little evidence of Jennifer's burial. That's excellent. The curtained area is still there too. Olivia, do want to start your preparations in there?'

'I'd love to.' This was the first time that Olivia had been to the barn, and she now felt very apprehensive.

'So, is that the place that had been your prison Tegan?'

'Yes. Just get on with it will you,' she replied with a smile.

Tegan watched James set up some mini cameras that he had originally bought for perfecting his mime routines, and then she checked the whole barn for anything untoward that the gang may have left as booby traps for them. By 5.30pm their preparations were completed, so they sat on the floor and talked through their plans again. None of them had seen any sign of a police presence and they hoped that that meant that they were well hidden, rather than that they hadn't been able to turn up at all. Sunset wasn't expected until about 8.30pm, so it was still daylight.

At about 6.15pm, Mister DiMarco appeared at the barn doors. Remembering that he was apparently scared of women, Tegan asked James to let him in.

'Good evening,' said Mister Dimarco, staying near to the doors. 'Do you have the money?' Tegan picked up a cloth bag and held it up for him to see. She opened it and waved wads of cash at him.

'Shall I bring it over?' she asked.

'No, no, that's fine, the money will be carefully checked before we hand over the weapons. Those are just behind me by the way, and they, and the rest of our team, will be here soon.'

'Good,' said Tegan.

'Are there just two of you? I was expecting the man calling himself Philippe to be here.'

'Just the two of us,' said James. 'Philippe is a busy man and he won't be joining us tonight.'

A peaceful quiet then descended on the barn until the sound of a large vehicle broke the silence. Mister DiMarco opened the barn doors as wide as they would go and three men entered, each wearing holsters that they obviously positioned so as to make them as visible as possible. They began to approach Tegan and James but James stopped them.

'Stay over by the doors. We want to watch you just in case you try any funny business. We are armed too so be aware of that. I want to see the first crate.'

'Certainly,' said one of the three.

'Are you the boss then?' Tegan asked him.

'Are *you* the boss?' he replied.

'I am,' replied Tegan.

'Likewise,' said the man.

'Not very talkative are you?' said Tegan. She got a grunt in reply.

Two of the three returned after a few minutes bearing a wooden crate. One of them opened it and James carried out an inspection. He nodded to Tegan.

'You three, stand by the doors. I just have some arrangements to make,' said James.

'Better not take long,' moaned one of them as the three wandered petulantly back to the doorway. There was a short pause and then the "play" began.

'Jennifer!' shouted Tegan. Olivia pulled back the curtain and walked, very slowly and gracefully, towards the men. All three of them stared in amazement.

'Jennifer, I thought you were dead. What the fuck is this? How can you still be alive? We saw you fall, you were riddled with bullets and there was a pool of blood. Look, the stain's still there.'

'Remember that night then do you? There I was, unarmed and only partially clothed, and you just took aim and fired. You didn't say anything to me, you gave me no chance to run, you just opened fire. You, the tall one, you shot first, then you, the ginger one and then you, the balding one. Like a slow motion firing squad. I remember all three of you as clear as if it was yesterday. But you didn't expect to see me today did you? The look on your faces! Now its you three who look shocked. I have waited for a long time to meet you three again, and I wish I had brought my camera.'

'We'll soon rectify this!' said the "boss". All three men pulled out their guns and aimed at Olivia.

'We won't miss this time,' said the tall one.

'Oh yes you will.' A voice appeared from a man standing just outside the barn. He had a semi automatic rifle with him.

'Gustav, what the hell are you doing here?' shouted Tegan.

'What is necessary.' All three men turned, saw what they thought was a trap and re directed their weapons towards Gustav, but they were too slow. Six shots rang out, and the three fell to the ground. The only shot made by the gang was from the tall one, and that went very wide.

'Gustav, what the hell have you done? We had this all planned,' shouted Tegan, but she got no reply because he was already gone. Mister DiMarco had also vanished and Tegan, Olivia and James just looked at each other.

'That wasn't the plan at all! Where the hell are the police?' said James, now visibly shaking. At that point officer Storey and three others arrived. "Mister DiMarco" was with them, already in handcuffs.

'It certainly wasn't,' agreed officer Storey. Tegan began to speak to the officer but she was told to be quiet until they got back to the station. Tegan and her colleagues were then arrested, on suspicion of causing grievous bodily harm to three men, and an ambulance was called to pick up the three remaining gang members, two of whom were now unconscious. The weapons were taken away and James' cameras were retrieved.

Back at the police station, and some time later, the interviews began. Tegan was first.

'Well this is a bloody mess isn't it,' said Inspector Roberts.

'It is. We were genuinely going to wait for you to arrest the three of them. As you know, I had our next moves all planned out and I had no idea that Gustav would turn up.'

'And the trick with Olivia pretending to be the murdered Jennifer? What was that about?'

'We knew that you wouldn't approve of that, but we thought that the shock of seeing her would delay the men long enough for you to catch them, *and* that we could get them to admit that they had shot her. That actually worked incidentally, so you should have it on the little cameras that James installed.'

'We are currently looking at those, and we'll see what they really do show in time. They had better confirm your story or all three of you will be in for long prison sentences. One of those men shot by your colleague is already dead, so your friend Gustav is now wanted for murder. Where can I find him?'

'I have only ever met him in Spain, in a town called Badalona. He won't be there now though, and you won't find him. I have no idea how he got to know my plans for tonight and he will have fled.'

'We are watching all of the airports,' said the inspector.

'He will likely stay in Canada. As Mateo Reyes' brother he will have friends here, and he will probably already have a new identity, and a new home. Ilef's lot were, or rather are, very capable. Don't forget that they are still operating.'

'Unlike the crooks that you met today. DiMarco has spilled the beans and it turns out that though they were a ruthless gang, they were a small gang. We have been to their various lock-ups and we are confident that we have all of them, at least all of the Canadian arm. They might have members elsewhere.'

'So it's over then,' said Tegan

'Not for us it isn't,' replied the inspector. 'We might still be charging you three with murder.'

'But it is over for me. It's time to go home, just as soon as you release me.'

'You sound very confident.'

'Wait until you see the footage from the cameras. It *is* all over.'

* * *

A few days later, the inspector was sitting in front of Ilef. 'Alright Mister Reyes, you've just heard what happened in that damned barn the other night, so it's time for some truth in this business. I'm frankly fed up with people trying to piss me off, and you are the worst culprit, so it's time to "spill the beans" as they say on TV. Begin at the beginning, and tell me who this woman you call Jennifer really is.'

'No.'

'Really? After all this bloodshed you still want to sit there and play "The Godfather"? Jennifer is dead, Gustav, your brother, is missing, presumably in hiding so he might as well be dead, Tegan's boyfriend Akmal is dead, Jean Belanger is dead, and three members of your rival gang are shot, one dead and another unlikely to pull through, so get on with it. If you won't tell me who Jennifer is then where's Gustav?'

'Genuinely, I have no idea where Gustav is. He will be somewhere that you won't find him, he's very skilled at that.'

'We have the airports covered so he won't get away.'

Mateo laughed.

'Gustav could hide in the middle of a supermarket aisle, and you wouldn't find him. I would like to bet you anything you want that he will never be found, at least not as long as you are still an inspector. How long have you got before retirement Inspector Roberts? Fifteen years? I'll likely still be in a cell then and you will be a free agent, but you won't have found him, and it will still nag at you, even then.'

The inspector stared at him for a while. She didn't reply to that comment.

'We are prepared to let you attend Jennifer's funeral. You can either watch her be buried in an unmarked grave, or you can tell us who she was.'

'Oh inspector, you are good. Cool as a cucumber, but I admit that I hadn't thought about her actual funeral.' He paused and examined his fingers for a while. 'Alright, I will tell you who Jennifer was, and you will need to do some checking to confirm it, but you won't believe me.'

'Actually, I already know who she was, I just want you to tell me.'

'More classic stuff inspector. Then perhaps I will wait until *you* tell me who she was.' The inspector lost a little of her cool at that point.

'Tell you what, if I prove to you that I do already know the identity of the dead woman, will you confirm it?'

'Maybe. Why don't we do as they did in Sherlock Holmes novels, and each write a name on a piece of paper, put it in a glass, and then allow the other to read what we have written.' The inspector sighed.

'Why not. I'm getting thoroughly bored with this anyway.'

Two scraps of paper of different colours were brought in, along with a ridiculously decorative glass. Names were written, sheets were folded, and the glass containing them was given to Officer Storey. The inspector asked her to read them both out.

'That's not what I suggested,' moaned Mateo.

'Officer Storey, what do they say?

'They both say the same name Ma'am. Jennifer's full name was Jennifer Erica Trumpe, owner of the RUMP organisation.' The inspector and Mateo both smiled.

'So what was all this about then Mr. Reyes?' Mateo sighed, then began again.

'Jennifer thought that her weapons division needed some publicity and, quite frankly, the weapons division was flagging financially, so she got the manufacturers to supply her with those weapons that weren't quite up to scratch. It's in the nature of manufacturing methods that there are quite a lot of those. They usually get destroyed, but Jennifer employed a few tech savvy people to set her up on the web, as a less than savoury dealer, where she would sell them. This worked and sales, both legit and not so legit, improved. But then there were a few exploding weapons which caused a minor slump. In the meantime she met me, and we formed a sort of alliance. That's it really, I expect that you are disappointed. She wasn't head of a mafia style organisation or anything remotely like that, and you haven't rid Canada of a massive gangland group of villains either.'

'So she was defrauding herself?'

'I don't think that's actually possible inspector, since she got all the profits anyway. She had nothing to do with the audio stuff fraud. That really was all down to the crowd that you tell me have now been found by that poor chap Akmal. Her own deception was going well until those three goons that are now very poorly set themselves up against her. You know the rest.'

'Indeed I do, and I will have to check to see who is running the RUMP organisation now. Do you know who that is?'

'No, genuinely I don't. *You* will need to find that out inspector.'

'Officer Storey, take this man back to his cell, and ask Tegan to come back in.'

'Tegan is here? Could I speak to her?'

'No.'

'Please, explain to her that what happened to her car and to her boyfriend, was nothing to do with me, at least not directly. I am so very very sorry, please tell her that.'

'Officer Storey, take this wretched man away before I lose my sanity.'

'Before I leave, how did you find out Jennifer's real name?'

'Deduction, Mr. Reyes. The only company experimenting with adding lead to lead free explosives, such as those containing tetrazole azasydnone salt, is Erica's South London explosives research department. The answer seemed obvious then. They were trying to save money by the way, didn't work though did it.' Mateo just sighed.

'Shall I take him away now inspector?'

'Please do so, and quickly.'

* * *

'So Akmal is dead just because the owner of RUMP industries wanted to increase her profits! If she wasn't dead already I would find her and shoot her myself. I assume that you have confirmed that she is indeed dead inspector?'

313

It was three full weeks after the showdown in the barn, but Tegan was still in custody. The inspector had waited until some loose ends had been tied up before confronting Tegan with the news that she knew would upset her.

'That just about sums up the whole situation Tegan, and yes, we have checked, and Erica Trumpe is indeed dead. Her company is currently being run by her deputy until shareholders can arrange a meeting. It was only recently that it was realised that she was no longer available. She had very little in the way of family, and those members that she did have didn't keep in touch, so it was really only our mister Reyes who new the full truth. Remember that both of the gangs who really were defrauding RUMP have been put out of action, so you have achieved what you set out to do.'

'Maybe, but things didn't have to be this way. It's been a very costly mission and the lives of quite a few people will never be the same again. I wonder whether it was worth it.' The inspector didn't reply to that.

'Have Olivia and James been released yet?'

'Yes, over two weeks ago. Olivia is now back in the USA and James is at home, a home which is up for sale by the way.'

'Thank goodness. Let's hope that this saga is all over for them, now.'

'What will you do now Tegan? Now that we are able to release you, will you return to the UK?'

'That depends on what James wants to do. He is unemployed now and he is selling his current home, so maybe I will go home, provided that he will come with me.'

'Well good luck. The papers are all signed so you are now free to go. I'll say goodbye for now because I want to ring my mother.'

'During work time, and during a high-profile investigation like this, you want to ring your mother? Is it to tell her that you are pregnant?'

'Tegan, I haven't even had it confirmed yet, I can only be a few weeks. How did you know?'

'I worked in a maternity ward when I was a student! Will your mother be pleased?'

'It will make her day, her week or her year even. She's been nagging at me for years, and now I'm forty-two it seems that it's finally happened, all courtesy of an exercise machine!'

'Well, I don't think that I want to know anything more about that, but good luck anyway. Whatever James and I end up doing, I'm having a holiday before I do anything else!'

Chapter 41: Epilogue

Ten months after they had arrived back in Iver Heath, Tegan and James were enjoying a quiet Saturday morning when there came a knock at the door.

'Now I wonder who that can be. James, are you expecting anybody?'

'No Tegan. Shall I get it?'

'No, I will.' She put down her newspaper and headed for the front door. After undoing the many recently fitted bolts, she opened it and there, to her absolute astonishment, stood Akmal. He was leaning heavily on two sticks and he smiled, but it was a fairly weak smile, and he looked a shadow of his former self. Tegan almost fainted and just stood hanging onto the door frame, gaping.

'Can I come in?'

'Erm, what? Erm yes, yes of course, come in, certainly, yes of course.' She almost recovered her composure and then opened the door wide enough to allow him entry to the house but, once he had stepped inside, she just stood for a while, door wide open, thinking. As he struggled in she didn't know what to do or what to think, her mind was all over the place, but once Akmal had sat down she suddenly woke from her dream. She had no idea what to say to this "ghost" and simply said 'Oh, sorry Akmal, do you need a hand or anything, shall I make some coffee?' She felt really odd speaking that name again and she was almost speechless.

'Yes, if you want to, or you could ask your new boyfriend to make it for you.' Tegan gave Akmal a look.

'Don't worry, I know all about your exploits and that you thought I was dead. I thought I was dead too, so don't worry about it. I want you to be happy.'

James made the coffee and then joined them, and Tegan made the introductions. They then sat for about half an hour drinking coffee and chatting like old friends that hadn't seen each other for some years, though Tegan actually said very little. Akmal explained that, after a week in intensive care, he was sufficiently recovered (though still very *very* ill) to be taken to a private hospital in a coffin that had been modified to allow his life support paraphernalia to be included by his feet. He spent two months or so there, and was eventually well enough to move to a convalescent home, and from there he moved to an assisted care home, where he still lived. He had been back at work for just over a month, and he was looking into buying a small flat for himself. Tegan was still shell shocked and her emotions had gone through the roof.

'You didn't think to tell me any of this?'

'I'm sorry Tegan. I wasn't really back in the land of the living until a few months ago and my care was being handled by the organisation anyway. It was they that insisted that nobody knew that I was still alive. I got clearance to let the world know that I was still around about six weeks ago, and you are the first member of my old life to find out. Anyway, it was made clear to me that you were back in England as a pair, so I knew what to expect when I came here today. It's nice to meet you James.'

317

Tegan said nothing but James gave Akmal a nod. James and Akmal chatted for a while, Tegan still not quite back in the real world. After a while Akmal said 'I'll leave now.'

Tegan replied 'But not yet. We still have so much to talk about. I need to know....'

'No you *don't*,' said Akmal, 'and *we* don't.'

'But what about the house? It's half yours.'

'I will write to my solicitors about that and they will sort it out with you. It's not important at the moment. I'm happy just to be back at work now, and eventually I will be able to walk without the sticks. So in a few years time I'll be almost back to normal, but my abdomen will remain heavily scarred. You must live your new life, but please remember ours.'

'But there's so much I want to ask you about.'

'Tegan, you once told me, nearly a year ago it was, that once a job was done it's done. You have to leave our life together where it is, which is in the past. That's how it is now.'

Akmal got up to leave but Tegan barred his way. She gave him a massive hug, which he returned, his sticks falling to the floor. James picked them up for him.

'Will you keep in touch?'

'Maybe, but remember what I just said,' and he smiled that smile that had melted her heart four years ago. With that he hobbled out and headed for his waiting taxi.

Printed in Great Britain
by Amazon

24776032R00182